stuck up a tree

stuck up a tree

jenny mcLeod

A *Virago* book

Published by Virago Press 1998

A CIP catalogue record for this book is
available from the British Library

ISBN 1 86049 314 9

Typeset in Bembo by M Rules
Printed and bound in Great Britain by
Clays Ltd, St Ives plc

Virago
A Division of
Little, Brown and Company (UK)
Brettenham House
Lancaster Place
London WC2E 7EN

To Lil.

She'd been on this road before. Truth is she'd been on this road her whole life and in the darkness it stretched out before her, incandescent lines jag-jag-jagging along, working with the headlights to keep her straight.

When she had first arrived in London she used to run this story to anyone who'd listen, that she'd been born on a road. She was born on a road in the back of a Zephyr in between two towns she couldn't remember the names of. Some place up north, nearly off the edge of the map, nearly falling into the sea even. For some reason it suited her, it made sense. In fact she had never been told the story of her birth. She suspected it wasn't nice since Brownie had never once spoken of it, at least not to her.

From way back when, Ella's mind was like a black box devoid of any light. From way back when, she had the will to keep the hinges tight, not allowing even one ray of one beautiful light beam to enter. As the years rolled on, so the hinges weakened, and every now and then a burst of light would flood through to her mind and hurt her eyes. She could take the odd involuntary burst. What she could not take was complete surrender, and she spent her energies working against this.

She reached for her cigarette lodged in the car ashtray and inhaled like a needy thing. She smoked Marlboro, not because she liked them but because she always had from way back when.

If she could pick the day it had started, perhaps she would pick some day way back in her childhood. Perhaps she might pick that day eighteen years ago. Or perhaps that day thirteen years ago when she'd finally left the House. Or perhaps it was just some innocuous day when the sun had looked just like Brownie's bread fresh from the oven. Or some day when rain had been falling on and around the Pink House. She recalled the time she'd snapped a string of Aunt Julie's pearls. Yes! That was how it rained in her home town, Hanville. Heavy. Like pearls.

Truth is, the day had already been charted, but not by her.

Yesterday two nasty things had happened. She had got news of her mother's death and then Ludo had asked her to marry him. Now she was off, running north.

She had never known how she would hear or when she would hear, but she knew whatever she was doing the moment she heard she'd stop and immediately head north. She'd been waiting for this day all her life. Keeping the one person who had become a part of her life so far from her, she could go without explaining why to him. On the face of it she was going to see Brownie stuffed in her box and lowered into the ground. To poke a finger into the chest of the woman to see if her heart had really stopped beating, to see if that vast chest had really turned hollow. That was how she had lived these past thirteen years: waiting.

Ella owned a restaurant, BrightWell's. It had come out of a catering van she used to run ten years ago, three years after arriving in London, running around dishing out Jamaican food to black people who couldn't be bothered to cook it. Later she'd opened up this smart restaurant dishing out Jamaican food to white people who thought it was trendy and would pay way over the odds for it. She'd found the place and immediately had the door painted a stand-out red to match its location in a stand-out part of London. It was on a hill, halfway up a hill to be precise. That was what attracted her to the place when she first looked it over, not the great location in the right part of town for overpriced restaurants or anything, not the deal she managed to negotiate with the estate agents, nothing but its situation on that hill. Precarious. And until a year ago BrightWell's had been doing very well, keeping her living a smart life in a smart part of the city.

That day she'd breezed back into BrightWell's just before the evening rush and stopped her staff dead in their tracks with her announcement: she wouldn't be around for a few days. She didn't tell them where she was going and why, she just made her announcement and then huddled around her desk with the maitre d' and the chef, laying out detailed and explicit instructions for what she wanted done and how she wanted it done, and then she left. Immediately they all thought the rumours were true. Well, they weren't even rumours. The staff could see for themselves. In the last year everything was going down – reservations, food orders, prices – and the whisper had gone round the kitchen like a smell. Ella's taking a few days away from the restaurant, when she'd never even had a day off that wasn't planned weeks in advance, was like the end as far as they were concerned, and some of them had already decided to start ringing round contacts in the trade to see what was on offer.

Thirteen years, no real thought of family, no contact with Hanville or anyone in it, and three words broke the banks of her river and flooded her world, just like that.

'Pinky? Dat you?' said the voice on the phone.

In her red sports car flashing along the road, Ella took a final puff on her cigarette, stubbed it out in an almost full ashtray, and lit another. To the steady hum of the car, the road north before her and one eye cracked to it, Ella's mind flooded.

Ella Brightwell was the last daughter of the Brightwell family. They lived in Hanville, in a house, around a corner, on a hill – and it was all pink. The only Pink House in the neighbourhood, in the country, on bad days the whole wide world. And she lived in this House until she was seventeen years and ten days old.

She thought her family were strange, the strangest people in a whole town of seriously strange people. And she had never come to terms with their strangeness – even now as a big woman she could not come to terms with it. And at the head of this strangeness reigned first her mother and then the House.

The House had six bedrooms and three downstairs rooms, not counting her mother's kitchen. The pink was everywhere imaginable: walls and ceilings, settees and chairs, beds and curtains, tiles, carpets and rugs, bath and toilets, all pink. The only place that didn't have a pink carpet was the kitchen and dining room where Brownie would wax and daily buff.

The only place that didn't have pink walls was the outside toilet – the inside one did. Even the rooms of her four arse-tearing brothers, Lambert, Kellit and twins Patrick and Johno, weren't allowed any other colour but pink. Her brothers' rooms looked no different from that of her sisters Della and Donna. Their room looked no different from hers, hers looked no different from her Aunt Julie's and her Aunt Julie's no different from her parents'.

Throughout her childhood there had been two stories about where the pink had come from. The first was that Daddy Ned worked at a paint factory that one Christmas discontinued both the line and the factory. Daddy Ned was always smiling and saying he was sorry. If he found a hundred pounds in the street, he would smile and say sorry for the person who had lost it. If someone knocked him to the ground and stomped on his head, he would smile and say sorry for his head being in the way. Ella used to study him and think that if she could just find out what he was smiling at, then she could do everything she wanted to do. So that Christmas home comes Daddy Ned with a vanload of pink paint, instead of the customary turkey and half a pig Brownie had been expecting, and Brownie doesn't ask, 'What me going cook for a family of ten?' She just looks at the paint and the smiling Daddy Ned and says, 'Children, Aunt Julie, look what Daddy Ned bring home for we Christmas. Look like we going be painting this Christmas.' And she kisses him and he smiles and they all set off painting. All except Aunt Julie.

The second story had to do with Brownie. Apparently

one night, two months after her last daughter had been born, the child still had no name and had been referred to collectively as 'that It Child'. Brownie had tied a black string around the Child's wrist to keep her safe and that was all she had done for her daughter since her birth two months before. When people visited the House, someone from the family would say, 'Tell that It Child to shut up.'

The visitor would say, 'Who?'

And the family member would say again, 'That It Child!'

It was during this time of namelessness that Brownie had her most prophetic of dreams. The dream said, 'Name this child Pinkette and all that surrounds you must be pink, and all that she does will have a wonderful bearing on you and yours, and you shall be pink.' And so the last daughter of the Brightwell family was called Pinkette, known as Pinky to one and all, and the House was transformed pink.

The first time Pinkette – or Ella, as she renamed herself – ran away from the Pink House she was thirteen and three-quarters. She told herself she was running from her family and their strangeness, but she could just as easily have been running from herself. She made three jam sandwiches, packed three pairs of shoes and took off at three o'clock on the third day of the third month. On that day she had suddenly decided three would be her lucky number.

It had been a Saturday – that meant soup and the kitchen inhabited from dawn by a huge woman of six foot three who had a deep amber singing voice that shook the House awake every morning. The woman had a great lump of dangerous silver hair that was allowed to do anything and everything on

any given day. The story was her hair had been that way
since some shock had visited her when she was fourteen.
What shock Ella didn't know. All she knew was hair was a
major property with this woman because she had sprouts
flying from all parts of her face. Over eyes, below chin and
out both ears and nose. The woman was extraordinary. She
had forearms that looked like freshly dug yams and huge
breasts that juggled about in a bright multicoloured rainbow
tent that hung from the top of her great frame to the bottom
of it, and it was like she was the whole wide world. For Ella
all memories surrounding this great rainbow tent were great.
The best hiding place ever! Where large hairy thighs were
swathed in huge warm silky peach balloon drawers that
failed to muffle the smell that emanated from beneath them.
One of the best, friendliest smells in the whole wide world.
Then there was Daddy Ned putting his hand under there
and Brownie jumping back and slapping his hand away, but
then always guiding it back, guiding it higher and higher
and holding it in a place they both seemed to love. When
Ella had first begun to recognise her mother as this great
colossus of wonder and strangeness, Brownie Brightwell
would've been in her early forties, but to Ella her mother's
age was as nonexistent as Jesus Christ to an infidel. She was
just there.

   That Saturday Ella knew the kitchen would be puffing
and dripping with the efforts of the soup as the condensa-
tion rose and fell. And as Ella opened the kitchen door, so it
was. Degrees warmer and cosier than anywhere in the Pink
House, and there was her mother. Head coming out of a pot

of steam, nose shifting from one side to the other, sniffing out whatever ingredient the soup was lacking, sipping loudly from a large spoon to confirm what her nose told her. And as the steam left her, Ella thought she looked like a monster rising from the bowels of something somewhere. This was her mother's room, her mother's most sacred, secret, comforting place of passion. This was her mother's kitchen.

Some kids were taught to sit up straight at table, speak only when spoken to, how to cross the road and keep safe. Brownie taught her kids something quite magical and strange. When Ella discovered that all the other kids in Hanville weren't taught anything like this, it threw her. When she discovered all the other black kids were taught who they were, where they'd come from how they should go forward in a world that hated them, it threw her. When she discovered that all the white kids were taught the world was theirs and they could do anything they wanted as they went about attaining it, that threw her too. Because Ella believed all that Brownie taught her kids was that 'food had soul!' And compared to the other kids, both black and white, it never seemed quite enough to Ella. 'Food had soul!' Feelings of being cheated and mystified were a prominent feature of Ella's childhood, something she couldn't shake off no matter what. Something that followed her to this day.

Through food Ella learnt vast amounts about her mother one minute, then had to reconsider in the next when Brownie confounded her with something she said or did. Of no doubt, though, Ella knew as unshakeable fact that cooking was her mother's symphony and Ella knew this when she didn't even know what a symphony was.

That morning Brownie saw her daughter but didn't break stride and her singing continued as she moved to the spice and herb cupboard. She was singing a Sam Cooke tune at the top of her voice – tomorrow, Sunday, she would sing a selection of sacred tunes at the top of her voice. Brownie stuck her hand down her cleavage, lifted one of her huge breasts, pulled out a huge key and unlocked the cupboard. It was always kept locked. It had the biggest, blackest padlock Ella had ever seen, like one of those that held lost treasure at the bottom of the sea in the fairy tales Ella never really believed. It was the only place in the House that was kept locked and no one but her mother knew why. All Ella knew was that none of her friends' mothers kept their spice and herb cupboards locked. None of their mothers had a spice and herb cupboard that was ten feet tall and wider still. None of them had a spice and herb cupboard that creaked and groaned behind locked doors, that had ingredients that mixed themselves into the brightest, most excitable concoctions that ever were. Things went on in this locked cupboard, Ella knew. She heard them. She tasted them. And only her mother knew what things.

As Ella came into the dining-room area she saw the great oak table that jutted out into the kitchen laden with stuff for the soup. All morning Brownie had chopped and peeled onions, carrots, cho-cho, pumpkin, garlic and thyme into mounds and they were now waiting in some kind of natural order to take their place in the boiling water. Sometimes watching her mother cook was all the adventure Ella's young mind needed and she knew that as Brownie had prepared the vegetables in the early hours of the morning there would've been something named joy oozing deep from within her. The joy would ooze into the food, on to their plates and end up in their bodies.

'Folks say that you found someone new, to do the things I used to do for you,' sang Brownie at the top of her voice, head still in the spice and herb cupboard, hands still instinctively mixing from the heart. 'Just call my name, I'm not ashamed, I'll come running back to you.'

It wouldn't be difficult to slip out past Brownie Brightwell. Perhaps if it had been, Ella wouldn't have wanted to. All it took was this: as her mother's head went into the spice and herb cupboard, Ella moved to the back door and her hand reached for the handle. The singing stopped and the words 'Pinkette, where you going?' reached her ears.

Ella stopped, hand on handle, about to open, about to step through to her new life. She turned to look at her mother. Her head was in the spice and herb cupboard, her hands were preoccupied mixing up some concoction, how could she know Ella's hand had reached the door handle at that precise moment? Ella couldn't answer her own question so she answered her mother's: 'London.'

'Well, make sure you go far enough.'

And that was how her mother was.

Ella hitched as far as Denby, the next town, before she had the misfortune to run into a cousin. Poor Cousin Winston. Winston Montgomery Merton Brightwell. A big boy-man,

a few years older than Ella, who wore the same pair of corduroy trousers with his various T-shirts or jumpers,
depending on the weather, every day of the year. The story
behind the 'Poor' went something like this: Winston's
mother, Miss Bee, was married to Daddy Ned's brother
Thomas. The word was that Miss Bee was something of a
loose woman who slept out every night and Thomas, a weak
man who drank and pissed where he stood, let her. One
night when Winston was about three, this particular round
of whoring, drinking and pissing had been going on for a
few days and as was customary, Winston had not eaten but
what he could find for himself around the house. On the
third night hunger and thirst forced Winston out of the
house and he made it down to the garden, where he was
found the next morning by Brownie and Daddy Ned.
Brownie had apparently been told in a dream that things
were not well in Miss Bee and Thomas's household and she
should go and offer help. On arrival they found Winston
sucking on dirt, chewing on worms, his face as black and
bleak as a cold winter's morning. Apparently the first words
out of Brownie's mouth were 'Poor Cousin Winston!' Ever
since then, Winston Montgomery Merton Brightwell had
been Poor Cousin Winston.

In Denby Ella stuck out her thumb as she heard the car
come up behind her. She recognised it immediately. The
driver leant over and opened the passenger door. Ella's
shoulders dropped, her arms folded and one foot was
planted down and pointed outwards. Twenty miles from
home, in another town, where no Brightwell but her had

any business, she had somehow annoyed God enough to make him send Poor Cousin Winston. And she realised that the strangeness that soaked their lives was making its clammy way to her.

She fought all the way back. Nearly ran the car off the road, called him all kinds of names she had no right knowing at thirteen, and even reduced Poor Cousin Winston to tears as he struggled along with one hand on the steering wheel and another restraining her. It was only as the car rounded the corner to the road where the Pink House stood that she shouted out her final abuse, 'Fucking pussy!', and then quietened down. As the car started to climb the hill, the Pink House came into view, and she felt her life was over at thirteen and three-quarters, on the third day of the third month.

The second time she ran away she was fourteen. This time she had saved up eleven pounds, made eleven cheese sandwiches, packed eleven pairs of shoes and had plans to leave the House at eleven o'clock at night – three no longer being her lucky number. As she opened the dining-room door, the smell of sweet-potato pudding was everywhere, stroking and dancing with her, soothing her. Ella didn't know what being in love was, but surely this must be it. Ella didn't know what getting drunk was, but this must be it. She didn't know what believing in God meant, but it couldn't be anything more glorious than the smell of a baking sweet-potato pudding. Like syrup and honey, hugging you warmly and sweetly from inside out.

'Hell a top, Hell a bottom, Hallelujah in the middle!'

Aunt Julie had told the young Brightwell children this riddle and just left it at that. That was Aunt Julie. Loved to believe she knew more than anyone else and it mattered not that the people she pitched her great wisdom against were children. It had been Brownie who had whispered and told them what it meant. Back Home sweet-potato pudding was always baked in a dutchy with live coals on the bottom and live coals on top, cooking the glorious mixture from top and bottom at the same time. The 'Hallelujah in the middle' then was the sweet-potato pudding itself. All Ella knew was that with a handful of sweet potato, yam, flour, raisins, milk, coconut milk, brown sugar, vanilla, nutmeg, sherry, rum and butter her mother could conjure nothing more divine than sweet-potato pudding.

Ella's eyes went to the open window where two huge ones were steaming and puffing cool on the sill, a suspended curtain tent around them keeping flies from them. In the oven two more were cooking, slowly, ever so very slowly. And at the table Brownie was standing, stirring up another. For ages she didn't appear to see Ella watching her; she was off walking up some Jamaican hill, eating guineps or plaiting her hair, the sun on her as she went. During her mother's reverie Ella saw on the table, next to the huge mixing bowl that was jerking under the rigours of her mother's efforts, the large black key that fitted the great lock of the spice and herb cupboard. Ella had never touched the key before; she had never seen it separated from her mother's person before because Brownie wore it in the bath, in church, in bed and in her meetings and memories. Now it was on the table. Ella wanted to pick it up and unlock the mysteries of the spice and herb cupboard, and she would if her mother remained a girl on that hill in Jamaica for even a moment longer.

But then from nowhere came her mother's voice. 'Pinky, what you doing with you coat on?' And the question was wrapped in the movement of Brownie's hand as it reached out for the key that then disappeared under the tent, under her breast.

'What?' Ella dragged herself from her fantasy of discovery.

'What you doing with you coat on?'

'I'm going to London.'

'Then all I can say is . . .' Brownie stopped midsentence. Had she forgotten what the all she could say was? Surely she remembered the speech she had for her youngest daughter on leaving home? Ella thought she should wait a moment in case Brownie remembered what to say. Then Brownie finished, 'All I can say is make sure you happy.'

Brownie didn't think she would go, that was what Ella thought. Her mother was working her brain, but she'd be sorry because this would be the last time she would see her. Ever! Because when she went, she would go, and go for good.

Ella banged the back door shut, then the gate behind her, and set off into the night. She had been out and about on her own at eleven o'clock and beyond before, because Brownie wasn't the type of mother to lay down curfews on her children, but on stepping out of the front gate Ella immediately discovered the difference between being out at eleven o'clock and beyond and actually running away at

eleven o'clock. Eleven o'clock was dark. As she walked further and further away from the Pink House, it seemed to get
darker and darker. The trees seemed to be having some kind
of conversation she couldn't understand. The tops of them
were meeting in the middle over the road and holding the
darkness tight above her. Front doors were being bolted, curtains drawn, lights going off. Cars were quiet and men were
home to beat their wives. This was eleven o'clock on the
run and something strange was moving across the road from
her. She couldn't see what it was. She knew it went on four
legs and had the most piercing eyes that had ever searched
and fallen on her. It wasn't a dog – she was on stoning
acquaintance with all the Hanville dogs. It wasn't a cat, it was
too big to be a cat. As it came into view she saw it was a fox,
though she had never seen a fox this close up before. It
stopped and so did she. Someone was trying to strangle her
and she couldn't fight them off. Her entire will was fixed on
the fox as it stared her out across the deserted street. This is
what running away from home gets you, was all she heard.
This is what being a big mouth does for you. This is what
eleven o'clock is all about! It brings you face to face with
foxes and a strange darkness. She wanted her Brownie and she
realised she was sobbing. Maybe the fox realised too because
then it went on its way, sloping off like a thing in charge.
Once the danger had passed, Ella was deeply ashamed of her
fear and started to tell herself she couldn't turn back just
because of some stupid fox. She had to carry on. What
would she be if she didn't? Who would she be if she didn't
take this moment to get away? And how would she ever face

her Brownie again? But thank God almighty, at the bottom of the road she turned the corner where she thought all light would begin to shine and she ran into Nathan Lewis. He was way past his curfew and sweating as to how he would escape the backsiding of his life. Bravely she took his hand, escorted him to his house, encouraged him to follow her as she climbed up the side of the house and into his open window, and lost her virginity to him. It would be the last time she would be scared enough to change her plans.

The next morning Ella returned to the Pink House and found Brownie chopping wood in the yard. Brownie only smiled at her. She didn't ask where her daughter had been. Didn't demand to know what she thought she was doing. Didn't even ask if her daughter thought she and she was companion. Brownie only smiled at her and carried on chopping the wood. Smashing the pieces to splinters and chunks with a rhythmically wielded axe.

In truth, all emotion that breathed and bubbled up and over in the Pink House was illustrated through food. It seemed to Ella that if she were deaf, dumb and blind, so long as her taste buds were intact she would be able to work out what was going on with the Brightwells and how far it had soaked into the psyche of her mother. What the family ate of a morning, afternoon or evening became the barometer of how they were feeling. What the family felt became the marker to what Brownie served up to them, so'til all three – her mother, food and family emotion – became intertwined and no one ever seriously asked 'Is what this?' or 'Why we eating this?' Not even Aunt Julie. Even she understood that

in the lives of her children, her family and the Brightwell
friends, it was Brownie who knew what they should eat at
any given time.

When her big brother Kellit wasn't patient about something – because that was his thing, he had no patience and
daily someone somewhere had reason to tell him he didn't –
there was a lesson to be learnt and learnt via food.

Brownie had gone walking in Badlands Woodlands and
Daddy Ned, spurred on by Aunt Julie, beat Kellit for not
having the patience to wait for Patrick and Johno after
school. The twins had wandered off down to the river,
Johno had fallen in and nearly drowned. Kellit said he waited
a good half-hour, looked for the twins, couldn't find them
and assumed Donna or Della had taken them home. He had
business across town around some engine he was interested
in buying just so he could look at it, strip it down, put it
back together and look at it all over again, and that was
where he had gone.

Aunt Julie had another version of the story. Kellit hadn't
waited longer than five minutes so'til she, who had just been
passing, had to jump into the river, save Johno's life and in
her best frock too. When Kellit was confronted with this
version of the story he had to admit it was true, and when
Brownie returned from her walk one of her sons couldn't sit
down, another was in a fitful feverish sleep and Aunt Julie
was strutting around the House like she owned it.

Brownie didn't demand to know what was going on, neither of Daddy Ned, Aunt Julie nor any of the other kids in
the House. She merely saw her children were as comfortable

as she could make them, put a piece of salt fish to soak and
went out to the yard to tend her herb and vegetable garden
by moonlight.

Brownie believed everything there was to learn was to be
learnt at a given time. The time would present itself and that
was when you learnt the lesson. This was the time for Kellit
to learn to cook salt fish and ackee, his favourite food. It
wasn't a complicated dish. All that was required was patience.
Early the next morning Kellit was roused and brought to the
kitchen.

'You can't just decide this minute you going cook salt fish
and ackee,' said Brownie.

Kellit was sore, had a pitiful feeling growing in the pit of
his stomach and he had no interest in anything his mother
was saying to him.

'You got to decide day before.'

It was true, until then Kellit had had a tendency to just up
and ask if they could have salt fish and ackee, and could they
please have it for that evening's meal. Brownie would always
say 'tomorrow'. 'Tomorrow I going cook you up a big plate
a it, you see!' And then she would kiss him. And Kellit just
hated waiting and fretted that tomorrow was so far from
coming he might just die waiting.

So that morning Brownie produced two pieces of salt
fish. One had been in soak all night, the other had not.
Where her hand went, she guided Kellit's, where her joy
appeared, she turned Kellit's eyes to see it. They skinned and
boned the salt fish, fried the onions, peppers and tomatoes,
washed the ackee and as an accompaniment Brownie

stretched a pot of rice. Simultaneously they were cooking two versions of the same dish, one with the soaked salt fish and one with the unsoaked. In the course of working with the food, Kellit forgot his pain and was soon well into what he was doing. When Kellit was finished he was proud to see and smell that the one plate of food looked as glorious as the other and the one smelt as wonderful as the other. He would have two plates of his favourite food and he just couldn't believe he had such a wonderful mother, who a day after he had made such a near-fatal mistake would allow him this. Only as Brownie placed both plates before him at the table and only when he tasted one, then the other, did Kellit understand. Only as he sat and began to eat from the two plates simultaneously, as Brownie had instructed him, did his lesson clang deep inside him and it clanged deeper than anything he had learnt from Daddy Ned and Aunt Julie the day before. He had to spit one forkful out, push away one plate and then watch mournfully as Brownie scraped the inedible food into the bin.

For weeks after Kellit talked of nothing but the importance of patience, of time and how everything had a place somewhere, because that was how it was supposed to be. He understood he wasn't wrong to want the engine more than he'd wanted to wait for his brothers that afternoon; where he had gone wrong was in not realising the engine would've been there whatever time he'd made it across town, but his brothers possibly wouldn't have been.

Kellit was overnight an aficionado of patience and all got sick of him. For instance, when Ella couldn't wait for her birthday to be over, he told her, 'Live every second of the day 'cause that's how it suppose to be!' and he said it so piously that she smacked him across the head and he didn't even mind, because that was how it was supposed to be.

Ella could feel her fingers sinking into Kellit's soft, warm afro once again. As her car moved along the road, she was sure she could feel his hair between her fingers and the feeling only left her once her phone started ringing in the car.

It was Ludo. She didn't know what to say to him. 'Hi!'

And apparently he didn't know what to say to her either.

There were parts on the road that were lit, parts that weren't. As the phone began ringing, Ella had hit a pocket of black darkness. She flicked her headlights and went back to hanging on to the tip of the beams, out there just beyond her car. That was where her mind settled once the feeling of Kellit's hair disappeared from beneath her fingers, not with Ludo or in the car, but on the beam, running after it.

Ludo wasn't sure whether her disappearance was due to the phone call she'd received earlier, or his marriage proposal. Only now had he found the courage to call her mobile. It was the early hours of the morning and it was just like Ludo to wait half the day and night before doing what he should've done first off. He wanted to find her but was scared.

'So!' Ludo said it like he expected her to fill in the sentence.

Even if Ella hadn't been peering through her windscreen at ninety-five miles an hour into the pitch black, watching two beams of light that held her life in the pick of their shafts, she would not have finished or filled in any sentence. She was peering because for a moment she thought she'd seen something out there. From the corner of her eye something had stepped into the light and stood before her. It shook her. She held the steering wheel like she expected to lose it. Whatever she was looking for, it wasn't there now. She looked in the rear-view mirror to see if she had left it behind her. It had been a feeling, she was now telling herself, just a feeling. She took a couple of deep breaths trying to hold on to herself as she stared out into the darkness.

'So. How are you?' he asked.

'In comparison to what?'

He checked her mood and tried to go round it, but he had never sensed it so wide before. 'Ell . . .' And he was tipping round it like a barefoot man over a trail of slippery stones, alligators circling all around.

'What?' she asked, no softness in her voice.

'About the proposal . . .'

'Not now, Ludo. I can't talk now.' And she pressed a button and ended the call, switched off the phone and tried to force him from her mind.

What did he think he was doing proposing to her? She felt like laughing. And if she thought she could ever have stopped laughing at the audacity of what he had asked her, maybe she would've.

On the other side of the road, a car was coming towards her. She knew she'd have to reach for the stick to dip her headlights, but for some reason she couldn't. The oncoming car had dipped its headlights in good time, but Ella couldn't dip hers. She wasn't being her usual obstinate self, she just couldn't bring herself to have less light guiding her way than she already had. The level of her fear of the dark was getting stupid. Would she run the risk of dazzling some driver off the road because she couldn't bear the dark? The oncoming car began flashing her. She tried not to look, tried to cringe away into a ball like she wasn't even there. It was one of the things she did when things weren't feeling right in her stomach. She would box herself off and try and swim through the mess without letting even one piece of it touch her. She held her eyes straight out in front of her, rigid and fixed to her light. She zipped past the other car.

Miles away, Ludo sat in his car, parked outside her flat, holding the empty phone like his life had just disappeared down it. He had been there for hours and had spent the time gathering himself to make the call.

Ella and Ludo! On and off they'd been together for eight years. From the beginning Ella had told herself he was never going to own any part of her. She wanted to hold him near, but on her terms. Whenever she had to go to him and apologise for some outburst, she would kiss him and hold him and tell him, 'It was just a bad moment.'

Ludo was the only kind of man that would put up with her and maybe she knew that from the start. He was attentive, had the money and time to be, dabbling only occasionally in his work, leaving most of it to his partner. He was white, plain-looking, but because of his money it didn't matter. The trouble with Ludo was that he didn't know how to be anything but a nice, steady, dependable guy, but then that was also the virtue of the man.

Yesterday's bad moment had started with a phone call. At Ludo's insistence they were at her flat having a late lunch. He was up for broaching the subject of offering financial help to BrightWell's. He had offered money once before when it was clear things weren't going well, but she had thrown the offer back at him – 'it's my place and I want to keep it that way!' But now he had it all worked out. He was offering a legitimate business deal. For a share in the restaurant he would put up as much money as she needed and he would leave all the decision-making to her, it would still be her place. To help, that's all he wanted.

Her flat was a huge place she had bought when she really couldn't afford to buy. A year after opening the restaurant, when all her money should've been ploughed back into it. She'd been walking past this estate agent's window, seen it featured and just stood staring at it through the window. It was set in one of those Victorian blocks, five or six floors high. Even through the pictures she could sense the feel of the place. Two huge bedrooms she could shape into little islands of their own. A reception room, a kitchen with windows all around, flooding it with light. Without even putting foot inside the place, by picture alone, Ella could smell the stripped floorboards that flushed naked throughout the whole place and sparkled where the sunlight hit them. She knew they smelt of sweet milky, warm oak. It would be a great smell to fall asleep and wake up to. She went in and bought the place straight off sight unseen.

Ludo had insisted on lunch at her place where they could talk, but they were in bed. She was sitting up, puffing on a Marlboro, looking down at him flat on his back with his eyes closed. He was still breathing heavily from their lovemaking and she traced a line of sweat from his hairline streaking down past his ear, running away into her sheets. She knew he wasn't at ease, knew he was nervously trying to pick a moment to say something to her and had been for over a week now. Weary of avoiding him, she had agreed to the quiet lunch at her flat. She had no idea what he wanted to say to her and as soon as she walked in, she'd kicked off her shoes, sat down and waited for him to speak. But he'd said nothing. She'd waited, but he'd said nothing. Instead he'd started a kiss that had ended up with them in bed.

She touched the sweat on his face and his eyes flew open and looked up at her. She smiled at him, but he was all over the place and couldn't smile back. Ella tried to ignore the panic she saw in him and tried to warm him by laying herself on top of him, taking care to cock the cigarette away from him when she kissed him.

'Looked like you were falling asleep on me.'

'No!' he said.

'I mean, we both have to get back to work, don't we?'

She was being obliging, falling just short of asking him what it was he had to say to her. Sometimes, when she knew she loved him, she wanted to accommodate him more than she wanted to accommodate herself. Now she wanted him just to stop and tell her whatever it was he was trying to avoid telling her.

'I'll get lunch,' he said.

'I'm not hungry,' she said, hoping to hold him with it. But he'd already shot up, grabbed his trousers and headed out through the bedroom door. Annoyed, Ella had to finish her cigarette before she could get up and get dressed.

She was pouring herself a drink when the phone rang. In the kitchen Ludo was praying she would let the machine pick it up. He had found some salad and bread and was putting it together with no ease at all. He knew what he was about to propose, but he was confused. Even he could-n't be that scared about suggesting a business proposition to her?

Back in the lounge, Ella was watching the banks of her river flooding. The box in her head had sprung open and everything had spilled out. All her terrors, all her precious thoughts fell slap bang on the oak floor, into the bright open light, and then disappeared between the cracks. She couldn't sit, couldn't put the drink down, she just stood listening to the voice on the end of the phone like she was commanded to do that and nothing else.

'You all right?' Ludo asked, standing in the doorway with the tray for two.

'Will you . . . ? I need to . . .' She was handing him the phone and pointing to the bedroom.

Ludo put the tray on the table, moved to her and took the phone from her, covering the mouthpiece with his hand. He watched her go into her bedroom and close the door behind her, listened for the click indicating that she had picked up the extension and then promptly hung up. If he had to pick the start of the moment that set her off this time, he would pick that phone call.

He sat pondering what could be wrong, then picked up his socks and shoes from where he had dragged them off when they'd started making love. He didn't touch a drop of the food or take a drink of the wine. He was waiting. When she came out, she looked as though life had played a dirty trick on the order of her world.

'Can you leave, please?' she said.

'I thought we were going to talk?'

'I have to be some place.'

'Where?' He stood up, full of concern.

Ella took a drink from the glass in her hand as she moved towards the front door. She was hoping that just like that he'd pick up his jacket and follow, but he didn't. He stood where he was and watched her trying to work out what was wrong. She opened the door and held it open for him to leave.

'Is it bad news?'

'Were you listening?'

'No! He sounded hurt that she could even think he would. Ella was digging deep to stop herself hurting him, she just wanted him to leave.

'I thought we were gonna have a chat?'

'Not today.' It was all she could give, because even with her news she was still thinking today was one of those days that opened itself up to her as a wonderful revelation that she loved him.

Watching her hand on the door, he thought he saw it

trembling. He got to thinking she was holding on to the door like that because she couldn't hold herself up any other way. He got to thinking she wanted him to hold on to her, because she could find no way of holding on to herself.

'Ell . . . ?'

The glass in her hand shot out, to the left of him and past him, in the direction of a very expensive vase. They watched the glass flying through the air and then smashed into the vase. Ludo had given her that vase. It showed two naked bodies spiralling round and round, fusing into one. Ella had never cared for the sentiment it expressed, but it was worth something, she knew. Everything Ludo gave her was worth something. Always sentiment, usually money. This once exquisite piece of unity split into shreds of separation that then began cascading down on the floor. Within a blink it was over. All that she had fought to stave off came crashing down on her.

She wouldn't look at him. She held her head straight, still holding on to the open door, embarrassed at her own behaviour, but refusing to admit it.

Ludo went over to the shattered vase, got down on all fours and began plucking the razor-sharp shreds into a pile. The vase had come apart in long slivers that had spread themselves into a rough circle. For safety Ludo was operating on the outskirts of this circle.

From the open door Ella could see sadness hugged around him like it was all he had. She was fighting with herself but still heard herself say, 'Leave it.' And she gave it as little oxygen as possible.

The sadness wouldn't let Ludo stop.

By the door Ella was growing angrier, watching his hands collecting the glass. His head was low and with every piece lower still.

'Leave it!' Ella screamed again, and this time she rushed towards him to the edge of the circle of glass.

Ludo, on his knees, watched her bare feet move about inside the circle and every time she moved, she somehow missed a piece of glass. Every time she put a foot down, it was an inch to the right of a sliver, it was an inch in front, behind or to the left. Ludo watched like a man sitting in a minefield, knowing one false move on his part would set it off. Fearfully watching Ella's nimble feet, he knew she'd realise her situation and the sheer terror of it would freak her out. Then he took a step inside the glass circumference, scooped her into his arms and held her like a precious thing he'd rescued from certain tragedy. He felt her settle into his body, like the end of a nagging ache.

'Marry me?' It jumped first out of his guts and then clean out of his mouth and he suddenly knew why the quiet lunch he had wanted had nothing to do with BrightWell's. It shook him that he could have hidden it so well from himself.

Usually Ella knew everything to expect from Ludo. But she hadn't been expecting that.

In the distance the lights overhung the road like lights above a stage. Ella was on the phone to her maitre d', but watching eagerly for a lit area of the road. She didn't know what time it was. Her maitre d' sounded groggy with sleep as his voice tried to reassure her her instructions had been carried out. He was reeling off the number of customers they'd had and who they'd been. She wasn't satisfied but she let him go.

A sign pointed out the north onwards and forwards.

'Pinky! Dat you?'

She wondered how easy it had been finding her. She liked to believe she was alone and that no family anywhere knew where she had gone or how she had made a life these past thirteen years. But someone had remembered seeing an interview in one of the black newspapers a while back – she had agreed to do it for the publicity it would bring her business – and that was how they had tracked her down. The voice was Poor Cousin Winston's. Her mother had dropped dead three days ago, the funeral was on Thursday and she was expected.

Ella's immediate reaction, as she had clutched herself on the edge of her bed, was had Daddy Ned died too?

'You Daddy Ned?' Poor Cousin Winston asked back, lost. Ella recalled Poor Cousin Winston was always lost. 'No! Aunty Brownie! I seh is Aunty Brownie drop dead!'

'Right,' was all Ella said and then there was a pause as she began to take it in and Poor Cousin Winston let her.

The truth of it was that Ella couldn't begin to imagine one without the other, but if she had to then she couldn't imagine Daddy Ned without Brownie. She could just about imagine Brownie without him. Brownie had resources to cope with all that the shift of life could hand her. But Daddy Ned! He was small. Like a distant star in a vast black sky. Brownie was the sure, full moon magnified a dozen times.

Ella couldn't remember how old she was when she first heard the story of her parents' first meeting Back Home in Jamaica, but she remembered always where she was on hearing it. Hidden under the huge oak table that stood in the centre of the dining area of the kitchen of the Pink House. She had learnt quite early that the best conversations were to be heard under the table, not sitting at it. When Brownie left the kitchen, the other women who congregated at the Pink House always poked around there, they were in and out of covered pots, and would always convene at the oak table with hot coconut drops and real Jamaican hot chocolate served with grated nutmeg on top. And then they would chat.

The conversation always started the same way and it always started with the same person. From the cold of Aunt Julie's mouth – her mother's one true blood sister – the words would fall into the warmth of Brownie's kitchen and the words were always these. 'How did a woman with the features of my sister Brownie manage to get a pretty man as Ned Brightwell?' Around her mother and father Aunt Julie had a jealousy that was so animated it walked and talked.

To Aunt Julie's question all that the other women could do was laugh. This was a family bitch. If anyone was going to badmouth Brownie, it would be her one true blood sister Julie, and Aunt Julie would tell them that if any of them tried. There was loyalty in this bad mind.

'And keep him too!' Aunt Julie always finished her question with those four words and they would send the congregation of women rocking and rolling with laughter. Six of them or more. Friends from Back Home, neighbours. One of them would fart and Ella would hold her breath, fanning the tablecloth like a bird trapped, but desperate not to be discovered. A hand slapped down on the table, upsetting something. It was a mug of chocolate flashing over the white cloth and then dripping through the linen, through a little knot in the wood, down on Ella.

Over the rocking, rolling laughter another voice: 'Them say, she see him, she want him and she have him!'

It was Miss Betty-Crow, the youngest of the bunch, who carried herself badly and had to be told every now and again that she needed to attend to her personal hygiene more frequently that she currently did. Miss Betty-Crow

was well qualified to utter such a sentence, after all back in
Jamaica she had more or less done the same thing: she had
seen him, she had wanted him, and she had had him! The
him being her first husband, Mr Gladstone Julian. Miss
Betty-Crow, who had simply been christened Betty, had
acquired the 'Crow' because of how she had married Mr
Gladstone Julian: on his deathbed. Mr Gladstone Julian had
earned a little money building houses and when ill health
forced him to stop work for the first time in his seventy-
odd years, he had taken a young nurse to assist him on his
way to his last breath. The nurse had been Miss Betty. Miss
Betty had not been in his service for more than two weeks
before she took Mr Gladstone Julian off his deathbed,
dressed him, strapped him in his wheelchair and invited
the pastor round to marry them. The piquancy of the tale
was this: she dressed him in his best black suit and in his
stiffest white shirt so'til he looked like John Crow. John
Crow was the colloquial name given to the huge scavenger
birds that circled awaiting some poor unfortunate. They
say the first John Crow was a preacher man who never
went anywhere without his dog collar. Some say he was a
schoolteacher who always wore a pristine white collar,
black bow tie and black jacket. Whoever the first John
Crow was, it was an appropriate appendage to Miss Betty's
name.

Then she moved to Hanville and got a new white husband, when white husbands for black women were unheard
of. And for the life of them, none of the women could work
out why, once Miss Betty-Crow had inherited all that Mr

Gladstone Julian had, she had left the island to come and struggle in a country like this.

'But Miss Betty-Crow!' came Aunt Julie's voice. 'How could a woman with the features of my sister Brownie even presume that such a beautiful man as Ned Brightwell would want she?'

And then another: 'But he did!'

And then another: 'And he still do.'

And then another: 'And passionately!'

And then: 'Oh, g-g-g-go on! Leave poor Bro-Brownie. All a you too bad!'

The last speaker was Miss Nugent, the woman from over the road, who washed the biggest, whitest sheets in the whole neighbourhood and had a husband who didn't think nothing of knocking her brains out over them – even before they were dry. They say she developed her stutter not long after marrying Sam Nugent.

'Obeah!' Aunt Julie threw at them.

'Nothing but that, sister dear!' Miss Tam. Three streets away, worked as a nurse. Four sons and a husband who had to bring his wage packet home every Friday and sit in with her until work on Monday morning. One time Miss Tam was absent from the congregation – on account of her husband, Mr Tam, had gone missing the whole weekend and the shame of it kept her inside. The story from above the table was that Mr Tam was holed up with some 'nasty white woman with draws as big as the town hall, that had been visited by more people than the said building!' Anyway, on this day, when Miss Tam was absent through shame, Ella heard

the story of how one of Miss Tam's sons, Wayne (pro-
nounced Way-On by Miss Tam), had been arrested for
burgling the richest white house in town. Expert knowledge
shifted between two scenarios. The first always began and
ended with a wink. It was that Way-On had been invited in
to do some chore by the lady of the house late one night
when her husband was out of town, only for the husband to
return and get the wrong end of the story. The second was
that Way-On had simply jumped the fence in an attempt at
a short cut home. Whichever piece of expert knowledge
was closest to the truth, there was no dispute, Way-On had
been caught where he had no business. As if these two
events weren't disgrace enough for one woman, when the
police came for the young man Miss Tam fought so bad and
so hard that she put two of them in hospital before they held
her down and got her into the car, where she lifted up her
skirt and shat on their seat. That was the disgrace!

'And I know the day!' announced Aunt Julie. 'I know the
exact day she work the obeah.' At this point she always
cleared her throat as if she believed she had something
important to say and she wanted her audience ready to
hear it. The women were hooked into her. It wasn't as
though they'd never heard the story before – they had,
many times before – but Aunt Julie was speaking and they
were listening.

'It was the day Ned come to Old Yard come ask Mamma
and Puppa for me. Him was such a gentleman, him bring a
whole bag a yam come throw down in front a Puppa.
Brownie did gone down banana walk gone pick banana for

the pot. When she come back, Mamma say to her, "Go put on the coffee pot." When Brownie come! Make me tell you what she have on.'

'Tell we, sister Julie.'

Aunt Julie stood up from her seat and took up a pose that Ella never saw. All she saw was Aunt Julie's feet turned inwards and her knees were knocking.

'Make me tell you. She have on a frock, you see! If it drop out on Bell Vue Road, you wouldn't even see the difference between the two.' Bell Vue Road had just had a new layer of tar laid. 'And the frock was suppose to be white.'

The table rocked with laughter again. Aunt Julie was soaring high.

'And how you did look, Aunt Julie?' It was a voice that could have come from a man listening to the love of his life as she related some unimportant fact, but he wanted to hear it just for the heck of hearing her voice and wonderful turn of phrase. It was Miss Tam's voice.

'Darling lady, me did have on a deep-blue frock that lick me here.' Ella saw Aunt Julie's hand halfway up her calf. 'Me spend two day pressing me hair, and then me have on a hat to match the frock. And some a Mamma toilet water. Me look good and me smell good.'

'That's right!'

'And, make me tell you! I had only to look into the ugly face of my sister Brownie to see the scorn. To me dying day she always been jealous of me. She look on poor Ned and I know! I know! Is like Jesus Christ himself come off the cross, bend down whisper inna me ears . . .' Only at Aunt

Julie's feet would Jesus Christ bend and whisper. '. . . and say to me, Julie Mundle, follow that bitch outta yard!'

'That's right,' one of them said.

'And I follow and I watch that bitch as the coffee boil.'

'And you see it?'

'With me own two eye them!' Ella saw Aunt Julie's hand swoop down to lift the tail of her frock before she continued. 'She lift up her frock, push up her hand, take out a hand of blood and mix it in with poor Ned coffee.'

'Obeah!' said one. 'Obeah!' Then another. And the word bounced around the women from one to the other.

None of the women ever asked why Aunt Julie hadn't stopped Brownie serving Ned with such a tainted cup of coffee.

'You see. You spit in the sky, and it shall fall in you face.' Aunt Julie finished most stories with this dictum. It never occurred to her that by the way she lived her life she was storing up buckets of sputum that would one day come pouring down from high heaven on her coiffed locks. And she made sense of her dictum with the line, 'That's why all but one a the pickney them ugly, bad blessing take her ras!'

'Bad blessing take her ras!' It wasn't this end piece that had captured Ella's mind. Sometimes when she recalled the story she didn't even remember Aunt Julie had said it and she didn't know what it meant anyway. It was the words before that that had struck her. 'That's why all but one a the pick-ney them ugly!' At the time Ella was left wondering which Brightwell child, in Aunt Julie's mind, was the one? Whatever age she had been when she had first heard the

story of her parents' meeting, that was the first time Ella
became wise to the notion that within the Brightwell
family there was such a thing as 'the one'. Previously they
were just the Brightwells who were all-enveloping and all-
overpowering. The minute she heard such a thing it began
to control her and she quickly decided she must be the one.
It made sense. It was the difference she had felt from the
beginning. This idea reared itself up before her as an explanation of why she of all the Brightwells stood alone, when
within the family of them, everyone else seemed to have
someone. Brownie and Daddy Ned had each other. Donna
and Della, eleven months apart, had each other. Lambert and
Kellit had each other as the eldest boys, a year apart. Patrick
and Johno were twins, joined by nature. Even the harridan
Aunt Julie could be said to have Brownie. But she, Pinkette
Brightwell, had no one. That was what it must be! She was
just too damn pretty to need anyone else and all the other
Brightwells were just too damn ugly to stand alone.

What it all meant, though, she had no idea.

For the past twenty or so miles, Ella had been aware the road was getting narrower. With every mile that took her closer to Hanville, the width of the road decreased until she had the idea that if she travelled all the way north, as far as this road could take her, past Hanville even, the road would squeeze her out and slam her life shut and over for ever.

Ten miles out from the sniff of Hanville, she began to panic. If there was one thing Ella could do remarkably well, it was panic. She like no one could panic the simplest thing into the most animated spectacle of 3-D proportions. She alone could shape drums and dark clouds which she could never control. And so, as she got closer to Hanville, the first murmur of a drum began to tap gently but menacingly inside her.

As if it was the next second, she pulled the car to the left and stopped on a grass verge. But it couldn't have been the next second, because now the town of Hanville was half a mile away, not ten, and the Bridge was there, just up ahead

of her. Ten miles had vanished just like that. Over the Bridge
and you were in Hanville. It was official. A few minutes ago
it had been dark; now suddenly, as she looked at the Bridge,
the sun was beginning to rise above it. A dimmer switch was
being turned up slowly and she sat at the wheel of her car
watching the transformation of the Bridge from darkness to
light.

She got out of the car, moved to the side of the road and
looked at everything laid out before her – it was all there for
no one but her. Standing on the bank of a high grass verge
that directly overlooked the town, she was standing on top of
Hanville. She didn't know what time she had set off from
London, only that it had been dark. She didn't know what
time it now was, only that the sun was rising. Deep into the
gully she traced it. Half the town was in darkness, half in
light. Her eyes followed the shadow as it crept over and
lifted from the sleeping town like a giant rising from its bed.
Down one hill her eyes traced it, across the flat, open town,
up the opposite hill, until it disappeared completely and the
town lay woken to sunlight. It was like a man falling off a
woman, leaving her hitched open for all who happened by.

Hanville was still the same. It was set in a gully either side
of two huge hills, it had a river running through it and
houses that fanned out around it. The church with its
crooked spire stuck out, the highest building in town. It was
set that way on account of the builders a century and a half
ago who couldn't agree how to finish it and had wrangled
for decades, until the elements had fixed the spire the way it
now stood. To the right was the Hanville School for Infant,

Primary and Secondary Education – three stages lumped together with no distinction or care. Then Badlands Woodlands, a dense patch where no sunlight penetrated. Over all of it swept the eyes of someone who knew it, someone who could put a story to each and every tree, each and every brick visible at this distance, and even to those that were not. She had been gone thirteen years and nothing had changed. She thought that, had she remained for those years, everything would have changed.

She had no way to make herself believe her mother could be dead and not already awake in the Pink House singing Sam Cooke and preparing breakfast for the Brightwells. Ella tried repeating the word 'dead' over and over to herself, but even that didn't make it real to her. She got to thinking maybe Poor Cousin Winston had made some mistake in ringing her up and telling her Brownie was dead. The sun had risen this morning! How could Brownie be dead down there and the sun have risen?

As her eyes stayed on Hanville, praying it would give up some explanation of how her mother could be dead, Ella heard her mother's voice in her mind: 'That's why the trees so big!'

Ella looked at the Bridge, expecting to see Brownie striding over it. In the years she had been gone, she had never heard her mother's voice with more animation, had not smelt her mother's smell more clearly.

She heard it again. 'That's why the trees so big!'

The murmurs of the drum were developing. But she'd stand her ground and try and force the woman away. She would not run. On that she was clear. If she could panic to exceptional proportions, Ella could also control herself to an equal degree.

She closed her eyes, trying to block the sight that had triggered such clarity of voice, and held the breath from her nose praying the smell would leave her. But it didn't matter, she didn't need the breath in her nose to know the smell, didn't need ears to hear those words again, to fix the moment in time when her mother had first said them. What she could not grasp, even now, was what they had meant or what had triggered them. She and Brownie had been out walking and were at the time surrounded by trees. There had been a silence of something like five minutes. Before there'd been some talk about something Brownie was looking forward to cooking, and then the statement: 'That's why the trees so big!'

They'd been walking through a field on the edge of the dense wood the locals called Badlands Woodlands, officially called Woodlands. It had gained its name on account of a notorious incident that occurred there seventy-odd years ago, long before the first black people arrived and settled in Hanville.

The incident concerned Anna Street. Anna Street was walking home one bright summer's evening when two men stepped out of the woods and asked the way to somewhere. Anna Street was the town free spirit before the town had the words to describe her. She had grand ideas about where she would go and what she would do. The two men, rumoured to be Barry Roses and Clive Armstrong, were young men about town who were just discovering that really and truly the world did belong to them and they could do anything they felt like as they went about attaining it. They asked the way to somewhere and Anna Street refused to answer, knowing them to be locals, and so knowing they knew exactly where the place they asked after was. Anna Street didn't get much further on her walk; she was dragged into the woods. The next day someone found her body in Badlands Woodlands. The day after that they found her feet on the Bridge as if they were walking. Even though they'd been severed from her body, they were up on the Bridge, one behind the other, planted in a walking motion – one way or another Anna Street meant to leave Hanville. To this day, out of fear or respect for Anna Street, most locals walked around or alongside Badlands Woodlands. Only Brownie and her children walked through it.

The sun was high and warm but as Ella followed her mother into Badlands Woodlands, she suddenly felt cold and the darkness of the place bothered her. Brownie was running from tree to tree, hugging trunk after trunk, looking up at each tree, and that was when she said it. She finished her nonsense statement with the explanation ''cause it always raining'.

This was the woman who was always embarrassing her, Ella thought. This was the woman who would think nothing of coming up to school with that morning's baking, to sit and have morning tea with the headmaster, and have it regardless of the fact that he was in the middle of teaching maths to a class of eleven-year-olds. This was the woman who would fart during parents' evening and then not have the sense to say, 'My God! Did you hear that? Can you smell that? I wonder who that could be?' If Ella and her mother got through a week, she could count anything between forty-three and one hundred and four times that she wanted to slap her mother or kick her in the shins. On this occasion, Ella's only stroke of luck was that the statement about rain and trees and the hugging of tree trunks came when they were alone.

Her mother's love, outside the family and cooking, was trees. Brownie felt trees were people who had died. In a tree she could find her dead parents, a dead friend or stranger. Brownie was what they called 'receptive'. Ella couldn't remember a time she didn't know her mother had this ability to talk to trees. What she did discover as she grew was when Brownie was more receptive to conversing with trees, particularly the one in their yard: usually after Brownie and Daddy Ned had had one of their louder, more combustible 'meetings' was the best time to find the channels between Brownie and the neighbourhood trees open.

Ella spent much of her time on the ledge of her bedroom windowsill just looking. The ledge couldn't have been more than eight inches wide, but Ella felt safe there and Brownie knew she was safe and would be even after she had taken the leap Brownie knew was as inevitable and necessary as a living breath. Ella's bedroom overlooked the back yard where she had always wanted a garden of grass and flowers.

Instead they had a garden of herbs and vegetables that Brownie had a tendency to work at night. But spectacular of spectacular! Overlooking the vegetables, the herbs, over-looking the Pink House itself, was an oak tree. Ella spent much of her time just looking at this oak tree. This oak tree had surveyed its domain for many, many decades, would do so for many more, and this oak tree was dazzling. Idiot or genius, someone had, decades before the Brightwell family bought and populated the Pink House, planted an oak tree in their yard – or maybe someone had built a house in the home of an oak tree, as Brownie liked to believe. On calm days its branches would brush up against Ella's bedroom window like a many-fingered, craggy black hand, and on stormy nights it happened a few times that the fingers would burst through the window and shower Ella and her bed with glass like it was trying to come inside. One time it happened twice in one stormy week and Daddy Ned got his tallest ladder, his biggest saw, his widest anger, and pre-pared to plant foot on the first rung. But something told him to look up. There was his Brownie, tent flapping in the wind, dangerous hair twisting like a mighty tornado, hold-ing on to the offending branch with great dexterity and seeming as at home there as Ella on the eight-inch ledge. Daddy Ned had never seen her more beautiful. And he had to admire. He had to withdraw, go into the House, up to Ella's bedroom and turn one of the two beds that stood side by side away from the window. It was into this tree that Brownie waited patiently for her youngest child to take her inevitable leap.

'Just listen. Give the tree a chance,' Brownie would say joyfully.

Ella just never believed it. She knew her mother was mad; what she didn't know was whether her mother knew she was.

'That's why the trees so big, 'cause it always raining,' she heard again, and her eyes snapped open like a lid on a box.

Above, the sky had gathered and flung itself together and settled over Hanville. That was how quick and fickle the mood was up here, and rain immediately began to fall. Ella hadn't seen rain like it since she'd left the place. As she hurried back to her car she could hear the rain chasing after her like footsteps. It spurred her on faster and she remembered it was one aspect of living this far from civilisation: people this far north had the power, by their very mood and outlook, to affect the weather.

Locked in the shell of her car, the rain beating down, threatening to smash her windscreen, Ella was shaking and realised she had been the whole time she'd stood on the verge looking down at Hanville. She was jumping and shivering like a habitual drunk the morning after. She closed her eyes, taking deep breaths, trying to calm down and screw the panic back into its box. But she found she couldn't or didn't want to. There was nothing she could do but listen to the drum swooping at an extravagant rhythm and banging it out through her guts. When it got this bad, when it got deafening like this, Ella knew what she had to do. It was what she always did. She started up the car, flicked the stick into gear and turned the wheel into a right-hand lock. The car went forwards and then spun into a perfect arc, driving back where it had come from, driving away from the Bridge and away from Hanville.

She felt the car was eating up the road, faster and faster; she was driving for her life, running from the place that just filled her completely. She'd been vindicated! She couldn't be expected just to walk back into all of that. She couldn't be expected, no matter who was dead. The further she went, the stiller the drum became until it slowly fell silent alto-gether. The second the drum fell silent within her, she slapped her mind bang shut and tight on it.

After an hour of clear, free-flowing road, her car got stuck in the jam of people dashing south. Just like her brain then, the road back to London was jammed. Her car slowed to a halt and she searched for her last cigarette. Even in the boot she didn't have any. That was how fucked up she'd been since hearing the news. She never ran out of cigarettes and though it looked like she chain-smoked, she never smoked more than a pack a day. She'd have to stop and get more, there was no way she could stay in this traffic, which looked like it was backed up for miles, without cigarettes. Thank God almighty, just up ahead she could see a service stop. As she noticed this, she also noticed that it had stopped raining. In fact, along the road it clearly hadn't rained for days or more. Ella knew the rain had stopped the moment she had pulled away from the Bridge.

She got out of her car and walked towards the service

station. The weather was bright and breezy. As she came out, ripping a packet of Marlboro open, sticking one in her mouth and lighting it, the light was now fading quickly. Ella threw the spare packs in the boot and got back in her car. Cigarette in hand, she watched as the sky opened and it began to pour. It had taken roughly one hour, but it had caught up with her. Miles from the Pink House, miles from where no Brightwell but she had any business, it had found her. She started the car and headed back to Hanville.

The Bridge took her down to the edge of Badlands Woodlands and for some reason she wouldn't discuss with herself, she avoided looking directly into it. The funeral was at three. She'd turn up, crack her face, see Brownie lowered into the ground, swim elegantly through the whole thing, allowing not even one iota of mess to touch her, and she could be gone and satisfied by five, half five the latest. She kept her head straight on the road that ran parallel to Badlands Woodlands and drove. If she remembered rightly the road would take her away and past Badlands Woodlands and deposit her in town a mile later. The road was narrow, wide enough for one car only. It was more a track than a road and Ella couldn't believe that this was still the only road Hanville had to welcome a stranger. She couldn't quite believe they hadn't chopped into Badlands Woodlands, made some of it theirs and widened the road – even for commercial reasons. Instead she knew they'd left it there intact as some kind of monument to nonsense.

On the track up ahead, a young woman was walking with her son, right in the middle, holding hands and walking like they had the whole day. Ella did not. She honked her horn and she did it in good time so they would fall to the side and give her right of way. As soon as Ella's palm fell on the horn, a flock of crows in a tree took to the sky like bad news. Ella's eyes followed them up and away and wondered what it meant. Nothing was inconsequential in Hanville, it all meant something. The woman and boy hadn't moved, they just carried on walking in that same all-day way. Like they didn't hear Ella and her car behind them. Like the crows hadn't signalled her return. Ella honked again, longer, harder, and still they either didn't hear or ignored what they heard and carried on. Ella could not believe it. They weren't going to move. She could travel slowly behind them, swing the car into the edge of Badlands Woodlands and go around them, or run them down. Tempting as the last option was, she swung the car out to the left of them to pass. As she came alongside them, Ella looked angrily into their faces for some kind of explanation, but they only smiled and carried on walking like they had the day to do this and nothing else. Ella shook her head and tore up the track.

Hours and hours of fear was what she had lived through so far. Fear that almost stopped your breath, fear that once it got bigger and braver would know how to stop your heart. Fear that could make you see fleeting shadows through your windscreen. That made you dam up memories that were just too awful to live. Fear like that was exhausting and needed a strong will.

Ella hit town, gathering herself for the fight. And immediately she didn't know which way to go. After standing looking down at the whole of it not two hours ago and picking out this landmark and that landmark, in the face of it, she was lost. She had come to a halt at what looked like the main Hanville Road. There was only one Hanville Road when she lived in the place, but this didn't look like it. And if this wasn't it, where was it and what was this? It was quiet, four or five people going about their business, a couple of cars trundling this way and that way, midmorning and one of the handful of businesses was just opening up. So Hanville!

But, she was reasoning with herself, Badlands Woodlands looked like Badlands Woodlands, the Bridge looked like the the Bridge, so this must be Hanville. It had a feel to it that she knew and remembered, but for the life of her Ella couldn't pick which way to go with any certainty. She could go left, right or carry straight on – or she could go back the way she had come. She scanned up and down looking for something, anything that would help her and she saw the Old Yew Inn, which she remembered all the black people called the Hole You In. The last year Ella had lived in Hanville she'd spent every Thursday and Friday night wiping tables for Mr and Mrs Dougie.

Mr and Mrs Dougie had what the locals called 'an eternal argument around bread!' Specifically how much to order for the following week. She always thought four loaves, he always thought three, otherwise they would have one loaf left over at the end of a week that was turning out, like all weeks past, particularly slow. The thing about the Dougies was that if they ever stopped arguing about bread, the inn would've been packed daily – by Hanville standards anyway – and they would've needed more bread than either of them could fathom, but because of the inclement atmosphere in the inn, hardly any Hanville local could stomach even a cup of coffee there, much less a slice of bread.

When Ella was six, she witnessed her first Dougie bread argument. She was out shopping with Brownie, Donna and Della when a commotion lit up the Hanville horizon. Between the locals commotions were apt to explode out of nothing. Hanville, both black and white, was like one big family, members of which every now and then got on each other's nerves. Someone had to stamp and shout out just how much they got on each other's nerves, before they could quieten down. Only after this could the world according to Hanville continue turning. Rarely, though, did any commotion explode with such spectacle as that of the Dougies. The result of which was that the back of the Old Yew Inn blew clean off.

The Dougies had forgotten the stove. Their argument had brought them out of the inn and deposited them in the middle of the Hanville Road in front of any local who cared to stop and look, and they all did, because Mrs Dougie had a gun on Mr Dougie. Mrs Dougie was a small woman who couldn't even look you in the eye when she served you her speciality of fried bread and blood sausage, but somewhere, somehow, she had got herself a gun and was aiming it at Mr Dougie and backing him out of the inn arse naked. Mr Dougie was protesting, trying to calm her, but every time he tried she fired off a shot and it made him quieten down until the next time, which Ella observed came too quick and fast for a man who was in serious peril of losing his life.

'This is the last time you go behind my back and change the fucking bread order! You hear me, Mr Dougie!' Mrs Dougie bellowed.

The Dougies were so angry and caught up in their domestics they had no idea where they were and under what circumstance. 'And I told you, you keep on ordering one loaf too many and in ten years' time we gonna be bankrupt out in the streets, flat on our behinds!'

Someone laughed, Ella didn't see who. It was then that Mr Dougie suddenly became aware that behind him he had an audience and the audience was swelling.

Mrs Dougie fired off another shot and most of the spectators ducked for cover. Mr Dougie ran in the direction of the inn, trying to save first his life and then what little dignity he might have left. With the firing of the shot, Donna and Della started to cry and simultaneously both reached for Brownie's hands. Ella, though, was bug-eyed with fascination. As Mr Dougie made it to the inn another shot rang out; the bullet flew clean past him, through the inn, through the open kitchen door and lodged itself in the stove. The stove blew up and the back of the inn shot up into the air. It was the loudest bang Ella had ever heard, and the first time she had seen a fire flare out of control. It looked like flickering fireworks leaping into the air, like chattering tongues looping the loop, each vying for the wildest tale. For Donna and Della, once they had stopped crying, the main features were the gun, the argument, Mr Dougie's arse! What Ella loved and was fascinated by was those fireworks. Brownie knew this before her youngest daughter knew it herself.

Years later the Dougies were unmasked as brother and sister. After the initial scandal, Hanville left them alone to conduct their lives in the privacy of their home as only Hanville could and would. Ella observed that Brownie alone never seemed shocked by the Dougie revelation.

The last time Ella had stepped through the Old Yew Inn doors and out into the Hanville night was the last night she had spent in Hanville. It had been a Thursday and she remembered it as a Thursday because the inn had seven records, one for each day of the week, and on that day it was Elvis Presley day: Thursday.

Elvis Presley was singing from the old gram. Ella was sitting at one of the tables reading some magazine. The inn was simply one room with a few tables. The room was dark so you never really saw the corners. Like stuff was hiding in those corners, even in bright daylight, that's how it was.

Into the inn, on that last Elvis Presley Thursday, walked Brownie. With her, was one of Ella's twin brothers, Patrick. Ella looked up from her magazine and looked at Brownie. She couldn't look at Patrick, it was how the two of them were since the accident. But she could feel straight away that Patrick wasn't comfortable. Ella had no idea what could possibly have upset Brownie enough to drag Patrick down to the Old Yew Inn when Brownie was the kind of mother who encouraged all her children to run wild like gardens and loved to watch them do just that. Standing by the door, both were breathing heavily. Brownie returned Ella's gaze; Patrick's eyes were fixed on his feet kicking at the mangy lino. Ella was waiting for one or both of them to say something. Then Patrick's fear infected her. She pushed the chair from beneath herself, stood up and faced Brownie. Ella had no idea how it would go but she knew from the feel between them that it would go.

Tapping on her car window. Ella dragged her eyes from the inn and looked to her right, through the window. A policeman was tapping and smiling at her. It took a moment for Ella to fall completely out of the memory, press a button and let the window glide down.

'You lost?' the policeman asked. He was being friendly.

'No.' She pressed the button, the window slid upwards and she drove off.

Inside the drum started up.

Ludo had left several messages. Ella couldn't believe he was the only person in the whole world who wanted to talk to her. She had other people in her life. She did! So why was he the only person who had left her messages over the past two days? Granted he'd left five, but still he was the only person.

The first was desperate, on a par with the three she'd picked up at the service stop. But the fifth, well, that was different! For a start it said he was leaving. Ella couldn't believe it; where the hell was he leaving to and why today of all days? Didn't he know she was returning to Hanville, the place she hated most in the world, to bury her mother? But of course he didn't. She hadn't told him anything. She'd told her staff she had to go away on personal business but she hadn't told Ludo.

She jammed her finger on the button again.

'Hi, Ell!' And once and for all she was gonna get him to stop using that stupid name.

'It's me Ludo.' And after eight years together, didn't he think she knew his voice by now?

'Just to let you know I've decided to leave you in peace. I'm gonna go to Australia for a few weeks and spend some time with Mother and her new husband. Sorry we didn't get to talk before I went. Bye!'

Bye! Ella sat staring at the phone in her hand. All she warranted was a bye and that was it? The end? After eight years? Ella began to punch out Ludo's number. She was miles away, on this most traumatic day, and he was about to hop on a plane to Australia.

'Ludo! Ludo!' she was yelling at his home answer phone. 'If you're there you better pick up. It's me, Ella.'

Either he wasn't there or he wouldn't pick up. She punched out his office number and spoke to his secretary Jodie, who tried to tell her Ludo had left for the day.

'It's the middle of the morning!'

Jodie repeated what she had just said, all gentle and polite, but Ella heard none of it. 'Put him on!'

Ludo's partner had to come on and tell her it was true, Ludo had left for the day to arrange his trip; after all, he only had a few hours to his flight.

Ella melted away and disconnected the call. No one else had called her for two days. None of her so-called friends, none of the men she sometimes cheated on Ludo with, none of them except Ludo had called her and he was about to leave her. Something soaked through her, spreading from the core of her to the extremities of her fingers and toes, and left her cold like a body passing by her grave. The anger came into her again and she was punching out his mobile number. She had to speak to him. She had never had to speak to him before. She didn't dare think what this new state meant. She just held the phone to her ear and didn't even realise the image of herself was akin to someone in prayer. The phone was engaged, so she left a message on his voice mail.

'Ludo, it's me. I've just got your message. You better call me, Ludo! You better . . .' She couldn't get her threat out, her voice was failing her and she didn't understand why. Her back stiffened and she pressed the button to end the call. She couldn't trust herself to continue and be heard that way, not by anyone.

So he was leaving her, backing away? She couldn't believe it. Hadn't their relationship always been guts and red and blood and stuff? Why had he suddenly gone soft on her, proposed and was running away?

As he had held her in the glass circle, she had felt him breathing on the side of her face. All Ella could think was that Ludo was trying to trap her, trying to do what she'd done to everyone she'd ever had a relationship with. No longer in control, she panicked, scurried off to her kitchen and started preparations to cook.

For a good few weeks now she had had her mind on something she wanted to cook – pepperpot soup. Callaloo, kale, okra, yam, coco, coconut milk, salt beef, pig's tail, green pepper, garlic, scallion and spinners – and whatsomore in this the most sophisticated of Western kitchens, she had them all. She set about the green soup, cutting up the salt beef into bits. Brownie used to call it her 'thinking dish'. Not because it required much thought, but because to prepare and cook it was so drawn out, it gave you time to think on whatever it was you wanted to think on.

Ella used to have the idea Brownie never thought about anything. Brownie just opened her mouth, or did something, and that was that. Surely if her mother thought about anything she wouldn't do or say a thing. Thought would surely send the idea straight from her mother's mind, since all that her mother said or did was so bizarre. The discovery that her mother had a 'thinking dish' was something Ella had difficulty with.

In Ella's lounge Ludo stood where she had left him on the broken glass. He didn't know what to do with himself. What he should say, if he should say anything. She hadn't bawled him out, maybe that was a good sign. Maybe he was in with a chance. He had decided to leave, picked up his jacket, shouted to her he would see her later and left.

'I'm going then,' Ella heard from the lounge as her head came out of the fridge, her hands holding a plate with a slab of salt beef.

Ella stopped dead and listened again. She was thinking on Ludo's 'I'm going then'. Did he want her to say something in response to it? Ella suddenly didn't know what to do. She had never not known what to do around Ludo before.

'I'll see you later then?' Ludo's voice came again in that same kind of rhetorical way.

Ella dropped the salt beef on the worktop. She wasn't

going to say anything, he'd have to leave and leave without a word from her.

And then 'Bye!' came in that same tone.

She could feel him in the other room, waiting, both of them holding the same breath between them.

She heard her front door bang shut. Quickly she had rushed into the lounge. Ludo wasn't there. Her eyes scanned the corners of the room where he could've been hiding but he wasn't there. As soon as it kicked into her brain that he had really gone, she had the feeling he had gone for good.

She was alone and always had been really. She took a step backwards and then she jumped in pain. She lifted her bare foot and saw a sliver of glass had punched through the tough exterior of her foot and made its way to the soft fleshy part. Immediately she dropped to her arse, cradled her foot and began pulling on the piece of glass. Her foot began to bleed and she was flooded with loneliness.

She played the message again – 'Hi, Ell! It's me, Ludo. Just to let you know I've decided to leave you in peace. I'm gonna go to Australia for a few weeks and spend some time with Mother and her new husband. Sorry we didn't get to talk before I went. Bye!'

Ella hushed herself with thoughts and promises until she felt brave. Her red car jerked into life and she went right. It was still very quiet where she was going and it felt kind of eerie because of it. She was on a road she remembered walking down as a miserable girl. She turned into a road and it was the road where the Pink House lived, would be, and seemed to breathe. It came into view straight as you rounded the corner. Sprawled slap bang, twice as big as any house on the street, it made you look at it. And there it still was, right where she had left it.

Big, pink and alive! As her car glided up the hill, that damn drum inside her started up again. It had returned with a vengeance, deciding this time against conventional beating, opting to perform great extravagant leaps in the pit of her stomach, clanging about like thunder. Ella began taking in great gulps of air as her body begged her to go faster, to please send more air to its lungs. She was doing her best but the sight of the House had thrown her. As soon as Ella clapped eyes on the House, it was like a person she had left behind when she never should have. She had read that people returning to a childhood scene were often struck by how much smaller the thing that had possessed them in childhood actually was now now they were adults. But not the Pink House.

Everything that had happened and was now happening in her life was about going back to what she had lived and left. Everything she had to make sense of was something she had lived through before. Around this mixing of the old with stuff masquerading as new, Ella knew she would flit until she stood and faced it down.

Ella pushed the door open and got out of her car. She threw her phone in her handbag, her bag over her shoulder, and locked the car.

At the gate Ella tried to gather herself. It used to be that when she stood on the pavement and craned her neck, she could just see the tip of the old oak tree in the back yard. But now her neck needed no craning; there it was, taller, more of an explosion over the roof, more commanding of an audience. Ella tried to stay calm. She pushed on through the gate and as soon as she did, people began jumping at her, touching her and running back to their cubbyholes before she could turn, see them and know them. All of them were real to her but to no one but her, all of them threatening to throw her to the ground in a faint. She ignored them. She pushed them away and ploughed on with the test she had set herself.

She walked on up the side entrance to the House, past the front door, which was never used, and through to the back gate, which was always used. Slowly her fingers went round the handle of the gate and her thumb pressed down on the catch. The gate creaked open in her hand and she was in the back yard. She stepped further into the yard and it was smaller than she remembered. Brownie's herbs were still in their corner, the vegetable patch in its place, and opposite them both someone had planted a much longed-for bed of flowers. On the far wall, piled high, were mountains of old newspapers. They were done up like they were waiting to be sent for recycling, only someone had forgotten them, leaving the mountains to grow and grow, sludging down into papier-mâché mounds by the seasons. Hanging on the line, for the whole world to see, like there was no shame in it at all, were Brownie's washed clothes. Ella stared at them. A pair of huge silk peach balloon drawers, a thermal vest Ella didn't remember her mother ever wearing, and a tent thing made out of kente cloth, all three flapping about in the warm breeze like Brownie herself were inside them. There was the oak tree in its place, making the place what it was. Which person had Brownie met in this tree? Every other tree she'd watched her mother acquaint herself with, Ella had found out from her who lived there, but never this one, and it seemed now a glaring oversight that she didn't know who lived inside the oak tree in the yard. Whoever it was, though, it wasn't anyone for Ella to be afraid of. And really, as she looked and wanted to be near it, it was the first time in years she had had no fear.

She was about to move towards the tree and do the most spontaneous thing she had done for a long time, she was about to climb it, when she heard something behind her. Without turning she listened to hear if it would come again. She knew the sound like she had last heard it only yesterday. She heard nothing. She waited for a good few seconds. There was still nothing but she was sure of what she had heard and slowly she began to turn. When she saw it she wanted to run and hide. The ease the oak tree had given her was gone and her fear was back. In front of Ella stood Brownie living large and doing a most natural thing. Brownie was painting the back gate. Up and down went her hand, dipping in the paint tin and emerging with a bright pink.

There and then, running was all it was about for Ella. But Brownie was blocking her escape, painting the very gate she needed to go through. Ella had an idea she could scale the fence, jump into next door's yard, head up the alley and escape to her car. She began to back away. Her brain was calculating: she would throw her shoes over first, rip a split in the side of her skirt for mobility . . . or no! She'd take the thing off. She'd go naked if it meant she could get away.

'Pinkette?'

The fear left her and was replaced by an old annoyance. How did Brownie know she was there? She hadn't turned. She hadn't seen. How did she know? The truth was Brownie always knew when someone was behind her and if it was one of her children or Daddy Ned, she knew which. Without ever needing to turn and see, Brownie always knew. One day Ella would tell Brownie how pissed she was by this omniscient ability.

'Pass me that fresh tin a paint by the shed,' came Brownie's living voice.

One day she would tell her; today was not the day. Ella looked by the shed and there was the fresh tin of paint requested by her mother. Without her eyes leaving her mother's back, Ella bent to pick up the paint and before she got it, she had the feeling someone else, other than her mother, was present. The back door was open and probably had been since the Thursday she had walked out. Standing at the back door, sucking on a sucker, half of it dribbling down her hand, was an ugly-looking kid, staring at her. It had great big uneven plaits that looked like coils of shit. Ella thought she knew the face the poor kid was forced to exhibit to the world for ever more, she thought it resembled someone from her past, but she didn't know who or what and she didn't care. The kid was wearing a sparkling clean summer frock that had been pressed to perfection. On her feet were extra-white ankle socks topped off with brown polished sandals – someone had turned the ugly kid out.

While she watched and was watched, Ella's hand was grasping for the tin of paint requested by her mother, but nothing was happening. Ella looked for the paint; the paint was gone. Ella looked for Brownie; Brownie was gone. Ella gasped, remembered where she was, realised she was making a fool of herself in front of the ugly kid, who found her too, too interesting, and straightened up.

'What you looking at?' Ella asked it.

It didn't answer. It just kept on sucking and sucking and staring and staring.

'Speak and understand English, do you?'

It continued to stare at her. Ella pushed inside past it and walked into the kitchen, half in pursuit of Brownie, half eager to get the whole Hanville/Pink House experience out the way. But Brownie had not rushed from the back gate to the kitchen. She was not now rising from some pot of steam, nose shifting from side to side, sniffing out some ingredient the pot was lacking, nor was she singing, coming through a door, opening the spice and herb cupboard, nothing. Brownie just wasn't there. Yet she was.

The first thing that hit Ella as she stepped into the kitchen of the Pink House was something fine indeed. It was something she had forgotten. Something that had somehow seeped from her mind and, now that she was face to face with it, something she had no idea how she could have forgotten. It was the thing that used to comfort her in a way that was second only to her Brownie. On the far wall of the kitchen, running into the dining area, from ceiling to floor, were shelf upon shelf and they were all crammed with one thing. The ultimate treasure box: red, yellow, orange, green, purple, black, brown, all kinds of colours fusing into a kaleidoscope that was like a gate to somewhere for Ella. Large bottles, small bottles, fat bottles, skinny bottles, round, square, sweet, savoury. Pickles! The shelves in Brownie's kitchen and dining room were crammed with home-made pickles. A wall of them. A giggle escaped Ella and she didn't even realise it. She couldn't believe she had forgotten this sight, she couldn't believe she had not gone to sleep every night for the past thirteen years thinking on it and dreaming on it. She just could not believe it.

Pickles meant one thing to Ella. One woman. They meant Aunty Rosa. It was from Aunty Rosa that Brownie had learnt the art of great pickle-making. Aunty Rosa lived in a house just off the Hanville Road, which looked like it had been built there by mistake. It just didn't fit. It was as weird and striking-looking as the Pink House stuck in its street. It was huge, bigger than the Pink House and all its occupants, the biggest black house in Hanville. All the white people, and some black people too, were perpetually flummoxed how an old black woman, living alone, with no obvious income, could afford such a house. Those that didn't wonder were Aunty Rosa's clients, Aunty Rosa's believers, the people to whom she gave her 'yieldings'. The house had three immaculate floors, was one of the first houses in the neighbourhood to have central heating, and it was 'kept up nice'. Aunty Rosa believed in firsts, but it wasn't that she tried to be better than everyone else. Her beliefs weren't from a position of bad feeling, Aunty Rosa just went her own way and did whatever she pleased, caring nothing for precedent, tradition or what anyone thought. What 'her spirit told her' she just did. In that way she and Brownie were the same. Thus she was the first black woman to both own and drive a car in Hanville – the drive part being particularly important because back then the fashion had been for black women to buy cars and leave them parked on the street, to admire from windows and to polish to a sparkle every Sunday morning so their neighbours could notice them as they made their way to the house of the Lord to thank and praise Him.

Brownie must have inherited Aunty Rosa's pickles, were Ella's thoughts as her eyes scanned the shelves. Brownie had been a great pickler herself, but this was surely the collection of Aunty Rosa. Ella recognised first one jar, then another and another. She smiled. Aunty Rosa had been a slight woman, as black as the night, who wore shoes that were so big they dragged behind her. The shoes had once belonged to her much loved husband Tandy, who had passed on only a week after they had married when she was a young girl in Jamaica. One child had been placed in Aunty Rosa's body during that week of love married to Tandy, a week she was for ever declaring to the world had 'kept her until the age she now was' – and when Ella knew her, she was ancient.

The child had been born strong and healthy. 'Like me love for Tandy,' said Aunty Rosa. But within less than a year, the child had turned sick and weak and died young. 'Like me love for Tandy', and Ella would notice that a part of Aunty Rosa died a little whenever she spoke those words.

The death of her child had been the final tragedy in Aunty Rosa's life. After that her joy was found in her pickles and the friends she made. She had never remarried. She had never had the need or desire since Tandy and her child had never left her. Some said she was alone in the world, but if she still had Tandy and her child and she was everybody's Aunty, she seemed to have more than those that indeed did have. Some said she worked obeah. Some said she was a fraudster who took people's hard-earned money and lived life on it. But whatever was the right or wrong of it, Ella remembered Aunty Rose as the maker of the most sparkling, wonderful pickles she had ever tasted.

The pickles were stacked on specially made shelves, row upon row of colour and vibrancy, all around Aunty Rosa's kitchen. Visiting her huge house Ella and Brownie always ended up in the kitchen, which wasn't unusual in itself, as in every black home you visited you sat in the kitchen. It was the natural heart of the home and where else were you going to sit except the warmest, most heartfelt place in the house? Ella had long believed there was nowhere on earth that came close to Brownie's kitchen, but Aunty Rosa's kitchen did and it was because of the pickles. Compared to the scale of the house, the kitchen was cramped, to say the least. It was tiny and intimate, a place of infinite wisdom where Aunty Rosa gave her 'yieldings'. It was green in colour, with hangings of garlic, citrus peelings and drying mackerels that gave the place a fishy smell that would've repelled any visitor, but that they knew what riches were to be had in Aunty Rosa's kitchen. There were chairs every-where, odd chairs, nothing matched in Aunty Rosa's home, but they all belonged. Yet the fact that Aunty Rosa lived alone but had all these chairs never quite made sense to Ella until the reason behind it was explained. Ella and Brownie had arrived one afternoon and Ella had sat counting the jars stacked all around her, as she did every time she went there. She had taken up a chair some rows back from where Aunty Rose and Brownie sat in conversation about some event they were remembering from their respective childhoods, some event that was obviously the same era after era, when Ella had asked the question why Aunty Rosa had so many chairs and yet she lived alone.

'Girl,' Aunty Rosa said in her warmest voice. 'Them is for the people that pass.'

Ella looked across at Brownie, who was sitting away from her. Ella had not understood the meaning of the world 'pass'. With a smile Brownie knew Ella would need once she did understand, Brownie mouthed the meaning of the word to her and Ella leapt clean out of her chair and jumped into Brownie's lap, where she hid herself. But for two things, Brownie and the pickles, Ella would never have returned to Aunty Rosa's house ever again.

A step had taken her into Brownie's kitchen. Ella now had a jar in her hand holding it up to the light. It was one of

Brownie's jars. She knew what was in it, what always went into this jar. She stood swilling its contents around: green tomato pickle with a little sugar.

'You first find a tomato grower who grow more than him can manage,' Brownie used to recite to Ella as she sliced the tomatoes around the table. 'You take the tomatoes when them green and fat, slice them up, sprinkle a little salt to draw out the water, as water and pickle don't mix. Get sugar, vinegar, cloves and cinnamon and boil them up.'

And that was it! Ella placed the jar back in its place and her hand dragged away from it. That was all there was. How it worked was as much a mystery to Brownie as everyone else. Brownie would cast salt over the sliced green tomatoes like a fisherman casting bait into the precise spot in the river that will give him the greatest yield. Brownie had no recipe book, no weights, no measurements; she went by touch, by feel, by something that was Brownie. Whenever Ella and her sisters came home with the recipe from that week's cookery class, Brownie could never get her head around the fact that they brought a list of exact and precise ingredients that could not be strayed from. Brownie never cooked like that. As the jar slipped back into place on the shelf, Ella smiled.

Looking around the kitchen and dining room that ran into one, she told herself the place looked shabby. The place looked dark. The place looked cheap, but somehow Ella didn't notice the place felt warm. It was crammed with things, things that meant something to someone who knew what things meant. There was still the large oak table in the dining room and it was still beeswax-polished with a fresh bowl of fruit as its centrepiece. The floor had been mopped and waxed that very morning and a line of shoes snaked around the skirting board out of respect for a home well kept.

Over at the stove four large prison pots were simmering away under a gentle heat. Things were cooking in them, things were happening in them, but were they stirring the way Brownie could get them to stir? Was it Brownie conducting this? Ella had a desire to see her mother standing at her stove cooking one last meal, just one more time. In the corner of the kitchen her eyes rested on the spice and herb cupboard. She went over to it. It still had the same great padlock on it. She tugged at it, but it was well and truly locked. She smiled and wondered whether anyone had remembered to take the key off Brownie before they took her to the mortuary. She placed her palm on the wood of the cupboard. It felt like something she had touched before. It felt as if it were welcoming her. The cupboard began to breathe up and down, like a big friendly giant. If she were lying on it, she would be this one insignificant dot that it took up and down like a hair on its gut. If she were lying prostrate and spread-eagled on it, it would be as if she were lying on Brownie, safe and secure as Brownie breathed up and down, up and down, up and down . . . She had forgotten the pickles, the smell of the Pink House, the layout of the place, many other things, but she had never forgotten the magic of Brownie's spice and herb cupboard. As she listened to its breath, as she felt it alive against her palm, she heard singing.

'Across the bridge, there's no more sorrow. Across the bridge, there's no more pain. The sun will shine across the river and you'll never be unhappy again. Unhappy again!' And so it went on and on. The singing was coming from beyond the dining area, led by a single strong female voice and backed up by something like half a dozen or more voices. All of them held a strange kind of happiness.

'Follow the footsteps of the king, till you hear the voices sing, they'll be singing out the glory of the land. The River Jordan will be near, the sound of trumpets you will hear, and you'll behold the most precious thing ever known to man. Across the bridge there's no more sorrow . . .'

With this ringing in her ears, Ella made her way past the dining room and stood at the door of the sitting room. The child was following her, but she didn't really have time to be with the child even if she had actually liked the child. The ugly kid offered Ella a hand as she stood at the front-room door pondering, building courage to open and go through, but she turned away from the ugly kid's hand, found her guts and pushed at the door. The door opened bravely before her. It opened before she really knew she was going to do it. Ella was face to face with a room of women dressed in black polyester dresses, white cardigans, hats of various sizes, all drinking tea with a couple of large carrot cakes in their midst. All of them shoeless. And by the looks of them she could imagine they'd been there the whole night. Eyes were looking at Ella, and even though her head was held straight and facing the room, she wasn't looking at any of the faces where the eyes lived. The singing had trailed off to a stop once they'd seen her. Then someone, out of nowhere, said a name that was dead to her.

'Pinkette!'

Ella couldn't turn her head to find the voice. She kept it straight and rigid, her will wouldn't allow her to turn. But the voice chased and found her, emerging from the group of women, and came and stood in front of her.

'Pinkette!' The voice with the body was now all face and the face was forcing itself into her eyeline, forcing her to look at it. Forcing her to look at herself, but still she refused to look, to see, to acknowledge, to embrace.

'Pinkette! I hear you come! I hear you come!' The face was fat and round and pleasant. It was friendly. It had beauty. It had innocence. Reverence. And from every pore poured love of kin and universe. Brownie had taught this face, nothing under the sun was clearer if you simply cared to look.

Ella held out her hand to shake the woman's. But the woman threw her large frame at Ella so enthusiastically that Ella stumbled back and would've gone over, but for the strength of the woman, who was able both to force her back and hold her up, all in the one embrace. Ella's flesh began to creep and tingle in a most uncomfortable way. It was like someone had sliced her skin open, pushed chilly weevils inside and roughly stitched her back.

'Pinkette!'

'Is me. You sister Donna!'

Ella hadn't forgotten she had a sister, she knew she had two of them. But she had thought nothing of what they

might look like now. The woman. Her sister. Her sister
Donna let go of her and looked at her with a beaming great
pleased-to-see-you smile on her face. There was a non-
plussed I-don't-want-to-be-here-and-I-honestly-don't-know-
why-I-am smile on Ella's.

'God forgive and pardon me, but if I was a man I could
fancy you meself, Pinkette. You looking well and gorgeous
'pon top.'

'Thank you!' Two words and Ella delivered them like she
were trying to stop shit coming through her mouth.

'Come in. Come in!' Ella felt herself being dragged
forwards and soon found herself in the midst of them.
'Everybody, you remember our sister Pinkette?'

'Ella!' Ella added quickly.

'Oh, yes! Yes! Pinkette! Pinkette!' And there came a
chorus of 'Pinkette's' as the women around her remembered
there was indeed another Brightwell daughter. This was the
Brightwell daughter they all remembered in her absence and
not the other two, who had remained. And in the space of a
few seconds Ella heard the dreadful name of Pinkette a hundred times more than she had in the past thirteen years.

Before she knew where she was, she was sitting with an
enormous glass of home-made ginger beer and a large
whack of carrot cake. She could only look at them and
wonder what consuming such things would do to her finely
chiselled thighs. As she looked around the congregation of
women assembled and staring at her, she realised it was a
question none of them had ever asked themselves or each
other. Ella discarded the glass and the plate, crossed her legs

and her shoe shot into her eyeline. She was still wearing her shoes! The only one! She swallowed hard, telling herself point-blank she would not remove them. Whoever she was, whatever she had come from, she would not fall into line for no one. She jutted out her shoed foot further than it needed to go for comfort and held it there right under their noses.

In all the reacquainting that followed, Ella did her best not to remember who the women were. After all she didn't come for any of this, she came to see her Brownie lowered into the ground and then she would leave. But one by one the women sat forward, said their names and recited some memory from their vast lives to help Ella verify that yes, she had once known them, known them intimately, that yes, she was of them through blood and through a shared history.

'Miss Tam! Remember me?'

'No.' It was a lie. Ella remembered her only too well and she remembered her before the woman began her story.

'Of course you do. Me is Miss Tam!' And she said her name again, louder, with more pronunciation, as if she thought Ella was deaf. 'Miss T-a-m!'

Still Ella shook her head.

Miss Tam was not deterred, she continued with a golden smile that left Ella staring in amazement into the mouth of Miss Tam. For in there was a perfect set of full gold teeth. Miss Tam held her mouth open a smile longer, a smile wider, a smile shinier than Ella had ever seen a person hold a smile for. And as she was doing all three, she twisted her head this way and that, searching for that perfect angle from which a person could gaze and see that yes, she did have this extraordinary set of teeth. Ella was mesmerised, she wanted to reach out and touch them. The only thing that stopped her and brought her back to her senses was feeling a damp drip on her skirt soaking through to her leg. Sitting next to her, staring and sucking, was the ugly kid with the shit plaits. Ella stared at her and pushed her away but the kid wouldn't go and came back. Something about Ella was fascinating her.

And then Miss Tam was away with her story, reciting some incident Ella had long forgotten.

'Remember how you used to come to mine and Mr Tam house?'

Ella tried not to remember. Her ability to stay on top, the skill she had built herself, had momentarily left her. She told herself she could've coped with being abandoned anywhere else except here and now to these women.

The story began. 'One day, not long after Way-On did gone way. Me one was in me house, kinna depress, kinna thinking 'bout Home, thinking 'bout Way-On. When ring-ring. The door! When me go, guess and tell me is who?' Miss Tam's eyes cascaded over the congregation of women and she spread her hand over them as though she were casting seeds into a field for germination. The women sprang up, gleefully feeding off a story they knew would sustain them till the last.

'Pinkette!' And the name flowed out of all the women except for one lodged in the corner who wouldn't meet Ella's gaze.

'Pinkette!' Miss Tam confirmed to the women and there were squeals of delight as their guess was confirmed.

'Pinkette come in and say, "Miss Tam, I hear you got a little trouble. I hear you in a little trouble."'

No way, no how, did she ever talk like that, was all Ella was thinking.

'"How you like me take off a little a the trouble off you? How you like me do you washing?" she ask me. Then she say, "For a price, of course."'

More squeals. This time the slapping of thighs. The rubbing of hands. The pinching of another woman's flesh. Ella began to realise that this was obviously what constituted entertainment in these parts.

'The price did cheap! So I see one less job. Anyway, Pinkette say she going start nine o'clock a morning. She will bring her own powder, don't ask me where she going get powder. Anyway, bright and early the morning Pinkette turn up with the powder and her little apron. I give her the boy them washing, Mr Tam washing and I give her me own. In fact, I give her the whole family washing for the week and I gone shopping. When me come back! When me come back, you see, me find Pinkette a hang out the last of me washing. Done and clean! Ladies?'

'Is what?' All the ladies were in unison, asking 'Is what?' at precisely the same chorus moment.

'No, my washing alone Pinkette do.'

Some of the ladies got the joke and were laughing before the story had ended, before the last line, and were now marvelling at the intelligence and guile of the twelve-year-old Pinkette. But then some of them just didn't get the joke.

'Is what?' those that didn't get it began to ask. 'Is what?'

'That's why the price was so cheap, 'cause is my washing alone Pinkette do!' Miss Tam explained further for the slower ones. And she found the joke so sweet she cracked up, clapping her hands so sharply she made Ella jump.

And then all of the ladies began to look at Ella and realise that in all the years they had been on God's great creation they had not had the guts, sense or will to think of, never mind execute, such an audacious deed. And one by one they all remembered why this was the Brightwell daughter they had all missed and remembered.

In the corner, quietly staring at a battered hymn book, still unable to meet Ella's gaze, sat an old woman. This woman had not yet introduced herself, but Ella knew her immediately. She was fatter, had lost her looks, was still clinging to what little poise was left and – sacrilege of sacrileges – she was wearing a wig. The woman's coiffed locks had been replaced and a smile was spreading over Ella's face as she remembered. Ella used to help her dress. At least once a day Ella used to be made to sit and hand her items of clothing that would be tried on, discarded and demanded again minutes later. Once a day this ritual took place and it always took place with poor Ella in attendance. It was this woman more than anyone who had taught Ella that there was something to be had away from the Hanville that had trapped her own two feet like a mosquito in amber. She had taught Ella that if there was something to be had you gritted your teeth, got

on with plundering it, wiped your feet and headed off into
the sun. It was Aunt Julie.

Aunt Julie was a few years younger than Brownie and she
lived in a room in the Pink House next door to the bedroom
Brownie and Daddy Ned shared. She lived there mainly
because she had never had the guts to strike out on her
own. Her life, over the years that Ella had known her, had
become nothing but a ritual and her room, her domain, was
the seat of that ritual and it was something to behold. The
entire place was in worship of her and her means of pre-
senting herself to the world as the beautiful person she craved
to be. Everywhere there were dresses, skirts, blouses, cardigans, hats, coats and more, and though they hung from
hangers around the picture rail on every wall, from curtain
rails, or lay folded in boxes, trunks, under the bed, in cupboards and wardrobes, Aunt Julie knew at any given time
where any piece of clothing she desired was. Beautiful
things – not beautiful to anyone other than Aunt Julie – had
become Aunt Julie's life work.

On the one side of her room, so huge it was holding up
the wall, was a dresser stacked high with the perfumes, oils,
creams, powders and potions that assisted Aunt Julie in
'keeping her looks'. Every time she entered Aunt Julie's
room, Ella went through the genuine ritual of amazement
looking at Aunt Julie's dresser. It was a wonder! She mar-
velled at it at least once a day as she helped Aunt Julie dress,
and sometimes more often if Aunt Julie had somewhere special to go and she had to change again and again. If Brownie
was positively the biggest woman that ever walked the earth,

then Aunt Julie's dresser must have been the biggest dresser
that was ever made for the face of the earth. Worst of all, the
dresser had to be cleaned every Saturday and even that was a
ritual. Ella wasn't trusted with the chore of cleaning, having
broken a couple of rare bottles that could not be replaced.
The cleaning was the chore of Donna and Della and it went
something like this. Donna and Della were marched in in the
morning while Aunt Julie could supervise from her vast bed,
from which she generally did not rise before noon. The
girls would take off every bottle, jar and tub and lay them
out on the carpet in the same order as they had removed
them, so they could return them to the dresser in that order.
This was important because Aunt Julie needed to be able to
find anything 'with her eyes slam shut'. As they worked, the
girls were not permitted to speak because of the headache
this would induce in Aunt Julie so early in the morning.
There was to be no clanking of jars and definitely no spilling
of the contents. Once everything was removed, the dresser
was wiped down, waxed with beeswax, left for thirty minutes, during which time Donna and Della would dust the
jars and tubs, and then the dresser would be polished. Once
the jars had been replaced, the whole ritual had taken the
best part of two hours, or two and a half if the girls weren't
on song.

In one far corner of Aunt Julie's room, amidst all that
lodged there, a dark foreboding double wardrobe struggled to stand tall and keep shut. It was so crammed with
clothes that the doors couldn't close and were held by a
piece of rope knotted to link the handles. The rope looked

innocuous, but it had a past. Everything of Aunt Julie's had a past.

Once, apparently Aunt Julie had got it into her head that she would leave Hanville. She had actually found the courage to branch out and do something with her life. Off she went to London to stay with a cousin who vowed to put her up until she found her feet, no matter how long it took. That turned out to be three weeks, because that's how long it took the cousin to find Aunt Julie in bed with her husband. Before Aunt Julie could dress herself, the cousin had got the piece of rope and strung it high from the roof beam, where she was seriously ready to string Aunt Julie up 'like the dirty dog she was!' But somehow, between the husband and luck, Aunt Julie managed to escape both the house and the city of London with her life intact, and with the rope too.

After Aunt Julie's clothes, her dresser and the wardrobe with its piece of rope, the next thing that struck you on entry was Aunt Julie's shoes. But what shoes! Whereas the dresser was the bane of Donna and Della's young lives, the shoes of Aunt Julie were the tragedy of Ella's. They were her chore. Once a week Ella was charged with cleaning the entire enormous lot. Once a week Ella would be forced to rack her brains as she tried to contrive some story of why she couldn't clean Aunt Julie's shoes that week. But under the sharp scrutiny of Aunt Julie there was never any story cunning enough to rescue Ella from this most hated chore. The saddest thing was that it would've been perfectly easy for Aunt Julie to put her shoes under cover and protect them from what she called 'the terrible dust!' Instead she chose to leave them lined around the room in ever decreasing squares. Two hundred and thirty-three pairs!

As Ella looked across at her Aunt Julie huddled in the corner, Ella saw that time had shat on Aunt Julie and it had done it from a magnificent height. Her face looked like the backside of an ancient rhino and her neck was the spit of a turkey's, long, mangy and veined. Her gnarled black fingers were snaking around the black leatherbound hymn book and you didn't quite know where the one began and the other ended. Her nails were a sickly-looking dark brown. Ella had never seen nails that black and had it not been for something else about Aunt Julie she would've remained staring at those nails longer than was company decent. The something else was spectacular, something Ella could not but feast upon. It was an extravaganza extraordinaire! Aunt Julie was wearing a long black Diana Ross wig which, if she stood up, would hit her just above her expanding arse in the small of her back. Or maybe it was Chaka Khan? Yes, it was definitely Chaka Khan. Aunt Julie was a woman who couldn't have been more than five foot four, and that was pushing it. If Brownie had been an elephant, Aunt Julie was the mouse and this wig would've looked out of scale on even Brownie's frame. Aunt Julie was a walking, talking living duppy spirit and no one, not anyone, had had the nerve to tell her.

The world had come full circle on Aunt Julie as her nature had deemed it must. But she must've known it would, Ella thought. From her own mouth she had condemned herself. And it looked like maybe the spit was still falling.

As Ella recalled the voices, she was staring Aunt Julie out across the room. As Aunt Julie fidgeted and tried to deflect her gaze, she knew the voices in her niece's head.

First there was Aunt Julie's voice: 'Is a genuine mistake, I tell you.'

Then there was Daddy Ned's voice: 'Brownie, man! A thought it was you. A was sleeping!'

Ella and Larry had been out in the yard burning ants with a kettle of hot water when some commotion had started up in the kitchen. It was the second time Larry had been round to the Pink House and Ella had been up for showing him all she knew, but then the commotion started up and that was all that they were interested in. The commotion had to do with the fact that Aunt Julie had accidentally, on purpose, got into the wrong bed. After how many years living in the Pink House, knowing the layout like the back of her black hand on some black night, Aunt Julie had somehow managed to find herself in Daddy Ned and Brownie's bed and what's more, Daddy Ned had been in there on his own. Ella and Larry had heard the sobbing coming from the kitchen – it was the one and only time Brownie ever cried over anything Aunt Julie had done her – and they'd popped their heads up outside the window just in time to see Aunt Julie come through the dining-room door with nothing but a sheet around her. Not only had Aunt Julie managed to find the wrong bed, she had also managed to find the wrong bed with nothing on.

'Is a genuine mistake, I tell you,' Aunt Julie protested.

Brownie was hardly listening, Ella thought, as the two of

them watched. Her hands were dragging a sack of red peas from the food cupboard and she poured them into a huge stainless-steel pan, the sound of which was cracking to hear.

'You listening me, Brownie?' Aunt Julie chased after her, trying to make her hear, but it never looked for a moment like Aunt Julie was actually trying to catch Brownie.

When Daddy Ned came through the door bare-chested, barefooted and doing up his trousers, Brownie was around the table picking the peas. And when she saw him, that was when the sobbing began. Like a low moan from the pit of her stomach, from a place Ella didn't even know her mother had, a place Ella was deeply ashamed her mother had to exhibit in front of her new best friend.

'Brownie!' Daddy Ned was putting his arms around her. 'Is a mistake. A thought it was you. A was sleeping!' And that was Daddy Ned's defence. He thought Aunt Julie was Brownie.

There erupted a massive row between Aunt Julie and Daddy Ned and it erupted around, either side and through Brownie like she wasn't even there. Aunt Julie was eager to know how her petite and nimble frame could be mistaken for Brownie's huge, ungainly one. And despite the fact that it was a question steeped in vanity, it was a valid point and Daddy Ned would do well to counter it. He could not. He had stuck his neck in the noose Aunt Julie had so expertly spun and hung for him. Seeing him floundering before her cock-a-hoop sister, Brownie pushed the chair from beneath herself, went over to the sink and began to wash the peas, all the while a sound of pain moaning from her. Daddy Ned followed her, trying an arm around her again, trying to console her.

'Brownie, man! Brownie!'

But it was no use. She slapped his hand away. It was a warning. He would not get another. Great tears splashed down into the washed peas.

'Brownie!' Daddy Ned continued, trying his best to get close to her and make her see it from his side.

It was never going to be any use, though. Anyone could see that; Ella and Larry saw that, Aunt Julie saw it and needed no more. As she made her way towards the dining-room door that would take her back upstairs, she allowed the sheet to slip ever so slightly from around the top half of her body and in so doing took Daddy Ned's head with her. Brownie, though locked into her own misery, noticed this immediately and struck Daddy Ned so hard across the face he staggered backwards, arms flailing for balance, and clattered into a bag of potatoes that then fell out on top of him, covering him. Ella had never seen her Brownie do anything like that. She had never seen her hurt another living thing and here she was, actually! actually! hitting Daddy Ned to the ground! Ella was stunned. Larry took it in his stride and put an arm around her.

Brownie had no mercy. She stepped over him to the stove and proceeded to put on the peas in a big everlasting pot. Usually Brownie soaked the peas overnight. Now it was the middle of the day, and without having been soaked, the peas would take a while. From the fridge Brownie pulled out a huge dish of salted pig's feet she had been saving for the

night after next's meal. She was over by the stove with the
dish of feet, holding one after the other over the naked fire,
burning the hairs off each foot until the smell of burnt
gnarled pig's feet was everywhere in the kitchen. As the skin
and hair burned, each time threatening to take Brownie's
hand, she would move her hand just in time away from the
fire, and she would do this time and time again until there
was not a piece of hair anywhere on the pig's foot.

Behind her Daddy Ned pulled himself up. His passion was
high. His emotions were flailing just as his body had been
moments before. And Ella supposed he was about to beat
Brownie the way she had heard his friends tell him he should
beat his woman. The way Larry knew that men always did.
But Daddy Ned's passion couldn't have been as high as they
thought because all he did was stand a moment glaring at
Brownie's back turned against him, then he marched out the
back door, banging it as he went. With nothing on his feet,
nothing on his chest, in just his trousers, Daddy Ned
marched out.

Brownie didn't care. Something had taken her over, Ella
didn't know exactly what. All she knew was her mother was
cooking in a way she had never seen her cook before and it
was all because of Aunt Julie. She had a bank of anger and
this in a woman for whom such feelings were death. She
threw the feet into a huge bowl of vinegar water and began
to clean them with such vigour her hands would be sore
later. Once they had been washed completely, she dropped
the salted feet into the just boiling red peas, added coconut
milk, scallion, garlic, onions, red, green and black pepper

and stirred. The peas should've been in soak overnight, the salted pig foot should've been in soak overnight. Pig foot was not food you just upped and cooked. You had to prepare. Because of Aunt Julie reason had left Brownie and though the family could accept this in every other context, it was a shock to discover it could happen around food.

At four in the morning the whole hungry household, except for Aunt Julie, who remained stubbornly in bed, and Daddy Ned, who still had not returned to the House, was woken and served the pig foot. They were more tired than hungry, but even if that had not been the case, the pig foot would've been the same disgusting offering it was. The salt was still in the foot and the red peas were still little bullets and whatever Brownie had been feeling when she had pre-pared the meal, it was there in front of the whole Brightwell family at four in the morning. The meal had no soul, because Brownie had had none when she had cooked it.

Larry never saw, but at their next meet-up Ella felt proud she could report to him that at six in the morning she had been woken by the faintest tapping on wood. She had crept out of her bed, cracked her bedroom door and looked out on the landing. Daddy Ned had returned. He was on his knees, tapping on his and Brownie's bedroom door like a howling dog in season. He was cooled, he was hankering. The door opened and Brownie came out. She looked down at him, dropped to her knees in front of him and her hands cradled his face. Then and there Ella observed that Daddy Ned's face was the most precious thing to Brownie. Nothing in that split second could've meant more to Brownie than the thing she had between her hands, because no other thing could've cooled the temper raging inside her like Daddy Ned's repentant face. Once she saw this, Ella closed the door on her kneeling parents; kneeling there with nothing between them and that was that. That was what she'd told Larry, but what she hadn't told him was that she had closed the door in anger and jealousy that her Brownie could look at anyone else that way.

Ella's memories ran empty for a moment and she found her eyes still resting comfortably on Aunt Julie in the corner. Ella smiled. Every time she thought she had caught Aunt Julie's eye, Aunt Julie would bury her head in the pages of her hymn book and Ella knew why. Shame! Every time Ella thought she would say, 'Ay, you're my Aunt Julie, aren't you? What happened to you?' Aunt Julie just wouldn't hold her head steady. But that didn't matter; Ella's wilfulness was back, and that was all it took: someone in more pain than she, someone upon whom she could feed and rebuild her own strength. Just like Aunt Julie had taught her, Ella now happily turned it back on her. Ella would savour waiting for Aunt Julie to meet her gaze.

'Look who's here!' said Donna, wheeling a woman forward. 'Go on, look who's here!'

From the side of the woman's twisted mouth there was a slow dribble that was collecting on the bib of her frock. Her hands were twisted inwards and held high on her vast tits. A belt around her gut held her to the chair and two smaller ones held her ankles. Before Ella could say anything, Donna, with great force, was holding the woman's face so Ella could

see her and she could see Ella. Ella looked into the woman's
face and started to feel like Aunt Julie: she couldn't sit still,
she couldn't hold her head still to even look at the woman.

And then from Donna came the words that stuffed Ella
into a little ball and shoved her violently inside herself: 'Is
our sister Della!'

Ella looked again at the woman in the wheelchair. Head
back skywards, strapped into a body Ella could not understand or know. Strapped into a world Ella felt appalled by.
Out of nowhere a hand was wiping the dribble from Della's
mouth with a baby's bib. It was the ugly kid with the sucker.

'She take a stroke when she have Mirabel,' Donna was
saying, her hand resting affectionately and proudly on the
ugly kid's head. 'This is our Mirabel.'

Ella stared at her and Mirabel stared at Ella. For the first
time Ella realised that the ugly kid looked liked her sister
Della. Della was the somebody from her past who the ugly
kid looked like.

'Mirabel, this you Aunty Pinkette.'

'Ella!' Even during trauma, Ella could remember what
she wanted to be called. 'She can call me Ella.'

'Whatever you say, Pinkette,' came Donna's voice.
'Mirabel, say hello to you Aunty Pinkette.'

'Hello, Aunty Pinkette,' came Mirabel's voice.

Ella just stared at the ugly kid. No warmth, no love, no
acknowledgement of kin, of blood. No nothing. Ella just
stared at her and she wanted to run and hide and lie and
disown and shout, 'No way nohow!' 'You can kiss her, you
know,' said Donna. 'You can kiss our sister Della.'

'What?' Ella was confused with what she wanted to do and what she felt she could get away with doing under the glare of these women and in her Brownie's Pink House.

'Our sister Della.' For some reason Della felt she had to continue with her explanation. 'She like people touching her face. Especially with them lip them.'

Donna waited. The women waited. Ella showed no sign of moving.

'Make me show you.' Donna lowered her lips to Della's lips, and Ella noticed that a thin line of spit immediately established itself and held itself between Della's and Donna's lips and only broke when Donna wiped it away with her hand.

Ella felt sick and turned her face away from her sisters. But all were still staring at her, waiting for her to say something, show some reaction, do something. Waiting most of all was Aunt Julie. Apart from Ella herself, Aunt Julie was the only other person in the room who knew exactly what Ella would do. Only Aunt Julie would know the debate that was going on in Ella's head and she knew it because it was the same God almighty thing she herself would be doing.

'No thank you, but I won't kiss her. And please, all of you, call me Ella. My name's Ella.' And her mouth slammed shut after that as she waited for them to digest what she had said.

So there came a hiatus during which the women, for really the first time, began to check out this strange creature that had landed in their midst. She was from the same stock as they, but was different. Her neck and head were inflexible, held high and straight out in front of her. She had once had the smell of them, but now she was perfumed, permed and coiffed into an odour they hardly recognised as theirs. Her hands were slender and soft, their own were ripped and hard-skinned. She had on a suit of clothes, down to her shoes, that would've taken them a year or more's disposable income to possess – the phrase would be hers and not theirs. And though bad mind and loose tongues sometimes over-took these women, when things blocked their way, things that could harm and divide them, there was a warmth and understanding that held them together and helped them find a way through together. There was a unity, a cast of mind, an identity Ella did not have.

She closed her eyes to her surroundings for maximum concentration but still she knew they were watching her. She was startled by a ringing sound. Something was ringing on her, and this really confirmed to these women that the last daughter of the Brightwells was the strangest person they had ever met. They were already exhausted by her, but they were fascinated by her too.

Ella wrestled in her bag and pulled out her mobile. The ringing phone was like a little puncture in her skull and through it gushed steam as from a pressure cooker. She pressed a button, listened and she was away.

'What the hell do you think you're doing? Where are you going?' she shouted. As soon as the questions had raced out of her and down the phone, she felt the release as the last of the pressure left her. But as soon as it was out there, she remem-bered where she was and in what circumstances; the hole sealed itself and the pressure began to build all over again.

'What time's your flight?'

'Eleven. Ell–'

'I'll be back before then.' And she ended the call.

The women were still looking at her but now the impression they gave was graphic. In unison, like they were one and the same creature with one body but many heads, they turned their heads this way and that trying to get an angle on her. They would cock their heads for the best angle from which to view and understand. But they couldn't understand her, it was no use, and only when all realised it was no use could they right their heads, simultaneously.

Donna was in silence. They were sitting around the table face to face, except that Ella could hardly look at her. They were sitting there, with the wall of floor-to-ceiling pickles to the side of them, the great oak table between them, the waxed floor, the shoes snaking around the skirting board, the spice and herb cupboard creaking in the corner, and outside the oak tree stood tall. It was just the two of them with a fresh pot of tea and a plate of uncut cake. Ella was thinking hard on something to say. But Donna had no interest in any explanation her sister was knitting together. Donna didn't work the way Ella had grown used to seeing people work. She had no need for the truth, she had no need for a lie. Whatever her sister needed to get by, her sister needed.

Then Donna was off speaking in a calm, deliberate way, like she was trying to make sense of what was what and what had happened to make it what it was.

'She wake early the morning, like she always do. You

remember how she always wake early?' Donna was just going over it in her mind, even Ella understood that. 'She wake early the morning, come down, set about mixing up some fritters for breakfast; she take sick, she sit down round the table, and she drop forward.'

Donna's head proceeded to demonstrate just how Brownie's head had dropped forward around the very oak table where the sisters were sitting. Donna's demonstration was slow, it was deliberate. All Ella knew was that Brownie was dead. She didn't need to see how, or know in what state she had been found; the fact that she was dead was enough. After the longest moment, Donna's head lifted and her chin rose off her chest where it had rested and her hand fell on top of Ella's. Ella guessed that at that moment Donna needed some kind of comfort or she wouldn't have been able to go on.

Ella was looking at Donna's hand on hers. The longer it remained there, the more it became clear to Ella that the reason it had fallen there didn't matter. All she knew was how she felt; sick from the contact. Ella began to get the distinct feeling someone was putting her through test after test and standing back and watching just how badly she could fail them. Thank God there was tea, there was cake. Ella slipped her hand from under Donna's as casually as she could and poured herself a cup of tea she had no intention of drinking.

'Is the face, you see.'

Ella had no idea what Donna meant and just sat staring at her, looking puzzled. Looking stoosh. Looking down.

Looking removed. Looking like she was calling on God to once and for all cut the crap and deliver her back to her life and out of this place.

'The face!' Donna continued like it was obvious what she meant. Ella remained staring blankly at her sister.

'Brownie! The face drop clean inside the fritter mixture and she drown. Right here, round the dining table, in that very seat. She drown, you see!'

Donna was pointing right where Ella sat. Ella was sitting in the very seat where life had left her Brownie. And Ella thought the way the day was going there was nowhere but in the dead seat that she could've found herself. She began to shift uneasily and her movement was not unlike the time in Aunty Rosa's kitchen when she had leapt for fear into Brownie's huge lap of protection.

'The doctor say is heart attack she take.'

Ella had no idea Brownie had had heart trouble. It surprised her that something could've happened to her Brownie without her knowledge. Life had gone on for Brownie, and it had done so without Ella.

'The doctor say she might a recover from the heart attack, but the drowning, you see. Is the drowning!'

It was bizarre. Ella had never heard of anyone drowning in fritters mix before and she thought it was just like Brownie to go out that way. Ella had to smile to herself.

By the time Ella had returned from her smile, Donna had gone again. But this time she wasn't rooting in the sadness of the death, she was running through a field of happy memories. Ella didn't know what to say or do as she waited for

Donna's return. She didn't belong there, watching this woman sit in front of her reliving memories she wasn't a part of. That affected her. It slapped her hard and she did what she did around anything that reached her – she covered it with something harsh.

The clock on the wall was saying nine thirty. The funeral preparations should've started by now. Ella wondered why nothing was happening at the Pink House and heard herself asking, 'Shouldn't we be getting ready?'

Donna came back and was as confused by Ella's question as Ella was, asking it. 'Getting ready?'

'For the funeral!'

'Oh, no! No!' Donna squealed, laughing. Is tomorrow is Brownie funeral!'

'What?' Ella pricked up and jumped into her skin.

The simple explanation was this; Poor Cousin Winston was out with his Aunty Brownie's funeral and out by a whole day. A whole square on the calendar! An entire day! Donna was sitting before her telling her Brownie's funeral was tomorrow. Friday. Someone was trying to ruin Ella's life. She wouldn't stand for it. So she stood, pushed the chair Brownie had died in from under her, gathered up her bag and herself and headed for the back door.

'You going?' Donna asked.

'I was told it was today.'

'Then you going?'

'I have to.'

'Already?'

Even if she wanted to be there, she couldn't be. She had a

legitimate, justifiable reason why she could not hang around the ghosts of Hanville while they fed upon her. In getting the day wrong, Poor Cousin Winston had left her no choice. It was his fault and that was the way she was playing it.

She held out her hand to shake Donna's goodbye. Donna wouldn't hold out hers because she just couldn't understand what was happening. Ella had arrived after thirteen years and now she was leaving after just, well, maybe an hour! Donna didn't know what to do but go after her, buzzing in her ear every step of the way. Through the back door, through the back gate, up the entrance and on towards the front gate.

Back in the kitchen, from beneath the table, Mirabel emerged and looked through the open back door where her aunts had just disappeared.

'But you don't see Daddy Ned yet!' Donna was struggling to stay with Ella.

'I'll send a wreath.'

'And you don't see the others yet!' Donna was panting. It was obviously the fastest her life had gone since the last time she had seen Ella.

'I'll send a card.'

They were ploughing on up the entry, past the garage door, down the drive, Donna step for step trying to catch, trying to match, to hold her sister with some word, some gesture.

'And we don't bury our Brownie yet!'

Ella stopped dead in her tracks. She was standing at her car with her keys in her hand, with her back to Donna and the

Pink House. Behind her Ella could feel Donna pleading with her, not necessarily to stay and attend the funeral and meet the rest of her family, but to understand how she couldn't. Ella turned back and looked at Donna and she had no answer of any kind for her sister.

Ella felt awkward and looked up the road for an explanation, and there, walking eagerly towards her, was Larry. He was twelve again. He was beautiful again. He was her friend again and he walked right past her, through the gate, up the entrance, through the back gate and she knew exactly where he was going.

Black or white, boy or girl, he had been her only friend outside the Pink House. Not because she couldn't get any more friends but because no one else was worth choosing. After Brownie and Johno, Larry had been the third and last beautiful influence on Ella's young life and had he remained longer in Ella's life than the two years he had, for sure her life would not have been the tornado it had become.

As she thought of him she didn't know if she was crying or what. She didn't know if she was a twelve-year-old girl or a thirty-year-old woman and that surprised her. And if she had ever before revived that memory from the maze she had sent it to, she would never have remembered herself crying. She remembered harshness, her harshness. She remembered feeding on him, unforgiving, when all he'd wanted was a gesture that they still belonged to each other. She put out a hand to hold on to the wall that surrounded the Pink House, trying to keep from sinking to her knees.

Something told her to look above and she did. At first she

thought she saw Mirabel in Brownie's bedroom window looking down at her, but when she kept on looking, Mirabel had either hidden herself or had never been there. Instead from the top right-hand window, the boys' room, a body was hanging. The body was hanging by the neck, from a rope, and as she looked up, it was hanging once again. It was Patrick hanging by his neck. It was the day Patrick broke both his legs.

Ella was thirteen the first time a member of the opposite sex physically prostrated himself in front of her. That member was Poor Cousin Winston, who was sixteen. Until then she had just had a sneaking notion he was in love with her – whatever that meant – but after that day she was in no doubt. Poor Cousin Winston was charging around the front yard with Ella on his back riding him like a horse.

It had been an overcast day threatening rain and storms since daylight, but the storm did not arrive until she saw her mother's face hanging over Patrick's body. That day Poor Cousin Winston had come over to play with them. From the back of the House Brownie's voice was heard singing some song with her usual grace, like a floating presence gliding up from the shadowy entrance at the side of the House, all warmth and softness lightly touching everything it surrounded. Meanwhile at the front of the House tragedy was afoot. Ella heard a great yelp as Patrick jumped off the ledge with the rope around his neck. The rope jerked him taught, stretching his neck and causing such pressure in his head that his eyes flung themselves back to the far dark recesses of his head. Poor Cousin Winston stopped dead and he and

Ella looked up in silence as Patrick swung above them, his feet steady and, by the looks of them, not missing the ground beneath them.

Poor Cousin Winston threw her hands from around his neck and pushed her off his back. Ella dropped to the ground like a stone and landed heavily on her arse. Before she could scream at Poor Cousin Winston, he had taken off at great speed down the entrance towards the back gate, shouting and calling like a madman, 'Aunty Brownie! Aunty Brownie!'

From the ground where she had been flung, Ella switched back to Patrick hanging above her. He didn't struggle. He just hung there like he had found what he was looking for and Ella was both angry and jealous that he had. She wanted to reach up and slap him down, not to save his life, but to stop him from looking so contented. She didn't care one bit about saving his life, she only cared that in this mess, in the prison they'd built themselves, she should have company: his company.

Poor Cousin Winston's wailings reached Brownie and her singing suddenly stopped. The moments of silence melted into each other like a long death. It was so quiet Ella thought he was dead, and she thought the silence was the mourning. She was just bricking up her prison anew when the rope gave way and Patrick crashed to the concrete. Up at the window Poor Cousin Winston was looking down, frantic with concern for Patrick, but unable to do anything but look.

Patrick broke both his legs, one in three places, the other

in two. Ella couldn't move as she watched Patrick fall like a doll and then lie there, a splash of blood oozing from his body. A couple of bones had burst through flesh like sharp knives slicing through meat. He was conscious and in pain and unable to do anything but lie there. Somehow Patrick's body wouldn't allow him to scream out and he lay there yards from Ella, who couldn't move towards him or away from him.

Poor Cousin Winston had got up to the bedroom and cut Patrick down faster than Brownie could get from the kitchen to the front of the House. When she did arrive, Ella saw the predicted storm and rain had gathered in her mother's face.

Now Ella felt a hand on hers on the gate of the Pink House. It was Donna's. Ella looked back at the ground in the yard, but Patrick had gone. She looked up at the boys' window; there was no body hanging there either. At Brownie's window there was only Mirabel now clearly looking down at her. Mirabel had no smile, no expression whatsoever. She was just lifting the pink curtain and stood framed in the window like one of the pictures that hung all the way up the wall of the stairs in the Pink House. Mirabel was looking down like she was studying her, like there was something to understand in her absent-for-all-these-years aunt, and Ella was under no illusions that Mirabel had already understood it. Anyone else would've gone under right then and there, but Ella, she . . . she opened herself up, reached into her guts, scrunched the drum tight with both hands until she heard it pop and smash into a thousand little drums that each went its own silent way.

Calmly Ella pushed at the gate and walked back up to the House. Behind her followed Donna, a smile on her lovely round face.

Fittingly the room had become Mirabel's, but it was still the room that was once Ella's. As soon as she walked in and saw the two single beds, toe to toe against the far wall, she suddenly recalled there used to be two single beds toe to toe and sickeningly everything was just how she remembered leaving it.

Mirabel was an exceptional child, it seemed. She hadn't broken any of Ella's dolls, pissed through the mattress, or stuck Sellotape on the wallpaper to hold up any drawings. And as Ella sunk down on the bed furthest from the window, the one she used to use, she couldn't believe it: Mirabel had chosen to use the same bed. Ella was right to think it, Mirabel did know something.

Ella had been the only Brightwell child to have a room all to herself. The four brothers had been stuck in two rooms where they were forced to lump, jump and sleep on top of each other. Donna and Della had shared another room; Ella had never worked out why, when received wisdom said the eldest of her siblings should've been given the privacy they craved. Once she asked Daddy Ned about it. A cool sadness had come over him and he went off blubbing into Brownie's loving arms, where she comforted him in just the way she knew how.

Through the window the oak tree was still threatening the glass. The only difference was the pink candlewick bedspreads were now pink duvets, with matching curtains and pillowcases. She began to feel as trapped as she had when she had lived there.

Donna was standing by the door smiling warmly at her, urging her through her smile to feel at home and remember that she belonged right where she sat. She finally left Ella alone when she felt Ella needed a nap to recover from her journey. Donna grabbed hold of her and giggled, looking at the floppy Ella in her arms. And then threw herself around Ella again, as if trying to squeeze ease and joy into Ella.

'I just can't believe you here!' She was stroking Ella's hair off her forehead like a man who had last seen his one true love years ago and had missed her for all those years. Ella did not feel ease, did not feel joy.

And just before she closed the door and left, Donna told her she should come down when Daddy Ned got back from wherever it was he had gone, whereupon the family would discuss the final arrangements for the funeral. Ella couldn't believe they were including her in the final arrangements for any funeral. She hadn't come to be included, she'd come to . . . well, she didn't know that either, but it wasn't for this. But Donna, the stupid happy woman, was telling her it was only right and proper she should have her say in what they did with their Brownie.

As soon as she was alone and the door had closed tight on her, she began to feel that whatever was spooking her and making her run was tenfold in this room and she didn't care to remember. Immediately then she was regretting her weakness in staying.

As she looked through the window, the old oak tree was there, strutting in her face. Down into the yard the drop looked scarier than it had ever looked when she was a child, the branches weaker than they ever were, the ledge narrower than it could ever have been, but nonetheless an idea began to form in Ella's head.

'If you hand inna tiger mouth you must take time draw it out!' Aunt Julie's voice told her.

When everyone was asleep she would climb through the window, down the oak tree, run through the back gate away from the Pink House and drive clean out of Hanville and back to London. That was what she would do! The only problem was in waiting for darkness, which she would need as she remembered how difficult it was actually to creep out of the damn place. She would not only have to see the rest of the family, but she'd have to see Daddy Ned too.

The bed gave her a kind of peace and confusion. She was home and she was afraid. The bed put its arm around her in a warm smell of camphor and rum as Brownie washed her hurt body when it had fallen out of a tree, not broken any part of itself, but sent such a high fever racing in her head she thought she would go blind with it and deaf and mad with the buzzing in her ears. The bed moulded itself to her body as if it knew it, as if it had been waiting all these years for the only body that knew its twists and bumps.

She thought of Larry, the time he had slept in the other bed with her in this one. Larry, her best friend, born in Hanville but spirited away when he was six by a mother who saw it as the only way she and her son could escape the tyrant that was her husband, his father, Harry Roses – the grandson of one of the men rumoured to have killed Anna Street. For four years Harry Roses looked for his son and wife. For four years he didn't know what to do; he couldn't go forwards, couldn't go backwards. The only thing for him to do was find one or both of them. Much to the agony of his wife, Harry was to find them on the other side of the country living life the way it should've been lived. Larry's mother had set up home with another man so Harry couldn't bring her back without a fight he had no stomach for. All he could do was drag his boy back home to Hanville, where he would regularly beat him. Once Larry had been returned to Hanville, all he could talk about was leaving again. Larry, now ten, had tasted life outside Hanville and as far as he was concerned no power under the sun was going to make him live out his days in Hanville farming Rose Farm the way his father commanded. No, when Larry had saved up enough money, or killed his father, left school, or his mum came for him, whichever came first, he was leaving Hanville for good, and once he crossed over the Bridge he would never look back. Ella liked that. It was what attracted her to him, and once he had caught her eye she decreed he'd be hers for ever.

Larry embraced the most glamorous and influential friend he would ever have with both hands. The fact that his father forbade the relationship between his son and the people who lived in the Pink House, but Ella in particular, only served to make the Brightwells that much more delightful for Larry.

It made no sense to Ella that Larry's father had spent four years searching for a son whose face he could not even bear to look upon. Larry was the kind of person everyone loved. Only his father seemed to be filled with a wild fury whenever his son strayed into his sight and his eyes reminded him of what he could not stomach. Regularly Larry would appear at the Pink House with a black eye, wales on his skin and even the odd broken bone. All of which Brownie would attend to, knowing that if the authorities turned up at Rose Farm it would be worse for Larry.

Brownie called Larry her 'Poor Little Lost Son'.

Larry loved hanging out at the Pink House. For Larry the Pink House had life, soul, good food, Ella and Brownie.

'Morning, Poor Little Lost Son!' Brownie would greet him at the back door.

'Morning, Brownie,' Larry would say, seeming to sparkle. Despite his life at Rose Farm, he was a tall, thin, warm kid with wet pink skin you could sometimes see through, who sparkled.

His mother was a black woman and he would proudly prove it by way of a picture he'd rescued from the fire his father had set to her things the day before she finally left him. He'd show that picture to anyone and everyone who doubted him, including Ella. His father was white and proud of it. On first sight Larry had none of his mother and all of his father, but that was only on first sight. He had blond hair, but it was kinky and the strands were always going to be too curly for some. He had a nose that had never seen the sense in coming together into a point and instead had settled on his face in a comfortable, homely fashion. Ella sometimes looked at him and thought he had something of one of her brothers about him, or any other black boy she saw walking around Hanville for that matter, but for one thing. Larry was red! And not just red, he was white! As white as any white man in Hanville and whiter even than some of them. And when the sun shone on him, his skin looked all dappled and his eyes danced like sparks flying from an open fire. On bad days his thin wet skin became so pink you could see straight through it to his vulnerability. On great, brilliant days, the sparkling warmth of him made him the kid everyone but his father loved. Nine times out of ten those were the days Ella and Larry spent together.

As soon as those seven words had passed between Brownie and Larry, it was his cue to come into Brownie's kitchen and usually he would be smiling as he did so. He would go straight to the table, sit and eat up his breakfast of whatever she put before him, and he would do it while keeping an eager ear for his life, heart and soul coming down the stairs. However, on an average of one or two mornings a month Brownie knew she would get no return greeting. Would get no smile. And he would have no appetite. She knew he would come, stand in her kitchen by the back door in some kind of pain, looking ever so vulnerable. On those mornings Brownie would set to work on him with camphor and rum. One day, Brownie knew, Poor Little Lost Son wouldn't be there. In the meantime she ate up her Poor Little Lost Son like one of her own, praising whatever she believed in for the second chance that had been given her.

Sometimes it bothered and puzzled Larry which Brightwell female he was more interested in, the daughter or the mother. Ella was his heartbeat, that was simple. But some days he felt he'd have no life if it wasn't for Brownie. His day would usually end with Larry rejoicing at having two such females in his life and he took care to nurture both relationships.

Brownie herself knew what Larry did for her youngest child and she knew what her youngest child did for Larry. Brownie knew the one without the other was lost, long before either of them had even the sniff of such knowledge. She knew to take care around their relationship, when the two of them took no care. And she knew all this because only when the two of them came together did something resembling harmony take place. Only around Larry was Ella the continual joy Brownie knew her youngest was fighting to be. No one else could induce in Ella the continual stillness that Larry could. Both Johno and Brownie could do it spasmodically, but only Larry could do it continually. It was as if Ella left Larry, went to the rest of the world, strutted her stuff upon it, shouted and exorcised herself on it, and then returned calm to Larry. It was not, however, a one-sided relationship in which Ella took what she needed and gave nothing in return. Ella had sussed, one second after decreeing that he would be hers, that if she wanted this boy in her life she would have to give of herself. She liked to believe she had a choice in the matter of whether he was in her life or not, but really she had no damn choice. It was just so. It was just how it was.

One morning, when Brownie had woken early to soak bammy for breakfast – because some dream had told her that bammy was what the Brightwells would need that morning, something sturdy and strong in their stomachs – there came no return greeting. Brownie's eyes looked up from the huge dish of bammy and saw Poor Little Lost Son squashed up by her back door. This morning he did look like her Poor Little Lost Son. He had a black eye and was holding his right arm carefully against himself. Straight away Brownie knew it was broken.

Usually Ella was the last of Brownie's children to make it down to breakfast but this morning she was there a whole hour early and in a mood Brownie noted was particularly bad even for her. It wasn't until she saw the look on the faces of her Poor Little Lost Son and her youngest child that Brownie understood the reason for Ella's mood and early appearance. They had argued. Or maybe it was worse?

Brownie stared at the state of her Poor Little Lost Son and watched Ella stare at him too. He stared back at Ella and every now and then his eyes would drop to his feet in pain and shame when he couldn't take the scrutiny she was subjecting him to. Something had put Ella in the most violent, noxious temper Brownie had seen her in and that was saying something.

Both Brightwell females watched Larry and at first nei-ther could say a thing. It was not that his injuries were particularly bad that morning, he had had his arm broken once before and had had both eyes blacked in one go before. What made them stop and stare was that they could see clearly that he had given up the fight for life. It was like it was the last beating he could ever take and the reason for this was what Ella had discovered the day before.

'Pinky, go pick thyme and bring two slat of wood,' Brownie said as she made her way over to Larry.

Ella continued to eat from one of the plates on the oak table. She wouldn't go and pick any thyme to wash him down nor would she go and gather any wood to splint his arm. Not for him and not for Brownie.

Brownie left it at that. Whatever had happened between the two of them, she left it at that. She walked Larry to a chair at the table, sat him down and went out to the yard. She left them alone.

While she was gone all kinds of things happened. Ella sat at the table eating her bammy: a round, flat bread made out of grated cassava, which Brownie made weeks in advance and woke early to soak in milk until they were soft the morning of frying. She was eating it with goat fish and was enjoying it just that little bit too much. As she ate she was pointedly ignoring him, making him suffer and enjoying it. He was dying in front of her and she was loving it. Larry got down off the chair Brownie had put him on, dropped before Ella on bended knee and begged her to marry him. The two of them were twelve years old.

When Brownie returned she found her youngest at the table devouring and her Poor Little Lost Son on his knees almost dead with pain. Brownie herself began to tremble at the pain of it.

In the face of Brownie, Ella was ashamed. So she stood up from the table, stepped past them both without saying a word and went out. As the back door slammed shut behind her, Larry fainted.

Ella crashed to the floor. For a second she didn't know where she was. Then a smell began to swarm around her, the warm smell of fried fish. For a second, the moment between sleep and waking, she didn't know exactly how old she was. Then she remembered she was a grown woman, but she only remembered it because she looked up and saw Mirabel standing in the open door looking down at her.

'You drop off the bed, Aunty Pinkette!' Mirabel announced in such a matter-of-fact voice it wasn't real. Any other child would've laughed at such a sight. Any other child would be rolling about with her on the floor, Ella herself would've laughed if she'd witnessed it, but not Mirabel. Mirabel just stood there, serious as anything, looking down at Ella. Ella picked herself up, holding on to whatever dignity she had left. In ways she couldn't understand Mirabel was more an adult than she ever was. Mirabel was creepy, that was all she knew. Mirabel fitted neatly, the new generation to inhabit the Pink House.

'Aunty Pinkette, Aunty Donna say to say Daddy Ned come. Daddy Ned come and dinner soon ready.'

'Ella!' Ella corrected her, but it was lost on Mirabel, because Mirabel went, closing the door behind her, and she gave Ella the feeling that she wouldn't even shit on her.

There used to be moments in the Pink House when she was scared to leave her room. It wasn't that she was in trouble and anyone was after her, it was just this inexplicable fear that used to be with her. Sometimes it was because every time she opened the dining-room door to go through to the kitchen and out the back door where she belonged, Brownie was always there, preparing some kind of food with that look of happy acceptance. Ella would stand and watch her with a kind of horror that this could be all her mother wanted in life. But now she was afraid in case her mother wasn't down in the kitchen. The truth was that she had never, until this day, been in Brownie's kitchen without seeing Brownie there. That thought, and perhaps something else, kept her bemused in the room for half an hour after Mirabel had left her.

It took the half-hour for Ella to remind herself that her memories were just ghosts. Eventually she cracked the door and spied out on the landing as if she were an intruder and not supposed to be there. Most of the bedroom doors were open. They were always open, except for one. Aunt Julie's room was right where she'd left it, mischievously next door to the room her mother shared with her father. As soon as

Ella looked at the door, she didn't need to go in to know nothing had changed in there since she had last been in there cleaning Aunt Julie's shoes. It was the door next to it that intrigued Ella and it was there she was heading. At the door she faltered, half suspecting there was nothing different in there either, but she couldn't resist finding out. The door was half open and around it Ella could peep round and just see the well-made bed against the wall. She looked behind her in case someone, Mirabel, was coming up behind to catch her out. She looked the other way down the landing but there was no one about. Ella quietened herself and took a step towards the door. With every positive step her right leg took, her left leg followed fast behind it, planting itself down in fear – her whole life it had been the same. She took a deep breath, held her head firm and leant on the door with her shoulder. The door swung open before her and she smiled, relieved of the feeling she had been running from.

It was a big room, but not the master bedroom. It was ordered, clean and simple, had the usual stuff any bedroom had, and just that little bit more. It had the spirit of Brownie and the love of two people. It was pink and calm and Ella couldn't imagine a time when it had ever been fraught. Her eyes circled from one point all the way round the room and she could see her mother in all kinds of ways and situations, just there. There was a simple dresser on which lay a brush-and-comb set. In the brush Ella could see twists of silver hair charged with static electricity. When Ella was nine years old, she had decided the thing to do was to find out what had caused her mother to exhibit to the world this shock of dangerous grey that had sprung up in the middle of an otherwise black head of hair. Ella had to help her mother back to the normal, quiet, black hair she still had a right to expect in her early forties. Only then would Ella be able to live a life that was not permeated by Brownie's embarrassing hair.

The only thing Ella had to go on was that the hair had turned overnight, and turned when Brownie was a girl of thirteen. It would be difficult to discover what and why, but surely not impossible. Aunt Julie would know, Ella thought, since they were sisters.

'Aunt Julie?' Ella was holding up a plum-coloured dress for Aunt Julie as she considered whether this would be the dress for tonight's date – Aunt Julie had dates the way other women had responsibilities.

'Higher!'

Ella held the dress higher, stretching her arms above her head and losing herself from view of Aunt Julie behind the dress.

'Higher!' Aunt Julie bellowed. She was cracking the whip this morning.

The dress went a little higher. Ella couldn't go any higher without standing on a chair. And it occurred to Ella that maybe this wasn't such a good morning to ask Aunt Julie about Brownie's hair. But she had to know.

'Aunt Julie, why's Brownie's hair grey that way?'

Ella's voice resonated through Aunt Julie's plum summer dress and the question seemed to hang there for ages before

Ella felt her hands being lowered and she saw Aunt Julie standing there in her stockings, brassière and slip, smiling at her. It was like there were diamonds, the size and likes of which were a sheer delight to Aunt Julie, hanging in the air before her. Forget that the question had come from Brownie's own young, impressionable daughter. Aunt Julie lowered Ella's arms, took the dress from her and threw it on the bed in a way Ella had never seen Aunt Julie throw any of her treasured dresses before. Aunt Julie was about to glean those diamonds.

Aunt Julie took Ella's hand and led her over to the ceiling-to-floor mirror that stood in front of the window to catch Aunt Julie in the best possible light as she surveyed her appearance. The two of them stood in front of the mirror, Ella looking at Aunt Julie, Aunt Julie admiring herself.

'Well, you see, Pinkette, when me and you mother was little – if you can consider you mother ever was little – our Mamma and Puppa was poor. Old yard was nothing but a shack. No toilet, no kitchen. Just a cellar and a room with a roof.'

Ella became uncomfortably aware that, as she got further and further into her story, Aunt Julie was striking Ella's hair like a doll's.

'Puppa used to go Cayman go pick fruit. It was the only way we had was to manage. Brownie being the big eater she was, it was like having double the size family we did actually have.'

It was a lie. Despite the size of her and the fact that she cooked, Brownie wasn't in fact a huge eater. The universe

had just said, 'Brownie Brightwell, you shall be big', and she
was. Aunt Julie was lying.

'So 'cause a Brownie appetite me and Mamma used to
have to be apart from Puppa for months at a time. Anyway
one day Puppa come back after six months in Cayman.'

Aunt Julie was now sweeping Ella's hair off her forehead
and smoothing it down flat on her head, all the time staring
at herself in the mirror. Ella didn't know if she should get out
from under Aunt Julie's hand or just bear the feeling. She
wanted to hear the end of the story, so she bore it.

'Every time Puppa go and come, him stop inna Kingston
and buy me and Mamma a present.'

Ella had time to wonder why there was no mention of a
present for Brownie.

'One time Puppa bring a special present! A present him
know would full up me and Mamma with joy. Puppa bring
a mirror!'

Aunt Julie's voice hit a squealing high. It seemed that she
had found her brightest and most dazzling diamond to date,
and she sounded like Connie Sarason's pigs as she gobbled it
up.

'Nobody in the district, in the parish, not even Pastor
Moore Daisy, did have a mirror, and Puppa bring one home
just for me and Mamma!'

'Anyway, Brownie, she, jealous as always, couldn't help
but take a look when she think nobody looking. But I
catch her. And I come up behind her, knock her on the
shoulder, she turn, drop the mirror on the ground and it
gone!'

'It broke?' Ella's question was full of excitement. She was shocked. Aunt Julie was telling a story that would leave Brownie on the right side of something. Ella couldn't wait for Aunt Julie's answer to her question.

'And it broke!' Aunt Julie acknowledged.

A smile hit Ella's face and Aunt Julie let it stay there for the longest time. So it was bad luck on breaking a mirror that had made her mother's hair turn grey in the middle. All Ella had to do was find a way to bring good luck back into Brownie's life and so reverse the colour of the hair. It would be easy. But just as Ella was about to move away from the mirror with that satisfied smile on her face, Aunt Julie grabbed hold of her, placed one hand on her head and another on her chin and held Ella's face firmly in front of the mirror. The smile slipped from Ella's face as she saw just out of reach, just around the corner, the prospect, the glint of something that was enchanting and within Aunt Julie's reach. Coming slowly into view was the biggest of the diamonds. Aunt Julie picked at it like fruit from the Cayman. Ella knew now that Aunt Julie wasn't finished.

'Is the shock, you see,' Aunt Julie continued. She had deliberately paused, knowing Ella would draw a wrong con-clusion. 'Before the mirror drop from her hand, Brownie look on herself. And is the shock, you see! The shock cause Brownie hair to turn.'

Ella had to swallow her spit hard. She had heard of this swallowing trick from Aunt Julie. When you heard some-thing that was about to make you drop your stack, you must 'swallow you spit!' and as Aunt Julie stood smiling at her reflection in her huge mirror, and Ella stood watching her, Ella swallowed her spit.

Ella knew Aunt Julie's story couldn't be true. She knew Aunt Julie's story was shrouded in that strange emotion that clouded her relationship with her older sister: jealousy.

When Ella asked Brownie herself, Brownie's hands had been deep in ten pounds of flour and all she said was, 'One day . . .'

As Ella's eyes now looked towards the mirror, she saw that it had been spun around and was facing the wall. She marked it, it confused her, but she didn't dwell on it. Next to the dresser was the wardrobe where Brownie's one or two pieces hung. Clothes were never Brownie's thing, but Daddy Ned had the most suits and white shirts that Brownie used to boil, blue, hang on the line so that they puffed up like they were brooding or something and then she'd starch and iron them. There was a cot in the corner that wasn't a designated bed. It was like the spare bed in her own room. Maybe they were for visitors, Ella had once thought. But when visitors came they were never offered either the spare bed in Ella's room or this cot in her parents' room. Instead Brightwells were turned out of their beds to sleep on floors for any visitor and these two sleeping spaces were always left empty. Just another thing that made no sense and if you asked for sense, either Daddy Ned or Brownie or both would burst into tears, hug each other and be unable to tell you anything. Occasionally, whenever Ella had a nightmare and rushed along the landing and burst into her parents' bedroom, she would sometimes find Brownie curled up asleep on this little cot – that was the only time it was ever used. Daddy Ned was always asleep in the big bed, Brownie asleep on the cot. Despite, her size, she always looked to be having her most rested sleep there. Ella would crawl in beside her and snuggle deep inside, safe and at ease, and she too would fall into the most comforting and refreshing sleep. As she stood and looked at it now, she didn't know how the two of them ever fitted on it, but the cot was the best place the two of them had ever found to sleep.

Ella swept past the bed and came to the window. It was open and underneath it cushions were stacked. She used to lie on them sometimes listening to Brownie sing, sometimes just spending the whole day alone there doing nothing and being bothered by no one. Finally Ella was back at the dresser and the wardrobe. There was something disconcerting about the whole room, a feeling she didn't remember. She had felt it as soon as she had stepped into the room. It was the bed! The bed had been moved from the far wall where Ella remembered it. Beneath her feet the carpet by the door was worn and you could only imagine and remember what the colour pink had looked like when it was new all those years ago. Further into the room, there was a patch that shone bright and new in the midst of fading colour. Ella saw two depressions on the carpet where the feet of the bed had been. The bed had recently been moved. It occurred to Ella that Brownie had had nothing to do with the decision to move the bed. No, this bed had been moved as recently as Brownie's death.

The table was set for many. A pristine white tablecloth had been thrown over it, and the fruit centrepiece removed. Knives and forks, glasses and crockery, serving spoons, peppers and pickles, the salads, one at each end of the table, covered with mesh tents. A couple of jugs of carrot juice with ice floating on top with specks of nutmeg. And Mirabel was putting the last touches to the table. As she walked into Ella's view, Ella's eyes quickly left the table and settled on the kitchen, where a big man with a wrench was at the padlock, receiving instructions from Donna, trying to break into Brownie's spice and herb cupboard. They hadn't heard Ella come in. She just stood and watched them. She had seen nothing as full-frontal as this for a very long time and she could not believe the sheer injustice of Donna and the big man trying to headbutt something as sacred as Brownie's spice and herb cupboard.

'What's going on?' Ella asked with indignation.

Donna turned to Ella and her turn carried with it the big

man. Donna smiled at her that warm the-world-is-a-wonderful-place-and-I'm-glad-we're-both-in-it smile which was now least appreciated by Ella.

'Pinkette!' Donna gushed. 'You come down!'

'What's going on?'

'Daddy Ned can't wait to see you.'

Ella didn't respond. She was too busy looking at them and the spice and herb cupboard. She was too busy being genuinely affronted.

'Dinner soon ready,' Donna added as if she thought this would melt Ella.

'What's going on?' Ella continued.

'Finally we want to see what Mamma keep in her spice and herb cupboard.'

'She never wanted anyone to know what she kept in her spice and herb cupboard,' Ella said as if she had some God almighty right to say it.

The big man looked sheepish, not because of the statement, but because of who it came from. Ella looked at him and finally clicked who he was. The big man was her brother Patrick, and he, and all that he meant, frightened her into a stunned silence.

Patrick's twin was Johno. Ella and Johno had been closer than any of her other brothers and sisters, even closer than Johno and Patrick. As the youngest girl and youngest boy, Ella and Johno had had plenty in common. Though all her children were for ever Brownie's babies, Ella and Johno could by the law of the universe lay claim to being Brownie's true babies and the two of them, led by Ella, played it to the hilt.

One particular hot midmorning, nearly five years before Brownie dragged Patrick into the Old Yew Inn and Ella stood up to face Brownie, Ella, Johno and Patrick too burnt down house number 27 of the road where they lived in the Pink House. Ella was twelve and the twins were thirteen. She remembered it like this: Ella and Johno were bored that day and the Pink House was out of bounds because Ella had not done some chore Aunt Julie had set her and she knew if she went home she'd be in trouble and, worse, be made to perform the chore. Shoes! It must've been Aunt Julie's shoes! Johno had spent the morning walking around Hanville trying to find something of interest to occupy himself. He had yet to realise something Ella had long realised; there was nothing of interest to occupy you around Hanville. He found Ella sitting in a tree looking up at the sun, eating a lunch of fried snapper and hard-dough bread and drinking from a cool flask of carrot juice.

'What you doing up there?' Johno's words floated up to her.

'What you doing down there?' Ella threw back at him.

She wanted Johno, more than anyone else in her family, to realise that up in a tree, closer to the sky, was somewhere he too could be if he simply cared to climb up. But he wouldn't, or couldn't, and Ella found herself climbing down to join him on the ground. Johno had already eaten his lunch, probably the moment Brownie had placed it in his hand that morning, and Ella offered him what was left of hers. He was greedy that way and as they walked on to nowhere Ella heard nothing from him until he had finished it up.

They found themselves outside the Hanville Petrol Station where Patrick had taken up a part-time job at the insistence of Ella, who saw it as a way of keeping him away from her beloved Johno. Ella could not bear the twins spending time together. She had long had the feeling that their spending time together wasn't good for her Johno. Johno had a tendency to be overshadowed by Patrick, Ella thought. Patrick was more exuberant, more boisterous; Johno was quiet, sensitive, given to bursting into tears at the drop of a hat or at a punch of one of Patrick's fists. Ella saw it as her duty to protect him, the sibling to whom she was drawn.

Between Ella and Patrick there was an intense dislike. Of all her siblings, Patrick was the one she cared for least, probably because he had a wilfulness about him that was just like Ella's. As tiny children Ella and Patrick had demonstrated that of all the Brightwell children they alone had a heap of wilfulness their mother would never understand. What they then had to prove was whose will was the strongest.

Between Ella and Patrick, Johno quickly became the tangible thing by which the two of them set about proving themselves. He tried his best to stand firm but there was little firm about Johno. The tragedy for Johno was that he had to live with the knowledge that he had the ability to both please and anger each of them and if he was doing one with one, he was surely doing the other with the other. With this knowledge came the certainty that he would one day perish between his beloved siblings.

For Patrick, Ella was just a stupid, skinny kid who had somehow, at every turn, managed to upstage him within

the Brightwell family. Worse, she had Johno's love and attention when nature had deemed they should be Patrick's alone.
He had no doubt that if it wasn't for the fact that Johno was
his twin, Ella wouldn't have wanted anything to do with
him. She was in it because she was bad-minded, he was in it
because Johno was the only person he had ever met who
looked like him, the only person who thought the same
thoughts as him – they only expressed them differently – the
only person who would, on soup day, swop his piece of beef
for Patrick's dumpling. He felt he and Johno were gradually
being parted by Ella.

So it was Ella who wound Patrick up and let him go to
spin like a top. It was Ella who got him to think stealing a
shelf of Marlboros was his own very good idea. It was Ella
who got him to break into number 27 of the road on which
they lived in the Pink House so the three of them could
smoke them. The fire started in a bedroom, spread behind
their fleeing feet down the hall, down the stairs, lapped over
the whole downstairs and engulfed the house in the kitchen.
Number 27 burnt to the ground in less than an hour.

'You recognise him don't you?' Donna was saying to Ella
back in the kitchen of the Pink House. And though she
couldn't say she did, Ella had recognised more in her brother
Patrick than she wanted to.

Even though she was trying to, Ella couldn't take her eyes
off Patrick. His face was full of hair. Hair grew from his
cheekbones, just under his eyes even, down his throat into

his chest. It looked like he was hiding from something underneath all that hair. It looked like if he were ever required to shave it off, say join the army or something stupid like that, he would die from the exposure. It looked like if whatever he was hiding from ever demanded he face it, he would just curl up and die. Patrick had locks that sailed down his back and beyond his arse even though they were twisted and tied up to take away from the length of them. At the front of his hair were flecks of grey that were truly Brownie's. All around him there was a strange darkness that blocked and deflected all kinds of wonderful light sources that were desperate to burst through and warm his soul. Patrick had the smallest eyes Ella had ever seen. She didn't remember their being that small when they were growing up. Over the years they had grown darker too. Perhaps he needed glasses. As they stood in front of each other for the first time in thirteen years, Patrick wasn't able to look Ella in the face.

'Hello,' Patrick mumbled, and for him that could've been it. He and Ella understood that it couldn't be any more than 'hello' without spilling over into territory neither of them wanted to visit. But Donna didn't.

'Hello!' mocked Donna shocked. 'Hello!'

Patrick's eyes had fallen slowly to his feet. Ella's eyes were able to hold up, but only just.

'Thirteen years you don't see our sister Pinkette and all you can say to her is hello? Hello! Hello! Hello!'

Ella began to shrink at how many times Donna would say that one solitary adequate little word.

'Patrick, man, hug up our sister.'

Patrick's eyes shot up from his feet, not far behind came Ella's, and three sets of eyes rested on Donna. Mirabel, the silent witness, who sensed the distance between her aunt and uncle and was a way further to understanding the enormity of what one aunt had suggested to her uncle, was observing all.

Patrick's mouth had fallen open. He didn't know where to put himself. He didn't know how to begin to 'hug up their sister' and he didn't want to begin to know. He didn't even want to touch her in a shake of hands, never mind anything else. Donna saw his eyes drop back to his feet and once she realised he was making no move towards their sister, she shouted out his name, 'Patrick!'

'What?' Patrick shouted at her, his head lifting from his shoes again. He was acting like a child; truth is he had never really grown past age thirteen.

Donna began to hit him. 'Thirteen years and all you can say is "hello" to our sister? Man, gwan better!'

'Hello. You looking . . . well,' Patrick added under pressure, lifting his eyes to look at Ella and then dropping them before he had come to the end of what he was saying.

'Thank you,' Ella only said. And that was her greeting and meeting of Patrick.

As the whole town gathered to watch the operation to try and save number 27 Patrick pissed his pants. Worse for Patrick, Ella saw him piss his pants. As Ella's eyes left Patrick's crotch and travelled up to his face she saw it was full to the brim with fear. Ella had never seen fear like this and seeing

it on the face of the brother she despised, brought her her
greatest victory to date. Her will was soaring higher than
that of the enemy. That for Ella was what life had become.
As Patrick turned and fled in the face of his sister's gloating,
she knew he'd never stand over her again.

It all turned bad, though, when Johno was picked up
trying to leave Hanville by a member of the Hanville
Constabulary. Ella was under the kitchen table listening to a
late-night conversation between Daddy Ned and Brownie
when she heard. She had not gone to bed that night because
her Johno had not been seen since they'd been separated running from the burning house. She'd looked for him but hadn't
found him. And how could she sleep when her Johno had
disappeared? She sensed he was in trouble, wrestling somewhere with the conscience she didn't seem to possess. She had
sat up under the oak table, waiting to hear the conversation
she knew would be had around it just as soon as Daddy Ned
and Brownie returned from the police station, where a phone
call some hours ago had ordered them to attend. There, they
were told, was their youngest son Jonathan Clive Gladstone
Brightwell. As Ella listened, fear and shame were laughing at
her. She felt so much these two emotions she thought they
would swoop over her life and take it. Indeed it got so bad as
she listened that Ella prayed that they would. For Jonathan
Clive Gladstone Brightwell had been so petrified by the situation he had found himself in that when Daddy Ned and
Brownie arrived at the police station to discover what was
what, they found their son had been struck dumb. Below the
table Ella heard that not only did the Hanville constabulary

suspect Johno of setting fire to number 27, they were also holding him on a charge of stealing from the Hanville Petrol Station a whole shelf of Marlboro cigarettes which they had found on his person. Somehow Patrick had managed to leave Johno holding the Marlboro!

Daddy Ned and Brownie were devastated. Brownie particularly could not believe that a seed of her and Daddy Ned's bodies, conceived, born and reared with nothing but love, devotion and goodness, could have created such a woe as emerged over the next six months. Refused bail, Johno was held by the authorities as he awaited trial. And every couple of weeks some new charge would filter out and be told to Brownie and Daddy Ned. The gist of the whole thing, according to the Hanville Constabulary, was that Johno was responsible for almost every unsolved juvenile crime that had ever taken place within their jurisdiction. The charges ranged from stealing flowers from Mrs Whittaker's front garden to cleaning out O'Leary's, the local gents' outfitters, and selling the clothes on to Tommy 'Twelve Fingers' Bowers, the local fence. And it all raged with Johno unable to say a thing in his defence.

Ella and Patrick kept their own counsel throughout the whole affair. They could not face each other or anyone else. They found places within, places where they went to seal up their part in what had befallen Johno. Only occasionally did the two of them emerge when they had to take part in some family event, answer some question they couldn't avoid, but always they would scurry back with more bricks, more cement.

Throughout Johno's detainment, his trial and sentencing, a look of death had come over Brownie's face. Ella had never seen such a thing in her mother before. There was always something of the sun about her mother and here she was wounded by something that had started as, well, as nothing. It was the darkest time for the Brightwells, but for Brownie it was really a death. Amazingly she didn't cook for the whole time Johno was locked up, and only started cooking again once he was sentenced. It was the longest time Brownie had spent away from cooking. In fact she had never not cooked for a single day since her adolescence, until this time when this thing had happened to her youngest son. That was the way Brownie felt: this thing had happened to her Johno. She knew her youngest son could not have done these things he was charged with. They had happened to him. Brownie knew her children expertly, she had studied them. She knew them by the foods that were their favourites. Johno's favourite foods were almost rotting fried plantains, a peg or two of breadfruit, roasted on an open fire which Brownie would rise and light out in the yard in the early morning so the breadfruit could spend the whole glorious day roasting, giving it a smoky tang that enveloped its whole delicate taste. Cho-cho, a green vegetable that you had to keep an eye on so that it didn't overcook, so that it was ready in the shortest time, the way that Johno liked it. Fish fried in the hottest oil, so that it fried quick and crisp, sealing in all the flavour, sprinkled with vinegar, onion and peppers and set out with fried dumplings for a feast. They were foods that took a delicate, knowing hand to prepare, and Brownie prepared them with joyful reverence for the gentlest of her children. Brownie, then, could not believe she had misread one of her children in so drastic a way. The only answer was that this thing had happened to Johno. She didn't understand now, but she knew the universe would one day give her the answer.

Johno was to be detained at Her Majesty's pleasure. No one had any idea how long Her Majesty's pleasure might be for a frightened, unfortunate little black boy who had burnt down a house and more, and really that was the whole point. The sentence was devastating for everyone, but particularly for Ella and Patrick.

Before Donna had decided which way to go with Ella and Patrick, the back door sprung open and two women came cursing into the kitchen of the Pink House with a brood of a dozen or more children.

Princess was a large woman who would have run the size of Brownie a close second. She was the older of the two. She was wearing a large flounced tent thing not unlike the ones Brownie used to wear. She had a large scar that ran from just above her right eye and ended beneath the bottom lip of the left side of her face. Her right eye didn't move. It was dead. Over each arm was a tattoo: a great big bird of prey on one and a lion on the other. They were tattoos from a previous life, a life she could not get rid of. A life she had once been quoted an extortionate price to remove from her psyche when she had been piss-poor. But now, with the love and support of Patrick, she had decided to keep them and show them off to the world.

'As a lesson,' Patrick had told her. 'Wear them as a lesson.'

'Listen,' Princess was saying to the other woman, 'if you think because is your weekend, I not going come pay my respect to Mamma Brownie, then you make a sad mistake!'

And the other countered with, 'You hear what you say, though? You hear it? From you own mouth sprung the truth! My weekend!'

Althea had a warmer spirit, as if once she settled her mouth down she would do anything to make a stranger's life easier. She was wearing a miniskirt and a top that showed off her midriff, and her belly button was pierced and the belly itself was snaked with stretch marks from being pregnant many times. Her nails were painted a bright look-at-me orange and Ella did. Her hair was permed straight and cropped short. Her lips were red like blackberries and they had fastened themselves to a mouth that would've swallowed any face but her own. No one, anywhere, had a face like Althea's. Her eyes were big, watery and soft. Her nose was big, but it took no air that wasn't its by right. Althea's gargantuan facial features fitted her face perfectly into some kind of prettiness. God knew what he was doing when he created this woman, but only just. In fact, what Althea wasn't some kind of prettiness, it was beauty.

Ella was trying to decide which face she wanted to feed upon when Princess sprung at Althea, got her down on the kitchen floor and began fighting her. Princess's former life had evidently not been banished to the hell it had once been as completely as she liked to believe. A stack of pots went crashing to the ground as the downwards chaos took a shelf, all the pots on it, and the two women too. One large gleaming pot hit one of the kids. The result was a piercing cry that set off the brood of them like a tower of playing cards. Ella observed that one particularly vocal one stood on the step in the doorway screaming without breaking for breath. Patrick just stood there watching as though he had seen it before. Donna went into action, consoling the most distressed of the kids and ushering them all outside to the yard. Down on the floor the fight went backwards and forwards, neither woman having a clear advantage. This was the kind of stuff Ella understood. Brownie had not taught it to her, but she knew it. This was how you lived life. If someone pissed you off, you didn't like the way they looked at you, spoke to you or disagreed with you, then you wrestled them to the ground and fought and you did it anywhere and any time you so desired. And you so desired because in life, no matter where you got to, you had to have respect. If you didn't have that, then you had nothing. However, to see the struggle was completely disgusting for Ella.

Princess had rolled Althea and looked like her weight advantage might just pull her through. But then a cascade of cold water came over the two of them down on the kitchen floor and they fell away from one another soaked to the skin.

'Now the two of you get up, clean up this mess, and remember this is the home of a dead woman. My mother!' The action and voice of something called reason had come from Donna. Althea and Princess burst into tears at the state they had made of themselves and said sorry.

Ella looked down at her sodden shoes.

Princess and Althea were the two women in the life of Patrick. Patrick had the ability to keep two women interested and in love with him, and keep them well enough to disgrace themselves and each other whenever and wherever they came together. Over the years they had had to work out detailed plans, keep diaries about where one would be just so the other wouldn't be there at the same time. They could talk on the phone as they arranged their diaries around one another, but if they ever met, the scene in Brownie's kitchen was nine times out of ten the result. Their diaries centred on every situation that took them out of their respective homes: shopping, school visits, doctor, a spontaneous walk in the park, Brightwell family events. But on this occasion Althea had been calling Princess and had got no answer. Immediately she had felt cheated and the anger began to build inside her. She knew exactly where Princess was, she was off 'trying to nice up herself with the Brightwells' when it wasn't even her week to be with the Brightwells.

The two of them had approached the Pink House from opposite ends of the street. Rounding their respective corners at precisely the same time, the two of them spotted each other, with their respective children yapping behind and in front of them, at precisely the same moment. It was a dash down the street where the Pink House stood as the one tried to get to the House before the other. Bursting into the kitchen with the above result.

Ella looked at Patrick. He was evidently good. He was clever, bright, cunning. He might even have been better at it than she. One innocuous-looking man had built himself a life destined to keep from his ever so hurt mind any mention, any sniff of what they were both running from. That she had to concede, albeit grudgingly.

All had gone on and Daddy Ned was but a wall away.

Donna stepped over the two women, unhooked the Sheila Maid, lowered it from the ceiling and took several towels off it. She then got down on her knees and began dabbing gently at Ella's feet. Ella immediately tried to stop her hands. Whatever Ella was pretending to be, she didn't want this.

'No, let me, Pinky. 'Cause I'm so sorry. Let me, Pinky.'

And Ella could do nothing but let Donna serve something like a penance and dab at her shoes. Ella could see, from the height she was and the depth Donna was, that the fight, the scene, had embarrassed and shamed Donna deeply. Ella suddenly saw that this woman, who had settled for all this the way Brownie had, was in deep immeasurable pain. A look of failure came about Donna and it shook Ella. Had she been someone else, she might have made Donna stop dabbing at her shoes, helped her to her feet and hugged her up, just like Donna had wanted Patrick to hug her up. But Ella couldn't do that. And Ella knew Donna needed to kneel at her feet and dab at them more than Ella needed to stop her. And because they were sisters, Ella swallowed herself for the woman on her knees below her. It was the first selfless act Ella had exhibited for God knows how long, it dawned on her.

In the passage all she could now go with was the look of pain on her sister's face. She had only been back a few hours and she didn't understand or know her sister's life, but she had immediately thought that Donna had all she wanted and now finding out she didn't was an immense shock.

Ella was standing outside the sitting-room door where she was told Daddy Ned was waiting for her. To say she would rather not be standing outside the sitting-room door would be greatly to understate. She would rather have been soaking her head in a vat of vinegar.

There was a part of Daddy Ned that was called Brownie, a part of him that only Brownie could start up and she could start it at will – next to him, five hundred miles away from him, dead and away from him, she could start it up. Ella had never seen, didn't know she would never again see, a man love a woman the way that Daddy Ned loved his Brownie. Loved her Brownie.

Ella knocked on the door. There was no answer, and she knocked again. They were I-don't-want-to-be-here knocks, hoping the person on the other side of the door didn't want her to be there either and wouldn't invite her in. She told herself when she knocked a third time that if nothing came from inside the room, she would turn, walk out of the

House and never come back. She was just about to leave when she felt someone lift her hand and force it down on the door handle. It wasn't a hand she could see, but the texture and smell were familiar to her. She felt a body behind her, pressing her into the door; she knew it and yet she wanted to fight it. Whenever she was forced to do anything she didn't want, she would fight. But even before she'd begun, she knew this was a fight she had no stomach for. In a second the body behind her had pressed her through the door and she was standing on the other side, looking around a room she had earlier visited. All she could do was to stand there stunned.

The sitting room was still now. Many rooms in other houses, after a death in the house, would've been cold on a ninety-degree summer's day, but not the sitting room of the Pink House. Ella fixed on a high-backed chair, the chair that Brownie had made hers. The chair that no one sat in because you always had to get up when she came to make a rare sit-down in the sitting room, not because she told you to or made you, but for the simple reason that you weren't comfortable in the thing once she had entered. Even Ella had submitted to this one unwritten truth.

Now Ella took a step forwards and because of the stillness of the room, her feet squelched in her soggy shoes. She stopped dead, midstep, conscious of the sound against the calm of the room, and then became aware of something else. Something bigger, something scarier, something that hadn't been there when she had visited the room earlier. When the room had been full of life and women in white cardigans and black polyester dresses, singing and playing the 'do you remember' game.

Under the window, with shafts of sunlight inviting the occupant up to the place where she belonged, was a peach-coloured coffin. The coffin was open and was sprouting hair. Here was her Brownie laid out in a peach coffin. And in the face of seeing her mother after thirteen years gone, all she began to wonder was who could have chosen that coffin.

Ella swallowed hard. She didn't want to stare, but she hadn't been brought up to avert eyes, ears or anything else. She had been brought up in the freedom of Brownie and now she stared with that freedom. The coffin was long and it was wide. It was painted with flowers that swirled and interlocked and wound themselves around each other in glorious natural harmony. But it was the size of it that was doing Ella into the ground. It was enormous! In all the years Ella had been away from her, Brownie had remained the same size in Ella's mind as she actually was in body and soul: huge!

Hair! No other person in past or present life had hair like that: hair that was sticking up all over the place. Someone had forgotten to comb Brownie's hair. Or maybe someone had combed it, but just as it was in life, in death too it refused to do anything a comb asked of it and took off in any direction it pleased. To Ella it didn't look as though the coffin lid would ever be able to close with all that hair sticking up. It looked as though that could well be the reason the lid was off. It would be like a suitcase. Men would have to be sitting on it, while other men struggled to fasten it closed.

Ella could lay vast bets at the embarrassment as they tried to manoeuvre Brownie towards her grave – she could only thank God she would not now be around to see it. The embarrassment would be her family's. Embarrassment, after all, was what they were about and most of it had come through Brownie. Standing in the sitting room, looking at the coffin with Brownie's hair sprouting from it, all Ella could do was swallow her spit hard and wonder.

She could see him sitting in the high-backed chair with his back to her. Midstep, she watched him, as still as the room, and as warm as the room. He was smaller. He was quieter. He was slower. He was older. It never occurred to her she would have to hug him. She stood looking at him before he knew she was there in the room with him. Or so she thought. He was sipping on a glass of white rum. Every now and then he let out a little giggle in his privacy. She felt embarrassed at being there, but she just stood there. Waiting for him to finish the rum in his glass, trying to avoid the sight of Brownie's hair flying out of her coffin, feeling sillier than ever. No sooner had he finished his glass of rum than he poured more and began to sip on that. The bottle was half empty. It could take a while, or maybe not, the way he was drinking.

'Come forward, Pinkette.' It was Daddy Ned's voice.

She remembered Brownie's voice because Brownie's voice was inside her, but his voice was like a dead person's. Like a stranger's.

'Come forward,' came his voice again.

She found herself timidly doing as she was told. She sat.

There was a chair opposite him, next to the coffin, where she supposed he meant her to sit, but she preferred to sit to the side of him, on the edge of the sofa, hardly able to breathe now.

'You mother waiting to talk to you.'

Ella didn't know what to say. In her years of absence, madness had begun to rot every Brightwell mind, it seemed. Well, he was either drunk or off his head. And then she didn't know why she thought either of those things.

'She waiting,' he continued.

Daddy Ned had not once looked at his daughter. He had remained looking straight ahead, sipping on his rum, in his own privacy. His four utterances had come hard on the heels of one another. Now Ella sat waiting for the fifth, hoping it would come quickly, since she had not responded to any of the previous ones and was eager to cover the silence between them. But it didn't come. Daddy Ned went on to drink the glass dry, pour himself another glass full, drink that, and pour himself another glass, which he then rested on the table.

Sitting to the side of Daddy Ned gave a different view to standing a pace behind him. He still looked smaller, he still looked slower and older, but where before this had looked like despair and grief to Ella, she now saw that it was no such thing. Daddy Ned wasn't devastated. He was in a place where he looked like he had found the answer to whatever it was we all want to know. He had something of a glow about him that placed him first among men. Ella didn't understand. Surely he was devastated at the loss of the part of

him that made him beam? Surely he was absolutely dis-
traught and grief-stricken at the thought of having to put his
Brownie down some dark hole for ever? Surely? Yes! But it
was no. He had not grown to hate his Brownie in the years
Ella had not been around. He had not grown complacent
with her. And he had not found a new love in the days
since she had died. He had found something else, he had
found a way to do something, knowing now that not even
death could take his love. Daddy Ned had found that where
his heartbeat was concerned, death had neither sting nor
taste, and now he sat and laughed at it. That was what he was
doing, he was mocking it. All this she thought in the time it
took him to deliver his long-awaited fifth utterance.

'Go on, go look 'pon you mother.'

'What?' Ella didn't mean to be rude, the word just fell out
her mouth before she knew it.

Daddy Ned's head slowly turned from the coffin to look
at Ella for the first time. When she realised what was happening, she almost pissed herself with fear. When Daddy
Ned was full on her, he smiled. He knew her and would've
known her anywhere, but she would've passed him in the
middle of any street. She stared back at his smiling face
blankly. Daddy Ned reached for his glass of rum and Ella's
eyes were drawn to his hands. She recognised them
instantly. Around his black skin patches had been stripped
white and where the two skins collided, patterns had
formed and were continually forming, disappearing up his
sleeves.

Ella had been on the ledge one day. Heard splashing from

the bathroom. The Brightwells alone had deemed it unnec-
essary to have opaque glass for the bathroom window. She'd
shuffled the few feet along the ledge from her room to the
bathroom. Brownie and Daddy Ned were just emerging
from a shared bath. Brownie was facing the window, saw Ella
and smiled at her. Daddy Ned, his back to Ella and the
window, never saw her, but Ella saw him and when she did,
she nearly fell clean off the ledge for shock. His back was
practically white, like someone had thrown acid down his
back and arse and had stripped his black skin white. Like a
kid painting on a black canvas; abstract patterns forming and
dividing so'til you couldn't tell which colour came first, the
black or the white. It had spread to his hands.

'Go look,' he urged her.

'No. No, thank you.' Ella felt an utter wretch.

'Is not everybody want go look 'pon her. Some do. Some
don't. Make you wonder what some 'fraid of. Make you sure
wonder.'

After this long delivery he turned his head back to the
coffin and fell silent. Ella recognised she had been suitably
chastised and she shrank further away from her environ-
ment. It took half an hour before she plucked up the
courage, took off her shoes and crept to the door. As she
approached the door, she told herself she would fight any
force that prevented her from leaving and she would win.
But as her hand reached out for the door handle, the seal on
the door cracked as easy as anything and she found herself
face to face with a smiling Donna. Ella stepped back, startled
for a moment, before she realised it was Donna.

'You and Daddy Ned have you talk?' Donna asked as she came bounding past Ella over to Daddy Ned.

They had had all the talk they were going to have, was what Ella thought as she watched Donna go over to him. There was nothing more she had to say to him and nothing more he had to say to her.

''Cause dinner more than ready now.' Donna stood over Daddy Ned. 'Daddy Ned, come. We waiting dinner for you and Pinkette.'

As Donna stood over him, waiting for him to rise, Daddy Ned showed no particular urgency to drag himself from Brownie's coffin. All Ella could do was stand back and watch Donna. She knew how to handle him.

'Daddy Ned, come. Come. Come leave our Brownie to rest little.'

He got to his feet, dragged his eyes from the coffin and took Donna's arm. The two of them, arm in arm together like that, in their own world where Ella wouldn't go, looked like they were one and the same. Like they'd come from the same root. As they glided lovingly out past her, Ella made herself as small as she could against the wall, fearful they might touch her.

Before they disappeared into the dining room, Ella heard Donna confirm to Daddy Ned, ''Cause you know our Brownie need her rest.'

Ella was now alone in the sitting room, and still brimming with fear. Her eyes flickered like someone was shining a bright light in them. They fell on the coffin and once her eyes had found their way over there, she couldn't remove them. Ella was taking silent fretful steps, the one shrouded in hope, the other shrouded in fear, and she was taking them towards Brownie's coffin. As she went, there began a low, deep sob that only she could hear. To take another breath in life she had to make it to the side of the coffin and look Brownie squarely in the face.

At the side of coffin she looked at the face of her Brownie and her stomach immediately jumped into her throat. At first she thought it was going to jump out through her mouth and shower her divine Brownie with its contents, but somehow she held on and did so by holding on to the coffin itself. The deep, low sob was breathing inside Ella and seemed to be breathing inside her Brownie too. For a moment it looked as if Brownie was breathing up and down like the spice and herb cupboard. Up and down like Ella herself. She settled on her mother looking closely at her and it wasn't as scary as she thought it might have been. She needed to take her in, reacquaint herself if such a thing was possible now she was dead. Brownie looked no different to how Ella remembered her. People in death are said to look peaceful, but for Brownie, who had looked as peaceful in life as she now did in death, there was no difference. Her skin was slacker but that was age. They'd been thirteen years apart, and her head of hair was entirely grey now. It looked as if Brownie was smiling back at her, it would have been just like Brownie to have the capacity to smile in death. Only someone who was content and at peace with the life they had left could look like that. It was such a Brownie thing to have no hostility, no vengeance, malice, hate or regret. If Ella had had any doubt that her Brownie was really and truly dead, when she had long thought her immortal, there was no doubt in her mind now. The feeling that she had returned too late came washing over her until she suddenly couldn't bear it. Ella reached into the coffin, touched Brownie's hair and smoothed it down. As soon as she did it, it was like it had been waiting all these years for just such a touch. The hair went down and stayed down. It was smooth as anything and lay full on one side of her face. Ella was close to breaking her heart for the second time in her life. Slowly she began to withdraw her hand and then she stopped. Something sparkled before her eyes. Sticking out of Brownie's hand, right in front of her, was something indeed. It was clasped tightly in Brownie's left hand and Brownie's hands were on her chest as though they were clasped in prayer. She didn't know how it wasn't the first thing she had seen on looking into the coffin, but now it was all she saw. It was a key. She couldn't believe what it was, what it fitted, she knew what it looked like, but was it? It was the key to Brownie's spice and herb cupboard. If she had that key she could unlock the spice and herb cupboard, discover Brownie's secret, take it and know her. She had to have that key. She had heard that taking something from the hand of the dead was difficult. If they died full of regret and spite, whatever they had in their mind when they passed, bad feeling made them hold on to it as one last bad jig. But Brownie had no bad feeling, Ella knew that. So Brownie would be the exceptional corpse. Ella's heart was beating so loud from the excitement at what that key meant that she couldn't hear a thing of the outside world. She was sure that once she clasped the key this banging excitement would stop and she'd burst with joy. Her hand reached into the coffin again and her fingers snaked around the key. When they brushed against her mother's fingers, it was a sensation she did not even feel, she was so focused on what she was doing. The key was stuck! She pulled again. Where was the ease with which the key should have left her mother? Brownie was holding on to it. What spiteful, bitter thing was this in a body that had never even had a sniff of it in life? Ella didn't know. She was pulling on the key with both hands, excitement bubbling in her. Next she found she was pacing in front of the coffin and muttering to herself, wondering why Brownie needed to hold on to something to see her cross over and pacified on the other side. Such were Ella's mutterings that Mirabel was able to stand by the door and deliver her sentence five times before the sixth found its way into Ella's mind.

'Aunty Pinkette, we waiting dinner for you!'

Mirabel and Ella stared each other out the way their short acquaintance had deemed they should. God damn it, Ella didn't like her. God damn it, Ella hated her. And God damn it, Ella wanted to kill her. And the ugly kid seemed to know it because she turned out from the doorway where she had stood observing her aunt and went back to the dining room to wait with the others for Ella to join them.

Ella tried to calm herself, taking in deep breaths. Her heart was pumping, her brain was ticking, she was alive with as much vitality as the last time she had fucked, and she was going on deep, low breaths. Before she went, she turned back and looked at Brownie in her coffin. As she looked, she thought – and did not ask God to forgive and pardon her as she thought it – but Brownie was damn ugly!

While she was asleep, while she was in with Daddy Ned – all day in fact – food and drink had been arriving at the Pink House and now it was a cavern of food waiting to be prepared and cooked, of drink waiting to be drunk. A dozen or so boxes of fresh chicken portions, half a cow, a whole pig, a goat, goat fish and snapper packed in ice and chilling in the shed. There were sacks of rice, boxes of yams, sweet potatoes, green bananas and plantains, all from the West Indian grocer. Drink from the off-licence, mainly Wray and Nephew white overproof – 62.8 per cent – rum and then some whiskey, a few bottles of Martell brandy, some crates of Red Stripe beer, Mackeson and Guinness and then Cherry B and Babycham for the ladies who insisted on being ladies. Ella couldn't help thinking it might have all kept her in business for a good few months. Donna would oversee the lot.

Around all this, dinner had taken place and it had taken place with none of the free abandon of when Brownie was alive.

For a start, Ella walked into the dining room and it was pin-droppingly quiet. It was eerie. She had never heard the Pink House so quiet when full of people before. The silence hit her and left her totally motionless. Ella didn't know how many eyes were in the place, but they were all looking at her. She looked at them, swallowed and remained in the doorway. All the adults were sitting around the huge oak table immaculately laid by Mirabel, and all the kids were sitting in the adjacent kitchen area, around a table that wasn't there before, two benches running the length of it on either side. All were looking silently at Ella, waiting for her to join them.

The only child allowed to sit at the oak table with the attending adults was Mirabel, of course. And the only vacant chair at the oak table was slap bang opposite Mirabel. This kid would be in Ella's face all through dinner. There was nothing Ella could do, there was no other seat. She couldn't bear the attending eyes on her any longer, she didn't have the stomach for a scene, so she sat. As soon as she was in the chair, Ella realised something else about that chair. Not only was it directly opposite Mirabel, but it was also the damn chair in which Brownie had drowned.

As soon as Ella was seated, all the adults and Mirabel too lifted their hands on to the table and joined hands in something like a rippling effect. It started with Donna and fanned out either side of her at an equal pace. It was like the ripple of a Mexican wave. Ella watched the joining of hands sweeping simultaneously around the two sides of the table and it dawned on her that the ripple was on its way to her. Any second the two people on either side of her would reach out

left and right hands in search of her own hands. Ella looked
at her right and flinched. Some twist of fate had placed
Princess there. She looked to her left; some horror of an
entity had planted Patrick there. Before she was ready, the
ripple had caught up with her at the exact same moment on
either side of her. To her left, Patrick's right hand rested on
the table in front of her. Ella could only imagine what would
happen if she put her hand in his. It would be like placing it
in a vice that wouldn't stop until it had squeezed out her life,
because she knew he wanted her dead. Ella went back to her
right, hoping to find solace and a way forward. Princess's left
hand was on the table waiting, just like Patrick's right, and
for the first time Ella noticed Princess was missing a finger.
The little finger. Ella closed her eyes; it was beyond belief.
When she opened them Donna was looking at her and waiting. Ella placed her hands first in Princess's and then in
Patrick's.

'Our Father God. Bless you for this what we are about to
receive . . .' Donna's voice came out over the table.

Had this started with Brownie's death? Or had this been
going on for years? When they were younger, Brownie
merely placed the mountains of food before them and they
ate and chatted over it in their enjoyment. And they did it
that way when all the other black people in Hanville did it
this way, because the Brightwells understood that Brownie
had already worshipped and praised God for sending the
food in her cooking of the food.

At the head of the table sat Donna and not Daddy Ned –
it had always been the women, Ella remembered. She liked

that, she liked that very much. It was not something she had imagined, it was actually true. In the blessing, Donna looked calm, looked like she belonged, looked nothing like the desperate woman who had not long ago insisted on kneeling at Ella's feet, dabbing at them. Ella took her in. Not only did she have Brownie's ways, but she looked like Brownie too. She had a fat face with a mole on the side of her jaw, which had a puff of hair growing from it. Her hair, all black, no grey yet, was cane-rowed back into tiny rows that ended somewhere in her back. She had on a white blouse that was struggling to keep her huge warm tits encased beneath it and she had a still breath that was not dissimilar to the breath of Brownie's spice and herb cupboard.

On Donna's right was Daddy Ned. Eyes open, but uselessly so. He was smiling that same smile, miles away, gone with his Brownie from this world and loving it. Ella thought how appropriate that he should be placed next to Donna, who made him look like the mouse Ella had always thought him. She had loved Daddy Ned when she was growing up. She loved him as her father and the man her mother had chosen as her husband. But there was always something about the man himself that she couldn't get her head around and because of it, there was a part of her that had not understood something of Brownie. If Brownie could choose this man to be her husband, then what did that say about Brownie? If this was the man on whose life Brownie's heart did beat, then what complexity was there about Brownie? Yes, he was pretty and the women rushed him, but there was something weak about him that when placed against any other human being would not have shown up, but placed against Brownie it showed him clearly to be the little thing he had become in Ella's mind. This aside, though, he was still the father she loved and Ella didn't know it, but a smile was beginning not just on her face but deep inside her too.

By Daddy Ned, where she had plotted and manoeuvred to be for how many years, sat Aunt Julie. As her eyes travelled across to her Aunt Julie, Ella's smile was about ripe and warm and it remained so, because Ella knew there was nothing Aunt Julie could do to have her father. She could wear the highest shoes, the longest wigs and the deepest necklines, but there was nothing she could do. Daddy Ned did not want her. Ella could see one of Aunt Julie's eyes trying desperately to peep open, to see no one was getting one over on her. But she knew that what was actually out there was far scarier than not knowing and the eye stayed shut. And then Ella noticed some of what Aunt Julie was running from. Just under her wig, at the front, Ella could clearly make out a tiny bunch of grey hair. What with the rhino skin, the turkey neck and the grey hair, God had certainly done His jig on Aunt Julie and she looked like nothing but the vulnerable little old woman she actually was.

Then there was Mirabel. As Ella's eyes came round directly in front of her, she saw that Mirabel's eyes were not closed and she knew they had never been. Ella stared back at Mirabel, but then she had to pull out of the stare when she felt Mirabel was about to possess her, and Ella's eyes fell down and away in shame and fear and she closed them.

At the head of the table, Donna was finishing up the blessing. 'And finally, God, we ask you to take care of our
glorious Mamma Brownie, who we love and who we know
and trust you call at this time 'cause she give we all that she
can. We thank you, God. Amen!'

The chain was finally physically broken long after it had
already been broken, all eyes opened and a sudden murmur
of chatter began around the table, just like the free-for-all
Ella remembered. The Brightwells were about to eat.

Donna had cooked a feast and it was nothing special.
There were dishes on dishes on dishes and they were being
passed around and helped to as freely as they had been prepared and placed before the family. There were two huge
bowls of rice and peas, three of yam – two white, one
yellow – two bowls of green bananas, one of boiled breadfruit, two of sweet potato and two of dumplings. Then there
was the meat. Beef and pork today and both would have
been seasoned the night before with salt, freshly ground
black pepper, onions, scallions and thyme, the last two both
plucked fresh from Brownie's herb garden. Donna would've
woken at some godforsaken hour, put a little oil in Brownie's
everlasting dutchy and put on the beef under a very low
fire – that was the secret to keeping it soft – adding a little
water when it was required. The pork she would've slowly
roasted in the oven with a little oil. There was a plate of fried
snapper with their heads still on. They were garnished with
rings of green and yellow peppers and onions. Brownie's
thing was that half the joy of food was in the look and smell
of it. Ella could see clearly before her that Donna had not left

Brownie far. It was all done up the way Brownie would've done it, and Ella only had to taste it to see if it tasted the way Brownie used to make it.

Princess, who was closest to the kids at their table, first started to set them up – Ella still couldn't quite count how many of them there actually were, they just wouldn't sit still and every time she tried, one of them moved and confused her. So Princess darted between the oak table and the kids' table, eating huge mouthfuls from her own plate at the same time.

'I say!' As Patrick was talking to Donna, a piece of food flew out of his animated mouth and settled on Althea's hand just as she was about to shovel a fork of rice and peas into her mouth.

She stopped and looked at her hand in disgust. 'Patrick, man!'

'What?'

'Watch wha'you a do no, man!'

'What? What you see me do?' Patrick bristled.

'You just a chat an' the food just a fly outta you mouth, man!'

Patrick kissed his teeth violently. Althea threw back her own kiss of the teeth that was much more animated, had a greater arc than Patrick's lame-duck kiss could ever have, and she wiped the food from her hand and continued eating her food, only slightly vexed.

She impressed Ella, who had not seen a kiss of the teeth like that in years, had really forgotten such an action of contempt existed and loved the fact that Althea had reacquainted her with it at this precise moment by throwing it at the person she had. Ella was next surprised to see that in between her forkful of rice and peas and feeding Della a spoonful, Althea winked at Ella. And Ella didn't know it, but she smiled back at Althea.

'I say!' Patrick was back on Donna down the other end of the table. 'Mikey say, we can decide on the hearse or the cart up to tomorrow morning. 'Cause you know him got them two black horse a run round him field and so that's no problem really.'

'So what you say to him?' Donna pushed back at him.

'I say we going decide and phone him tomorrow morning. Don't that what I just say to you?'

Ella looked down the table to see if Donna would come back to Patrick, but she wouldn't. Ella looked to her left to see if Patrick would go back to Donna, but he wasn't about to. He was concentrating on his food.

The table fell silent, but only for a moment. Althea wanted to know something and she wanted to know it from Princess. Ella was surprised to observe that Althea had no qualms communicating with the woman who had not long ago charged her to the floor. Princess ladled Althea's plate with more banana, cut it up with her own fork, and then passed Althea's plate back over to her.

'Positive!' was all Princess said in response to Althea's question. And the way she said it, Ella didn't quite know if 'positive' was a good result or not, she couldn't quite pick up Princess's turn of phrase. But anyway a whoop of delight came from across the table and took Ella's attention. The whoop came from Althea and then Donna chipped in with equally delighted congratulations. Ella didn't quite know what was going on. Not only was the conversation a choppy flood of patois flying about her head, but she was not quite down with the family shorthand. That is, until Althea delivered her next sentence:

'So the two of we going have pickney new year!'

Though Althea looked much happier than Princess, Ella saw that the two of them were happy enough, but Ella didn't understand how. She glanced at Patrick, still buried in his food, apparently no part of what he had created; he didn't even look like he was under any stress. Ella pulled her head in. She could've told herself that they were simple people who had not lived, who had not done anything, did not understand the way of the world the way she did, were even women who thought they were at the beck and call of a man who was too weak to decide which one of them he wanted to make his wife, but for some reason she pulled her head in and she couldn't believe she did.

The table fell silent again. It was a periodic rhythmic thing, Ella soon understood as she watched someone help themselves to a second helping when she hadn't even helped herself to her first. As Princess reached for a bowl of yam, Donna cut across her, looking at Ella's empty, cold plate.

'You not eating?'

Ella didn't realise the question was directed at her and just sat there like an idiot. But before long she felt all eyes again on her and looked across at Donna.

'You remember how we stay, don't you, Pinky?' Donna asked her.

Ella didn't quite know what that last statement meant and smiled at Donna, hoping she would take her mouth and eyes off her and so pull the rest of the attention from her. But she wouldn't. She was waiting for Ella to answer her and Ella's head was some place else.

'Look like you baby sister think she too stoosh for the likes a we, Donna,' and it was Princess alone who cracked up at her own joke.

Ella's head returned to where it was born and reared, she understood that. She looked at Princess and with one look reminded her she was a Brightwell by blood whereas Princess wasn't even one by law. Princess quietened down and went back to her yam.

As she reached for a bowl of dumplings, the angst left Ella and she realised she hadn't eaten since some time yesterday. As she reached for a bowl of yam, the hell was somewhere, some way, way, way from her. All that she was running from was somehow healed around that table, among these people, and only here could it have been. She could smell Donna the way she used to smell Brownie, and now she wanted to taste Donna. Ella selected until she had a plate of food before her, the size of which she had not seen since Brownie used to feed her. Ella began eating and it was all that was Brownie.

'What you think, Althea?' Donna asked.

'Cart!' came Althea's response. 'And we walk behind!'

'Prinny?' Donna turned to Princess.

'Me can't walk far, you hear. Hearse! And we travel like royalty behind.'

Ella thought the next person in line for Donna to ask was her and she found she was strangely looking forward to having her say, but it wasn't her. The next person Donna asked was Aunt Julie.

'Cart or hearse?'

Before Aunt Julie could answer, she broke out crying. Aunt Julie hadn't eaten much – she never was a great eater, Ella remembered, on account of her figure – and she simply left what she was forcing down to concentrate on the blubbering she was engaged in. The blubbering was huge. The chair on which Aunt Julie was perched was shaking almost out of control. This was a genuine bawl. Donna and Althea, who were both one person either side of Aunt Julie, put out a hand on either of her shoulders in an effort to calm and pacify her. To acknowledge that yes! they were aware what she was going through at losing her one true blood sister. That yes! this was a genuine bawl. Ella looked at Aunt Julie and knew there was no way around it, it was true. And Ella could not believe she felt she was home.

Donna had taken it all on. She had become head cook and bottle washer. There was room for the other siblings, save for Ella, who didn't want to, but Donna was looked upon as the one who was running the show. It wasn't surprising really, since she lived at the Pink House. It wasn't Brownie's death that had brought Donna scurrying back, as Ella had initially thought. Donna still lived at the Pink House in her old room. The surprising thing to Ella was that after her the only two who had escaped the Pink House were Lambert to America and Kellit to Jamaica. Donna had just never felt like leaving and by the time she realised where she and her life were, she was in her thirties and had been left behind. She had slipped into a routine at home with Brownie, Daddy Ned and then again Della and Mirabel, and just never bothered to change it. Donna had thought she might become a nurse. She liked looking after people, she had that warm Brownie thing that was just open and honest, but with Donna it had more focus than it ever had with Brownie. So she was well suited to becoming a nurse, you would think, but they hadn't wanted her. Donna had applied all over the place, but with no luck. She had managed, say, three interviews out of the dozens and dozens she had applied for, but nothing. The most surprising thing of all, though, was there had been no man. From what Ella could gather from her sister, there had never been no man. Not ever. This, Ella thought, was the strangest thing of all.

'You think so?' Donna asked her as she handed her a plate to dry. They were alone after dinner, Ella drying plates in her Bond Street black suit that she had refused to change out of and save for tomorrow, even though she had been offered an alternative piece of attire.

'Not even once?'

Donna shook her head as though she saw nothing wrong in what she was saying, and really she didn't.

'You're telling me that you're . . . how old are you?'

'Me and Della going be forty and forty-one next birthday,' Donna said proudly. It was something they had always done; whenever one of them was asked how old she was Donna and Della would give the ages of both of them like they were twins or something. Ella smiled.

'And you never ever have no man?' Ella's syntax was changing.

Ella didn't know why she was interested in Donna's story. She wasn't there for that, but she just couldn't help herself. 'And Brownie never say anything?' Now Ella knew Brownie must have said something. Brownie believed in the natural order of things and it was perfectly natural and ordered to have sex, leave home and then have some more sex. But Brownie had apparently said nothing and left it to her daughter to find her own way.

Della, on the other hand, had done it all. She had got into everything Ella considered normal – drink, drugs, sex, thieving – and all apparently during one summer eight years ago. Eight years ago, aged thirty-two! Ella couldn't believe it had taken her that long. She shuddered; there was what her life would have been like if she hadn't discovered there was something to be had away from Hanville and the Pink House. But there was much to admire in Della's agility in fitting a whole adolescence of rebellion into one summer. The summer she had got pregnant with the dreadful Mirabel. Apparently Della had left the Pink House when she was twenty-eight, not long after Ella had gone, and gone and married some man Donna informed Ella she should remember because he used to call round for Della when she was still there, but Ella couldn't remember him. For four years Della lived with the man and for four years they were very happy. Out of no argument, fight or anything, during the fourth year of their marriage Della decided to pack up and leave him. She took herself off and went to share a house with a bunch of eighteen- and nineteen-year-olds on the outskirts of town, apparently 'just to catch a taste of something!'

' "To catch a taste of something!" That's what she call it,' Donna quoted with authority she didn't understand.

Everyone noticed the change in Della. No one could say she was happy, but no one could say she was unhappy. Two or three times that summer her husband went to drag her home, but Della wouldn't budge. She wasn't going nowhere with him.

'And it looked like him wasn't going nowhere without her.' Donna laughed and Ella laughed too.

It was rumoured that she was even having an affair with one of the boys down there, but for sure Della wouldn't say. At the end of the summer Della had fixed up to leave with her housemates on a round-the-world trip that would end in working on some kibbutz. After that she had made no further plans and Brownie was pleased to hear she hadn't.

'"If that's what you want, just go and see," Brownie tell her.'

And Ella knew that was exactly what Brownie would've told her.

However, with a week to leaving, Della found out she was pregnant with Mirabel.

'You could look on it as bad luck or you could look on it as good luck,' Donna announced, as though she wasn't sure which one she went with. 'Either way Della couldn't go.'

Ella knew which one she would go with, and her fascination and humour turned to anger that nothing seemed to work out for her family even when they were about grabbing life the way it should've been grabbed. Now she was angry she had let her guard down. She was nothing like them. They came from the same place, but in no shape or form were they alike. And Ella couldn't believe that these were the children of Brownie, held down and anchored when she had brought them up to fly freely and climb trees.

'The thing was,' Donna was continuing, none the wiser about where Ella had gone, 'nobody know who the father was – the young lad or the husband. In fact, to this day nobody don't know.'

After eight months of pregnancy at the Pink House with Brownie, Donna, Daddy Ned and even Aunt Julie joining in the anticipation of a new generation of Brightwells, Della had a stroke, her stomach had to be cut open and Mirabel was born.

For Donna, Della's case was just what she needed to bring purpose to her life and she took on her sister's tragedy with energy. Donna didn't need to be a nurse now she had Della. She didn't need to have a child now she had Mirabel. And she never had found the use of a man. That was it, Ella thought as she listened, it wasn't that Donna never had any offers, or she was afraid, she had just never seen the need of a man.

It was Donna's daily duty that she took Della for an after-dinner walk and after the dishes, she was fixing to do just that. Ella stood back in the passage as Mirabel and Donna squeezed Della into her light summer jacket. Della seemed to know where she was off to and Ella saw clearly that her eyes perked up and her limbs relaxed that little bit further. Except when Donna put the hat on her.

'She don't like hat,' Donna explained to a bemused Ella.

Looking at the hat, Ella was not surprised.

'But she prone to head cold and if she get a summer cold, you see! Poor me and Mirabel, that's all I can say.'

Donna rammed the hat down further over Della's forehead and her head began to move from side to side.

'Mum!'

It was the first involuntary word Ella had heard Mirabel speak and it took her by surprise. She looked at Mirabel, not afraid of her now the kid's attentions were tied up with trying to pacify her mother, whose head was still rolling around, banging on the sides of the wheelchair.

'Mum!'

'Now, Mistress Della, stop the showing off 'cause you see our Pinky.' Donna was telling her off in a friendly voice.

Ella was embarrassed.

''Cause you know you got to wear you hat.' And Donna held her sister's face between her hands, stopped her head from rocking and kissed her full on the lips.

Ella was truly embarrassed. But then, as she watched her sisters, she remembered they had hardly a year between them and really nothing between them. They had always wanted to be dressed the same and they wanted to be together. Ella had never had anything like what Donna and Della were now sharing.

When Ella was five, for some reason Brownie had neglected taking her to school at the beginning of her first school term and it was well into October before Ella did eventually go. Every morning of that term, the other kids would get up, eat up their breakfasts and go off to school. Patrick and Johno were six and had been attending infant school from the previous September, bang on the first day of term, and Donna and Della were at secondary school with a year to go. The Brightwells were well known throughout the Hanville School for Infant, Primary and Secondary. Ella had not been aware there was anything wrong, that she had missed nearly half a term, and really she didn't care. The days just seemed to be rolling along like they did for any five-year-old, that is until there came a knock one morning on the back door. It was pushed open and Aunty Rosa came through.

Ella was under the table. She had lodged herself there when Brownie's back was turned and was practising pushing her finger in and out of the little hole in the knot of the wood, the hole that was her view on the world.

'Morning, Aunty Rosa.'

As soon as Ella heard Aunty Rosa's name she was about to rush out from under the table and hug her, when Aunty Rosa's voice stopped her.

'The baby don't gone to school again?'

That one sentence kept Ella under the oak table and she watched as Aunty Rosa, wearing Tandy's big wide shoes, dragged her feet over to the table and sat.

'Brownie, I not leaving here till you see sense on this thing!'

Brownie had already that morning made a fresh batch of coconut gizzadas, or pinch-me rounds as some called them, as that was what you did with the pastry when you made them. The result gave them a kind of fluted edging. They were hand-sized coconut tarts made with grated coconut, light-brown sugar, nutmeg, water and butter and pastry and Ella had never met anyone who liked coconut who didn't like pinch-me rounds. Brownie placed a plate of them and a cup of coffee before Aunty Rosa and joined her at the table.

Before Aunty Rosa said another word, Ella heard her champing away, grinding her false teeth over the sweet tart, and then came the sip of the coffee as she rinsed the bits of coconut down.

'Them going prison you!' Aunty Rosa said with great definition to Brownie.

Her mother was upset. Brownie didn't cry or let out any sound, but Ella knew her mother was upset.

'What me to do, Aunty Rosa?'

Brownie had never not known what to do before, at least Ella had never heard her express it in the five years she had been with her.

'Send her to school!'

'Daddy Ned say the same thing.'

'And Daddy Ned would be right and correct in saying the same thing,' Aunty Rosa confirmed to her.

'Daddy Ned say I must put on her clothes and send her to school.'

Through the knot in the wood, Ella saw as Aunty Rosa's hand went out and rested on her mother's affectionately. Though she didn't quite understand what, Ella sensed that what was going on above the table was important.

'Him say she need nobody but her bigger sister and brother them.'

'And Daddy Ned would be right and correct in that too.'

There was a long pause, during which Ella had no idea what was taking place above the table. The pause was so long that Ella was getting bored, was about to come out and show herself, when Brownie spoke.

'Sometimes ah sit, and ah look, and ah watch her, and she know, Aunty Rosa. She know is she one. She know is she alone.'

Neither woman said another thing and Ella didn't understand what they'd said up to that point. The next pause made the first look like a second in the lifetime of a five-year-old and Ella crawled out between the two sets of feet and showed herself. Before she could get to her feet, Brownie had scooped her up and loved her just the way only she knew how.

The next morning a strange new thing happened. She was woken at the same time as her other siblings, instead of being left to rise at whatever hour she chose. She was washed and dressed, had her hair oiled and plaited, and was brought to the table by Della. In the dining room Ella found Brownie about her work and in a mood she had never seen her mother in before – Ella half understood the mood to be fear.

The strange new morning experience continued apace when Della began dragging Ella up the road as she and Donna chatted about something she didn't understand or care about. Ella was looking back at the Pink House, where she could see the shrinking figure of her frightened mother standing watching her go. Ella knew Brownie was calling her, but never heard her mother's voice. This wasn't Brownie. Brownie never had fear about letting her children go. She knew they'd go out into the world when the time was right and they would return when the time was right.

When Ella arrived at school, and Della had done her duty and delivered her up to the infants' class that was Miss

Cook's class, Ella thought she understood what Brownie had
been afraid of, what the previous day's overheard conversation between her mother and Aunty Rosa might have been
about, but she only thought so.

Miss Cook, on having the little Ella deposited in front of
her, said in an all-sugary and welcoming voice, 'You must be
the long-awaited Brightwell child.' And then with a touch of
humour, 'Where's the other one?' Miss Cook looked behind
Ella. It was Miss Cook's little joke, though she knew she was
no good at making jokes. Once Lambert and Kellit had
passed through her hands, Miss Cook had got used to
Brightwell children turning up in twos. She had had one set
of legitimate Brightwell twins and before that two
Brightwell girls who thought they were twins.

All jokey she said it again, adding an extra little grin,
'Where's the other one?'

It was the only thing Ella remembered from Miss Cook's
class.

Mirabel took her place, holding her mother's hand. The kiss
had pacified Della. Donna knew just what to do. They were
ready.

'You sure you won't come with we, Pinky?'

'I'm sure.' Ella jumped out of the way as Donna began to
push Della's wheelchair because it looked like Donna didn't
care one bit where she pushed the thing.

'Well, make sure I don't come back and find you do a
thing, you hear?'

Ella didn't believe there was any danger of that happening. Donna was past her and going through the dining-room door, on her way to the kitchen, still talking to Ella, who was slow behind her.

''Cause the ladies coming over to help me cook when I come back,' Donna was continuing. 'Now! Daddy Ned! Make him lay down up there. Even if him not sleeping, I say make him lay down up there! 'Cause you know when them man come on here later, that's the last a him. The last! And I warn him already. I warn him him must stay up in the bed. So don't make him give you no foolishness 'bout him a get up, you hear, Pinky?'

And Ella heard herself answer, 'Yes, Donna.'

Mirabel had run ahead of her aunt and mother and gone to the shed. Ella watched her closely; she didn't know what the kid was up to now, but she didn't trust her. From the shed Mirabel pulled out a wedge of wood and Ella heard the clang of something else fall out of the shed. A crowbar was on the ground near the shed. The wedge of wood in her hand, Mirabel casually kicked the crowbar back inside and proceeded to slot the wood up to the back step and then stood back as Donna wheeled the chair down.

'All right then, Pinky! See you in 'bout a hour.'

They were through the back gate and Ella shut the back door behind them. She was alone and thinking about nothing but getting the key and unlocking Brownie's spice and herb cupboard. She was still fixing to be gone and to catch Ludo before he left, nothing there had changed. What had changed, somewhere between dinner and spotting the crow-

bar, was what she could do with the contents of Brownie's
spice and herb cupboard. Not only could she solve a childhood mystery in finding out just what Brownie had in there
by way of cooking secrets, she could also use the secrets to
help BrightWells. Brownie would want that. It all began to
make complete sense to Ella now and she started to tell herself this was the reason she was back there. This was the
lesson the time was right for her to learn and she was ready
for it.

Directly Ella swept through the kitchen, through the
dining area, into the passage, through the sitting-room door,
closed it behind her and stood there staring at Brownie in
her coffin. In her hand Ella had the crowbar.

Ella did not move from the door for the longest time.
She stood there with the crowbar in her hand and it was
just like when she had been in the room earlier with Daddy
Ned. That all seemed like such a long time ago, but it
wasn't. It was only a second ago she had found herself right
where she stood to see her mother laid out in her coffin
with that dangerous hair, waiting for Ella's hand to smooth
it down. Here Brownie was again. Here Ella was again, but
this time she had a crowbar in her hand and was about to
do something.

In her head a crescendo was rising. It must have started at
the door to be this loud now, was what Ella was thinking as
she looked down into the coffin. It must have started by the
shed where she had first picked up the crowbar to be this
loud now, or was it when she shut the back door behind
Donna, Della and Mirabel? She didn't know. All she knew

was that her head was about busting with the noise in it and she knew too that if she didn't just do the thing, if she didn't just lift her hand and do it, the great noise in her head would kill her dead before it stopped.

She stalled. She just stood there, looking down into her mother's coffin. Looking from her mother's face to the key in her mother's hands and back to her face again. Still smiling, still content, still ugly, Brownie lay there. Ella was telling herself, Do it! There was no space in her head not to do it. There was no space to hear the door shut behind her.

'Aunty Pinkette, Aunty Donna say to give you this 'bout Uncle Lambert.'

Mirabel remained by the open door and she stretched out her hand offering something to Ella. It was a bunch of newspaper clippings. Ella hitched the crowbar high into her back, held tightly on to it and walked calmly over to Mirabel and took the clippings from her.

'Thank you!' Ella told her grudgingly.

Mirabel turned and walked out and Ella closed the door again. Stuffing the clippings into a pocket and quickly rushing over to the window, behind the coffin, she looked eagerly through. Maybe she would lose her nerve if she didn't just get on and do it. In the next moment she saw Mirabel hurrying down the drive, through the front gate and off up the road to catch up to Donna and her mother.

The crowbar was already at work, lodged in the little space between Brownie's thumb and index finger, straining mightily against the one so the other would give and surrender the key. It wouldn't budge. It still wouldn't budge with any ease. Ella went at it again; still it wouldn't budge. Brownie wasn't about to give it up without a struggle, and Ella being Ella wasn't about to be beaten. This time her mother wasn't going to do her, this time Ella was going to do Brownie, and with one final brutish yank against her mother's thumb, a crack exploded in Ella's ear. As the crowbar slipped out, her mother's thumb gave way, fell away from the fist and settled on her stomach. The thumb was attached now to her mother's fist by skin alone. Quick as anything, she reached into the coffin, lifted the key with all the ease she had previously hoped for and backed away.

As she stood a few paces from the coffin, clutching at the key, the noise in her head fell suddenly silent and in flooded questions and emotions. She had just broken the thumb of her dead mother! Who she had not seen for thirteen years! She had a key in her hand that opened her mother's spice and herb cupboard! It played on in Ella's head at least half a dozen times and even then she couldn't quite understand what it was she was trying to tell herself. She had just committed a violent act on a woman who had never, save for that one time with Daddy Ned, found any reason or need for anything of the kind. Maybe a dozen times she thought that one, and still it too meant nothing to her. The truth is, nothing she punched herself with could have meant anything to her, because she couldn't bring herself to piece together what she had done. Ella glanced across to the clock on the mantel and saw that forty whole minutes had gone by since she had first shut the sitting-room door with the crowbar in her hand. Forty whole minutes had passed her by and she still made no move to go to the spice and herb cupboard to get what she needed to leave the Pink House. She knew she was struggling when she went back to the coffin again. It was her mother! It was Brownie!

She knew this feeling. It was like everything she had ever done she was doing again and if Ella's heart had been broken before, it was now smashed to pieces and again refusing to sustain her life. It all laid itself open before her like a sore she had merely pulled the flimsiest of veils over.

She had arranged to meet Larry at the Bridge one morning, the morning before he would turn up at the Pink House with the fight for life beaten out of him. The morning before Ella would arrive at the breakfast table one whole hour before she needed to and in the foulest of moods. What it was was this: Ella's heart had been smashed to pieces.

The morning before, Ella had been late arriving at the Bridge to meet Larry, because Brownie had fried fried dumplings with salt fish and ackee for breakfast, and whenever this occurred, Ella made it her duty to stuff her face and belly with all she could carry. If she just hadn't been late, then maybe it wouldn't have happened. If Brownie hadn't made what she'd made for breakfast, then maybe it wouldn't have happened. But Brownie did and Ella was late.

She and Larry were going to skip school to discuss their favourite subject: what they would do once they left Hanville. She was only late by about twenty minutes, but as she approached the Bridge she heard the distinct sound of two

people meeting each other. She had never heard this outside
Brownie and Daddy Ned's bedroom before and she found it
most intriguing that it could occur anywhere else. She
stealthily got closer and saw Larry fucking Andrew Naylor,
the son of the first black teacher in the town. On coming
upon the spectacle of two people, never mind two boys,
fucking and in the wide open space, Ella stopped and took it
in. Her mouth fell open. Andrew was bent over on all fours
and Larry was on his knees behind him. To Ella it sounded
like pain, but the minute she saw them she knew deep down
it was no such thing. This was a moment of pure pleasure for
Larry, and her heart smashed itself into pieces. She was in
deep, deep trouble and so began her greatest cover-up.

It took her a few seconds to hatch. It took her a mere
moment to toy with the choice between confronting them
or walking away unseen and so preserving their dignity. As
soon as she had thought the latter, Ella did the former. She
came out from behind the bush, took a few more steps that
brought her into the full view of them, and she came out
singing, 'Yes, Jesus loves you, yes, Jesus loves, yes, Jesus loves
you, the Bible tells me so.' Ella had never sung any hymn
outside of church before and only sung them inside of
church because she was made to. As she 'saw' them and they
saw her, she let out a loud gasp and put her hand sweetly
over her mouth. There was something of a moment, fitting
for maybe a team of horses and several wagons, as the bent-
over Andrew Naylor held his breath and the flushed pink
Larry held on to Andrew's hips, his movement stopped, both
of them staring at the shock-feigned Ella.

Larry's flushed face dripped away into a sick blue, that then turned again to wet pink skin that Ella could see straight through. As Ella parked her eyes on him she thanked God he hadn't given her skin you could see through. Her eyes were on his face and they wouldn't leave it. She was hanging there, forcing back into him every piece of hurt and betrayal he had given to her. She had believed he was hers – not in any hearts and flowers kind of way, but in the way Donna and Della had each other, Lambert and Kellit, and Johno and Patrick had each other, in the way where for all her life, no matter who came, who went from it, she would always have him to fill the space that had been there right up until she had met him. He was suppose to be her special person. Either he was hers alone or he wasn't hers at all. Clearly Larry had made something with someone else. She set about smashing him back.

The hiatus between Ella and Larry looked like it would never end until Ella continued her walk on over the Bridge past him, singing her hymn loudly. 'Jesus loves me, yes, I know, 'cause the Bible tells me so . . .' And her voice disappeared with her over the Bridge and as it went she had only just begun to smash him back.

In the sitting room of the Pink House, Ella heard chatter through the window and saw the ladies on the road congregating in front of the front gate. Miss Tam, Miss Betty-Crow, Miss Nugent, Princess and Althea and three or four Ella didn't know. They had been home to wash and change and sort out any little thing they had to sort out and were back. The way they stopped in front of the House, it looked to Ella like there might be a moment, it looked like they were milling, waiting for something. Maybe Ella would after all have time to get to the spice and herb cupboard, check out Brownie's secrets and get gone. Maybe! And when one of the women Ella didn't know started to sing, right there on the pavement in front of the Pink House, Ella knew it was a definite.

'What a friend we have in Jesus, all our sins and grief to bear . . .' As Ella opened the sitting-room door she heard the singing from outside. 'What a privilege to carry everything to God in prayer . . .'

Ella was sweeping through the dining area and moving towards the kitchen. She could defeat herself, let Larry defeat her, Brownie, allow all to defeat her, or she could take the key in her hand and go and open her mother's spice and herb cupboard. She'd been given this moment for a reason. The women were stalling at the front of the House, having an impromptu open-air hymn sing for a reason, and the reason was all around her; if she didn't take the chance she would be a damn fool.

In front of the cupboard Ella stood with the key in her hand. Standing there with the key was worse than standing over Brownie with the crowbar. This was Brownie's real place. She reasoned: she could go through all that noise in the head again, she could go through all that stalling, or she could just get down and do it. Do it or be nothing and nobody, it had always been Ella's thing.

She pushed the key into the lock and just before she turned it she put her ear to the wood and listened the way she used to listen as a child. Up and down, up and down like Brownie's stomach.

Ella turned the key, and over the cupboard's breathing she heard the padlock click open and the latch flew up before her eyes. Quickly, with no ceremony at all, Ella slid the lock off, laid it down and opened up the cupboard. She wondered if she was about to be caught and shamed before the whole family of Brightwells and their friends, but she didn't care. She was inside Brownie's spice and herb cupboard.

The door didn't creak open like maybe it could've, like she always dreamt it would. It glided open. Both doors simultaneously in her hands, a crack of the way, a little bit more, half the way, a whole lot of the way and then wide open before her. Despite Ella's cut-to-the-chase attitude, she somehow found the ceremony such an event demanded. She was holding her breath, looking in with eyes as big as Brownie's empty plates waiting to be filled with the glorious things. But it didn't last long. As soon as she came face to face with what she was looking at, with all that her eyes could see, they shrunk away and her head popped forward nearly off her neck. She stood there with the cupboard open before her and couldn't believe what she was looking at. There were shelves. Regular shelves. Perhaps twenty or so, maybe six inches apart, and the shelves were stuffed with bottles, tins, bags, all of them crammed any which way. Ella reached in and took a bottle down. Allspice! Then another. Cayenne! And another. Dill! And another. They

were regular everyday spices that Ella had in her own cupboard at home. This was what Brownie had kept locked all
these years in her mysterious spice and herb cupboard? Ella
couldn't believe it. She went in among them again, plucking a bag or a bottle and sniffing and tasting at random.
Garlic! Nutmeg! Lemon grass! Thyme! They were just
what they said they were, there was nothing but what there
was in the cupboard and she banged the doors back to in
anger and lent against it, not knowing what to do next. Ella
stood there with her hands pressed against the cupboard,
shaking her head in disbelief. One of the cornerstones of
her childhood was just what it was. The thing that had so
intrigued her was just that. Then she felt it breathing
beneath her palms. Again! She felt the damn thing go up
and down like that giant she knew. Her head raised itself
from where it had fallen. There was something there, or
else how could it breathe? Cupboards just didn't breathe
and she wasn't imagining it. She flung the cupboard open
again and peered in. Something was in there, something for
her was in there.

Up the side entrance, moving towards the back gate and
door, Ella could hear the singing of the women getting
closer. Ella's head was still in the cupboard just like Brownie's
used to be, and her hands were working ten to the dozen
moving and shifting and replacing bottles as she searched for
Brownie's secret. She was only halfway through her shifting
and sorting and sniffing when she heard the catch on the
back gate go. She skipped a few shelves, maybe the vital
ones! There was nothing that struck her on the shelf she next

went to. Nothing on the next, or on the next. Whatever it was, she had to find it or she wasn't Ella.

'Rock of ages cleft for me, let me hide myself in thee . . .' came drifting into her ears just as she saw stuffed at the back of the cupboard, between the second to last and last shelf, a tatty old yellowing book. As her eyes fell upon it, they again took on the appearance of Brownie's empty plates, but this time they didn't remain empty. In one movement she grabbed the book, slipped it under her arm, slammed the doors shut, dropped the padlock back on and dashed towards the dining-room door.

The back door opened as the dining-room door closed and the kitchen was swamped with the women.

In the sitting room, Ella was forcing the key back into Brownie's hand and trying to adjust the thumb so it wouldn't look broken, but it was useless. It looked broken and the key was crooked. She opened the window behind the coffin, scrambled over her mother, even put a foot in the coffin, and she fell through the window. Once outside she could just make out it was fresh air, but it was Hanville air. Her eyes scanned around, trying to check there was no one about. She was moving hastily towards her car. She had had a time like this before trying to leave Hanville. She made it to her car, she was sure this time she would make it out. The car took off. On the seat beside her, her mother's tatty yellowing book.

Zooming away from the Pink House was like escaping all over again. She was after saving herself and she was again leaving her Brownie to do so. She didn't feel guilty; in fact, the nearer she got to the Bridge, the better she began to feel. She had the book and if she could just make it to the Bridge, her life would be all that it wasn't and she would've achieved it without facing down any of the old Hanville ghosts that were racking her life. She was about to get away with it. She was going to get away and she couldn't believe the joy that such knowledge buzzed in her head.

She was just approaching Badlands Woodlands when it suddenly got much darker. It was eight o'clock, it was summer! It had no business being this dark on a summer's evening. Unease floated into her. It was like she had hit the edge of Badlands Woodlands and it had gone extra dark. She put her foot further down and as she tore along beside the Woodlands and up the track, the sky was the same kind of Hanville sky she remembered from another night. It seemed to her that she had been scared in one way or the other ever since she had first left the place. Perhaps the fear was Hanville itself and the best way out of it was not to stand and fight, but in this instance to run and hide and never look back. And she began to rehearse in her mind this mantra; 'This is what running away from home gets you. This is what being a big mouth does for you. This is what eight o'clock is all about! It brings you face to face with . . .' something that was following her. That was the real unease, not darkness. Something was following her.

She thought it was another car, even though she couldn't see anything. No car lights, no lights at all, nothing except the darkness she was leaving. Her eyes went back to the track in front of her. The second her eyes were back on the track, the second she got the feeling that it was there again following her. She looked back into the darkness again, turning her head round to peer out of the rear windscreen, but there was nothing again except the darkness. She went back to the track, repeating the same thing a couple more times. Every time she looked back there was nothing. Every time she went back to the track, someone was tracking her. She was going mad. And what a right and proper place, Ella Brightwell, to go off your head! She put her foot down harder. In her rear-view mirror two red lights suddenly bored out of the darkness. It was a car with red headlights. Gradually they were getting bigger, gradually they were getting nearer to her. Her foot could go nowhere else, but she was still pressing. She had never driven the car this fast before. And then they were gone, the red lights behind her disappeared. She searched her rear-view mirror, but they weren't there. She swung her head to look out the back and they really weren't there. There was only the tight darkness with not a blemish in it. She turned back to the track, a wired, noise-filled wreck. No sign of the Bridge. Back and forth her eyes darted to her rear-view mirror and the track in front of her, back and forth desperate for the Bridge. She flashed her eyes back on to the track and something was in front of her. She was face to face with something. But it wasn't on the track, it was on the car, on the bonnet. They weren't red car lights, a car doesn't have red lights that pick you out, that punch holes through the night. They were red eyes staring in at her through the tight night, making the night their own. It had outrun her, come to the side of her, gone past her, climbed on to her speeding car and was now lying on the bonnet staring in at her. She swerved, startled, trying to throw whatever, whoever, off. But it hung on to the bonnet, looking in on her. It had the determination and drive to seek her out and face her down. The swerve took her directly into Badlands Woodlands.

This way, that way, the steering wheel was turning in front of her, threatening to break her arms if she so much as tried to control it. Whatever was after her wanted her dead like Brownie. But whatever had told her she could leave Hanville, live away from her family for all these years and now turn up like this, kicked in. She gripped the wheel as firmly as she could and her arms were not ripped from her nor were they broken. That was all it needed, within seconds – three, four max – it had ended. The car

came to a violent but controlled stop inches from crashing
sideways into a tree. The book shot off the seat next to her,
flew forwards and then backwards half under the front passenger seat. The engine flicked off. She was alone, deep, deep
inside Badlands Woodlands with the night closed in and no
one around for miles. Ella's ears were full of her breath and she
was jumping and shaking. She hung on to the steering wheel,
panting like an animal, looking around for whatever had
jumped on her bonnet, but she made out nothing in the dark.
Outside, the stillness was Hanville and nowhere else.

Inside was a seething space of fear and anxiety. Her hands
were locked around the steering wheel, her breathing still
heavy in her head, her eyes scanning outside, and all she
could see was trees and one massive clump of darkness so
broad it probably covered the whole planet. She pulled on
the hand brake making the car a secure stationary spot of
light blazing out in the middle of nothing. Then the radio
flicked on by itself, rupturing the stillness. It was Sam
Cooke. Sam Cooke was on the fucking radio! And all by
himself! Stunned, Ella began to fumble for the handle in the
door. She couldn't find it. She couldn't take her eyes off the
radio and she couldn't find the door handle. Then the door
opened and the car slung her out on the woodland floor.
Across the ground, on her arse, eyes not leaving the car, Ella
backed away into a tree and sat there, waiting for whatever
was after her to come and get her. The sound of Sam Cooke
blasted out into the darkness. The door of the car was open,
the courtesy light was on. Headlights, tail lights, all on. The
car was a spot in the darkness and a beacon for miles.

You're always told to stay in the car. She should've stayed with the car. Whatever was after her was going to get her now because she had made herself a sitting duck. 'Get back to the car,' she was telling herself, 'get back to the car, lock yourself in and drive away.' She found she couldn't even move.

Then, as suddenly as it had come on, the radio went off. There was silence again and she could hear her own fear resounding in her head. Ella could've pissed herself, but that same something that had saved her until now kicked in again, like her own personal generator, and she began to fumble around inside her pockets. It wasn't in the first pocket. It wasn't in her second. She had to fight. It wasn't in the third or fourth. She was beginning to fear she had left it in the car when she remembered she had left the book in the car. She couldn't believe she had just left Brownie's book like that and she was half in and half out, thinking up a way of getting it without getting herself killed. In her fifth pocket she found what she was looking for and it took her mind momentarily off the book. She pulled it out and began to punch out the numbers. It began to ring. As it rang, Ella was checking all around that what- ever was after her wasn't stealthily advancing on her without her knowledge. The phone was answered and she heard Ludo's voice.

'Ludo! Help–' The line went dead. The connection was gone. The battery was good for it. She punched the redial button. It was dead. She began to believe that if she didn't get up, so would she be.

Quickly she began to crawl across the woodland floor, crackling dry leaves and twigs with all fours as she went. Looking that way, looking this way. The car would save her. So she went towards it, crawling. Slam! Bang! went the door, went the central locking. She was in. She sealed the car. Checking all around, this way, that way, all the time, waiting for it to come and get her even now, as she turned the key to drive out of there. She had her right hand turning the key, her left hand feeling around the front passenger seat for the book, and her eyes on duty switching from window to window. She turned the key. The engine wouldn't start. Her hand groped all over the seat next to her. The book wasn't there. She switched off the headlights to give the engine a clear run at it. She looked across at the seat. The book wasn't there. Her head dropped, she saw it half under the seat and bent down for it. All the time trying the ignition key again and again. She dropped the book on her lap and determined never to let it out of her sight again. She was threatening to burn a hole in the starter motor, holding it longer all the time, praying it would kick into life. But it wouldn't start. It spluttered like it was half dead and then that was it. She would either have to walk back or sit it out till morning in a place where no one went, where something was after her.

Ella found she was climbing a tree. She had no idea where the idea came from, where the courage to leave the relative safety of the locked car came from, but she was now climbing the same tree she had moments before nearly smashed sideways into. As a child she had found it surprisingly easy climbing trees, it was only in getting down from them that the problems presented themselves. She had the book under her jacket, had kicked off her expensive shoes; her Bond Street suit was a wreck and she was climbing. At the top of the tree she felt safe. She couldn't see much, with the density of trees and the darkness, but it was safer than the car. Her head wasn't silent but given her situation there was no better place to wait for sunrise. She nestled in, scanning as far as she could.

Hanville was holding on to her.

'Pinky? Aunty Brownie dream me and tell me to come look for you.' It was Poor Cousin Winston.

He found her in her car, not up the tree. She had passed the time inside her car.

They were bouncing along away from her car, going back towards the heart of Hanville. Back to the Pink House. And Poor Cousin Winston was well into his chat. Ella sat there listening to just how well he could talk. Wrapped in her hands, out of sight under her jacket, was Brownie's book, beating like the little treasured heartbeat it was.

Poor Cousin Winston had on a new pair of black corduroy pants and a deep-purple shirt. He was a fine-looking man who had utter peace in his face.

'And I feel like a hand coming out to me. I feel like a hand, you see, Pinky. A hand just covering up me face and shaking me. "Wake up! Wake up!" That's all she saying to me. "Wake up and go look for you family."'

It was nearly midnight, Poor Cousin Winston was telling

her. Ella couldn't believe she had relaxed enough to fall asleep in the car but apparently she had.

She was looking out the window. She felt like she did when she was thirteen on the third day of the third month. Only as the car rounded the corner to the road where the Pink House stood did she see her final indignity. It was on the road, lining the edges in the cool night with the moon high above. It was just like the night when she had run away, aged fourteen. Her family were standing there in silence with the breeze playing in their clothes, looking, waiting for Poor Cousin Winston's car to circle the corner with her in it and trundle up the hill to the Pink House.

The car stopped slap bang outside the House and she stared at them. Poor Cousin Winston leant over and opened the passenger door for her. It swung open and stayed there for seconds before she decided there was no way round it, she had to get out and be among them. Not one of them took a step towards her. Not one of them made a move away from her. They all watched her, keeping their own personal counsel, waiting for some kind of movement from her. Ella wondered whether they'd found Brownie's broken thumb and knew what she had done. Mirabel was there and she knew that if any one of them knew, Mirabel did, and if Mirabel knew she would've told the rest of them. Mirabel hated her enough to drop her in it gleefully, of that Ella had no doubt. Ella swallowed deeply, her shoulders dropped, her arms folded and one foot was planted down and pointed outwards. She stepped out of the car and walked boldly past one and all of them and went back into the Pink House. They followed silently behind her.

It was another night of Set Up. She had forgotten that all this went on. That all this had to go on. Nothing was straightforward when a Jamaican died. You didn't just turn up on the day of the funeral, eat ham sandwiches, drink cold, sweet tea and recite platitudes in a cold, foreign church. You kept company from the first night or day of the death, through to the funeral and then on until the Nine Night – the night the duppy, the spirit of the deceased, was believed finally to leave its earthly home and pass completely over to the other side – and the company went like this.

Anyone – it didn't matter whether you knew the dead person or not, or you knew the family or not – anyone could knock on the door of the dead house and they would be let in and be fed and watered and all they had to do in return was to sing hymns, usually all the women, play dominoes, usually all the men, tell stories about Back Home, usually both men and women; in short, all they had to do was keep company.

As Ella stepped in through the back door of the Pink House, vexed and sulking that she had been brought back like a child, she saw the kitchen abuzz with the congregation of large and small, dark and red, short and tall black women she had run from earlier. All of them were clustered around her Brownie's stove, the sink and the worktops, preparing some food, and all of them loving it. They hardly noticed Ella. She leant against the wall by the back door, watching them go about their business. She was feeling exposed, feeling caught. Behind her, her family traipsed in through the back door. The women hardly broke stride. It was like a small industry. They were cooking and preparing the food for the Set Up. Yams, bananas, coco, carrots, turnips, cho-chos, peppers and scallions were being peeled and chopped. Each woman was assigned to a certain vegetable, a certain seasoning; each woman was well into her task. Someone was picking a huge bowl of rice, lodged between her open legs, secure and tight there. Someone was taking out an enormous tray of patties from the oven, and someone was shouting, 'Them cook already, darling?'

'Yes, me dear,' the woman with the patties answered with a joy that led her into looking at how well they had indeed cooked.

On top of the stove were the pots. Some of them were off and bubbling. One Ella knew without looking, without smelling, was a pot of curry goat. There was always goat, even she knew that. No Jamaican gathering of any kind was complete without goat. A woman was dipping a spoon into it and stirring and coming up with the gravy. She opened her palm, spread the hot spoon across it and tasted the gravy.

'Little more pepper, Miss Tam!' the woman shouted behind her.

Ella's eyes followed her and found the request had gone over to a woman that was indeed Miss Tam. She had before her a chopping board with the most amount of red and green Scotch bonnets Ella had ever seen. She picked up the board and went over to the pot where the woman stood and shovelled them in like she were shovelling treasures into a deep hole that was her secret.

'Mind we kill people, you know,' Miss Tam giggled to the woman over the pot.

'Them must dead! Make pepper kill them!' And the women laughed.

Ella thought they looked like witches who knew a secret. They were edging and elbowing each other to giggles of glee as the one stirred and the other shovelled. 'Go chop more. Chop more, Miss Tam!'

And Miss Tam went back to her spot and indeed began to chop more. As she went back, she passed the woman who was halfway through peeling the bananas. This woman had a pot into which she would drop the green skins and another pot into which she dropped the bananas. 'A what sweet you?' this woman asked Miss Tam.

Ella never heard the answer. She was now following Miss Betty-Crow. Miss Betty-Crow was moving towards Ella and the back door, carrying a chair. As she approached, Miss Betty-Crow smiled warmly and Ella only just managed to force out her smile in return. She planted the chair in front of the back door and stood on it and Ella looked up at her, curious as to what she was doing.

'I don't understand how nobody don't do this yet,' Miss Betty-Crow was chastising the women behind her. In her hand Miss Betty-Crow had a tape measure, some tacks, which she lodged between her lips, and a hammer. Ella wondered what it was no one had done yet.

'Nobody don't do that yet, cause Daddy Ned say him

don't want nobody do it,' the woman peeling the bananas told her.

'Seem like that man going love that woman even though she dead,' another woman threw in.

'Well, me and him if him ever make a move to take down this tape measure,' Miss Betty-Crow was able to threaten without losing even one tack between her lips. Ella watched as she began to hammer the tape measure to the doorframe.

It dawned on Ella. She remembered and that meant she was one of them. No matter where she ran to, no matter how many times she tried to take off the suit of clothes she thought were uncomfortable, they grew back and she had to remember she was one of them.

What Miss Betty-Crow was doing was just one of many ways of warding off the duppy. Among these women it was a firmly held belief that duppies couldn't count. One way of deterring them from returning to their earthly home was to put a tape measure over the doorframe. That way, when the duppy tried to return to their earthly home, they wouldn't get past the door since it would take them an eternity to count through the tape measure. There, at the door of the home where they had once lived, the duppy would remain frustrated until they gave up and left for the place where they now belonged. The same idea explained why the bed had been turned. Ella suddenly didn't know why it hadn't occurred to her as she stood in her parents' bedroom that afternoon. She had heard Aunty Rosa suggest it to people who had come to her on many occasions – usually women who came to her and told her that their husbands were

turning up every night 'to ride them same way'. Aunty
Rosa's suggestion was always that the bed had to be turned
so that if the duppy returned to where they had once slept
they would be disoriented by the bed being in the wrong
place, think it was not after all their home, and leave. And it
was the same reason you washed the clothes they had died
in, hung them out on the line and took them in after Nine
Nights: to allow time for the spirit of the dead to be set free.
Everything, then, was being done to keep Brownie from the
Pink House. Ella wanted to tell them that none of it was
working since she had seen her mother in every nook and
cranny about the place since she had returned.

Over at the oak table the men had gathered and were slapping down, with great ceremony, cards of dominoes. There
was a match going on. It wasn't a game, it was a match.
Milling around the four players were the men who were
waiting their turn. All of them had on porkpies.
Occasionally one man would hold up the game, scratching
underneath his hat, straining his legs apart as he tried to get
comfortable in a seat where he was finding no comfort.
Knowing that his partner, sitting opposite, would let him
have it if he put down the wrong card and gave the match to
the opposition. There was no room in a match for a man
who couldn't read the game. If you couldn't read the game
and took up a seat pretending you could, there was much
room for the most ridicule. There was much drinking of
white rum in shot glasses and bottles of ice-cold Mackeson.

On the outskirts of the match, a woman was having
something of a row with all of the men involved in the

match. The woman was Aunt Julie, with wig, with arse, with high heels on which to totter uncertainly. She was after something, she was always after something where the men were concerned, was the whisper among the women. This time it was the bottle of white rum the men had before them. She wanted it to add to her mannish water. No other bottle, especially one offered by the women around her, would do. It had to be that one, the one the men had, and it had to be that one precisely because they had it.

Mannish water was a kind of soup tonic made from the entrails of a ram goat. It received its name because it was supposed to assist you, through its healthy properties, towards strength or 'mannishness'. The ingredients and preparation of mannish water were just up Aunt Julie's street. Ella had once seen her prepare this dish and nothing had revolted and frightened her as much. In truth it was the only thing Aunt Julie could cook, that she wanted to cook. It was her favourite dish and, as Brownie would never cook it, she had to learn to do it herself. Give her her dues, Aunt Julie learnt the art of great mannish water to perfection. And the art was all, apparently, in the killing of the goat. Goats were old men, Ella had observed. It seemed to her, as she watched her first goat bleating in the yard of the Pink House, that the poor thing looked like an old man. It spoke like an old man, had the spirit of an old man bleating away to get out.

Whenever Aunt Julie killed a goat, the children of the Pink House were put right out of sight of this spectacle. None of them had yet seen it happen. Brownie would not allow it, it was about the only thing Brownie would not allow. All they knew was that whenever they and Brownie returned, the goat was always dead, Daddy Ned was always washing blood from the yard and Aunt Julie was always up to her elbows in it. What happened between the goat tethered and the washing away of the blood was a mystery to the Brightwell children but, Ella being Ella, she had to be the one to crack that mystery.

One day Ella somehow managed to escape the gathering arms of Brownie as Brownie gathered up her lovely things and led them up the entry, through the gate and away from the Pink House. Ella wanted to see and see she would. She had positioned herself on the ledge of her bedroom and was spying down looking at Aunt Julie as she sharpened a long-bladed knife against a cutlass. Aunt Julie was done up to the nines in a fine frock. She had done her hair well, had painted her nails – it was a ritual for which she should look her best. The goat was tethered to the fence. As the woman approached it, it began to wander this way and that; it knew its fate and set about a bleating that would haunt Ella for the longest time. The long-bladed knife was hanging by the woman's side from her hand. She straddled the goat, wrenched back its head and began pulling on it with an appetite Ella had only seen in a man beating his wife. The goat's beard hung over her hand and the goat struggled. For someone so slight, Aunt Julie was able to hold the goat firmly with one hand. Up came the other hand from her side, brandishing the long-bladed knife in a smooth, perfect arc. Quick and sure she dragged it across the goat's throat and that was that. Suddenly, at that moment, Ella understood

Brownie's reasoning. Both Ella and the goat jerked and startled at the same time. The result was that the goat begun to convulse with the last vestiges of life and Ella fell off the ledge for the first time and just had the luck, sense or insight to reach out a hand to the oak tree. She was caught. Aunt Julie, having heard her, looked up and saw her swinging in the tree. Aunt Julie smiled up at her. And Ella got to wondering which one she was more afraid of, Aunt Julie's smile or the sight of the goat.

Below her, the blood from the goat was pumping out into the whole wide world and running down Aunt Julie's legs and up her arms. It seemed like she was drenched in goat's blood from top to toe. The goat jerked its final movements of shock and spasm and collapsed beneath Aunt Julie. Calm as anything, this woman, in a frock she loved and valued as a favourite, roped two of the goat's feet, dragged it over to the oak tree and suspended it at a height that was beneficial to her. The goat swayed under the oak tree, directly below Ella, blood dripping into the yard. Aunt Julie turned the belly so it was in full view of the sickened Ella. She was about to begin her second stage of work. The knife went down the body, in a clean, straight, cold cut set against the dying warmth of the goat's belly. The blood and guts and intestines began to drip out and the knife went inside after what was needed for perfect mannish water. The woman had dexterity. The woman had art. The woman took pleasure in her work. Into a pot went the tripe, plopped the whole insides of the animal, and her hand emerged with a mass of red, some of which fell into the pot. Just when Ella thought she might vomit from a height, Aunt Julie picked up the pot and went inside. She had finished. As she went she was still smiling, still considering and living what she had executed. The animal was left swaying under the oak tree and Ella.

Now, as Aunt Julie stood arguing with the man for the bottle of rum, Ella knew what she had already done to be standing there arguing for it.

The men were having none of her. 'I say you must move!'

But she wouldn't. She made a grab for the bottle when she thought they were distracted by the match, but one in particular wasn't and he pushed her hand away, the result of which was to upset the disputed bottle over his trousers. There was much cussing of Aunt Julie from both the men she sought and the women whose husbands they were. And that had been Aunt Julie to a T; her pursuit of the opposite sex had always left her on the wrong side of her own sex.

'Move and go where?' Aunt Julie tried to save herself but she couldn't win this one. She was forced to withdraw and accept a bottle from one of the women and as she did, you could see the pain on her face as she looked to the far side of the congregation of men, on the opposite side of the room. Over there, where there was the most storytelling, much of it told a hundred times over to the same people at different Set Ups, a tale was developing. There was a disputed point, a disputed ending. There had to be a dispute of some kind or it wasn't a story. Between a tiny man of five foot something and a woman who had crashed the male company and was quite at home there, was a heated discussion on whether he

had got the date of the story he was telling right. It was on
her that Aunt Julie's eyes fell with much pain. The tiny man
was adamant that he hadn't got any detail of the story wrong.
The woman was equally adamant that he had.

'Miss Bee, listen me. Hear what ah saying!' said the tiny
man, loving the fact that he among all the men had her ear
and he would argue his corner with enough passion to keep
her ear.

Ella didn't know who he was, but she knew the woman
Aunt Julie turned away from with hate. Miss Bee was Poor
Cousin Winston's mother, who was married to Daddy Ned's
brother Thomas. That made her a kind of aunt to Ella. She
had worn well and sat at the table still beautiful, still warm,
still in the place where she genuinely belonged, among the
men. Miss Bee was a Jamaican Indian. She was red, tallish, had
a jet-black mole just below her eye and a head of hair that she
didn't know what to do with. Whereas Aunt Julie had to
work at being Aunt Julie, Miss Bee was just simply Miss Bee,
awake, asleep and in the dreams of all the men she enthralled.
Tonight she was wearing a floral dress with a plunge; an inch
lower would have been indecent and it might still be indecent, taking into account the occasion on which she was
wearing it. Her tits were crammed against this plunge and
they were fit to bust out. And she had the firmest and what
looked the finest breasts Ella had seen on a woman of her
years, and she must have been in her early sixties. Ella could
only watch and listen and marvel at Miss Bee as she held the
men with her version of the story. From the corner of her eye
Ella saw Aunt Julie snake away to her mannish water.

'Nineteen fifty-four!' Miss Bee shot down to the company, and the company rocked with her passion.

'Fifty-six!' the tiny man put back up.

'I say is nineteen fifty-four Mas Rupert dead.' Miss Bee pounded down on the table with her finger. And as her finger pressed her point, the men did not fail to notice that her tits jigged about and clattered into each other, and they loved it with a united passion.

'What year him dead, Miss Bee?' This came from a man Ella didn't know, sitting right in the eyeline of Miss Bee's tits. As Miss Bee prepared to come again, to deliver her version, the men gave silent but clear homage to the wonderful man who had not heard her first time round.

'Nine-teen fif-ty-four!' Every syllable Miss Bee pounded into the table. And on every syllable her fine tits jigged up and down and smothered the men with so much pleasure, one of them played the wrong card, lost him and his partner the match, and his partner didn't give a damn.

'How it could be fifty-four when Mas Rupert last child born fifty-six, the year of him death?' Tiny asked.

'Then, Big Man, you no hear the story?' a smartly dressed man sitting in the corner asked him.

'What story?' The tiny man called Big Man asked back, ready and serious to take a point that might help his version of the story.

'That Miss Rupert was elephant? You never hear?' The men who were with the story, even those that were with the domino match and were on the fringes of the story, erupted into laughter. Even Miss Bee couldn't hold herself.

'No two-year elephant go?' The smartly dressed man came again, taking a shot of rum before he started laughing again.

'Man, stop chat foolishness.' Big Man was ever so slightly embarrassed and bemused that he had become the butt of the amusement, when not a moment ago he had had Miss Bee in his glorious hands. And when he saw that no one was in any hurry to stop the laughter, he shot to his feet and it didn't look as though he had even left his seat. 'People over here a have a serious conversation and all you can do is chat foolishness!'

It only made the situation worse and they went again, laughing even more. It was no longer about the smart man's crack, it was now about Big Man's reactions.

'Big Man, stand steady no?' a man's voice threw into the company that again erupted in a body wave.

'Man, shet up! shet up!' But the company wouldn't, and the more Big Man protested that they should, the more the laughter went on. Big Man had had enough; he put on his hat, pushed out past them all and went through the dining-room door and out into the passage. Laughter bounced after him.

Ella found herself happy. She found questions had answers. But then she couldn't work out how because she didn't belong to these people. They had nothing to do with her. She didn't know them and they didn't know her. The truth of the thing was that nothing had changed since long before she was born, since long before the generation before her and the generation before that and before that and so it went on and would go on.

'Miss Pinkette!'

Instinctively Ella's attention shot over to the sound – and so she still knew who she was. It was the smartly dressed man, but she didn't know who he was.

'You don't remember me?'

She was about to be disgraced, the way you are when some old man relative grabs you up at a dance and makes you dance when you really don't want to, but to protest and refuse would cause greater disgrace. Ella smiled and had decided to submit long before he said his next two words.

'Is me!' Had 'me' become someone's name? 'You god-father.'

Ella remembered a godfather; after that, nothing. He was a smart man who never wore the same shirt two days in a row. He had on a pinstripe suit, a crisp white shirt and a blood-red waistcoat Ella had seen before. She didn't know where and was staring transfixed by it, but she had seen it before. On his head he wore a natty red felt hat with a long cock feather sticking out the side. It was a bravely put-together set of clothes, and he looked good. She remembered him now; Aunt Julie had once made a fool of herself over him when she knew he was happily married to his wife.

His name was Jackson. Just Jackson. He was a good friend of Daddy Ned's and Ella remembered that he was especially attentive, always remembered her birthday. He was her god-father. Her eyes dragged away from Jackson's red waistcoat and looked at him. He was standing in front of her admiring what he was looking at and then his arms were around her, hugging her to him. It was a warm, comfortable embrace, the first she had had in years. As the man held her warmly to him, he had a smell about him that Ella remembered from childhood. Morgan's Pomade hair oil had her floating away wrapped warm and secure around a sweet image upon which she used to be. Beneath her jacket Brownie's book was beating between them.

She felt another hand on her back. All too quickly Jackson was letting her go, was conceding to someone else, and she didn't want that. She turned to where the other hand had come from and there was Ludo smiling at her. Friction roared itself back into Ella's mind.

Her first birthday they were together, Ludo found her one cold crisp morning at the bottom of his garden naked, wearing his overcoat and sitting in the sycamore tree looking up at the sky. He'd watched her from his window wondering what it could be and whether he should go to help her. He was hoping she'd come in on her own, just find her way down out of the tree and come back into his bed on her own, but for the longest time she'd just sat there like she didn't even know where she was. After some time, maybe half an hour, maybe longer, he'd given up hoping she would ever come in, dragged on a pair of trousers and gone down to the garden.

'Ell?' Ludo was hugging himself.

He could see her feet bare and black with dirt and slashed red by the branches of the tree. He could see them tender and red hanging beneath the branch of the sycamore tree where she sat so comfortably she seemed to belong there.

He wanted her to trust him, that was all he wanted, but

from the moment they'd started he'd known that so far he could go and no further. All he had to do was decide whether he wanted to hang around for what she was offering. It wasn't much of a decision really. The little she was offering was always going to be tenfold what any other person had ever offered him and he reached for it, embracing her as the most glamorous gift he had been offered yet.

He had met her at a wedding. Some society wedding. Wearing a summer-green dress that fluttered delicately in the breeze like tissue paper, she was holding a glass of champagne. She was encircled by four men, each desperately trying to entertain and claim her bored mind for himself, and her nose started to bleed. She told Ludo later that ever since her childhood sometimes when she was stressed, her nose had a tendency to bleed. She didn't know when it was coming or anything, it just happened and she took it as a symptom of her life.

She told him that she had seen her mother fall dead and red and screaming to the earth beneath. Her father smiling red, an aunt for whom the colour seemed to exist, and a brother she hardly remembered. She told him she was alone in the world and the death that her family had met when she was a child was a death that haunted her because she should've been in the car with them.

However, she wouldn't tell him that since her family had gone he was the only thing she wanted to hold near, but she held him near nonetheless and he found it was where he wanted to be.

Ludo had never been in her flat without her. Eight years and he'd never been left there alone while she popped out to get breakfast for them after a whole night of love, never been asked to look after the place if work or whatever took her away. But today he was alone in her flat with her things and he began to worry about what he would do if she walked in and found him going through her things. Where was she? Luggage, passport, currency, he was waiting to see if she would return with anything to stop him boarding that plane. He was a couple of hours from checking in and he desperately wanted her to come back and say something to him. Something like 'Yes!'

'What time's your flight? I'll be back before then,' she'd said.

There had been optimism earlier in the day. Optimism he had grabbed with both hands to warm himself with. He'd called her mobile again and still it was off. He sat for a moment thinking and worrying.

It was eighty thirty, almost time to give up and leave for the airport, when: 'Ludo! Help—' And the line went dead. 'Ludo! Help—'

In her bedroom the bed was as they had both left it only the day before. He traced her imprint where she had lain. At the door he stood and scanned round the room. On the floor by her wardrobe a small bundle of black clothes had been frantically dropped. Like she'd been trying on outfits to finally settle on one to wear. At the bottom of the bed, the briefcase was open and there were photographs in and around, black and white mainly. He sat where she had sat

and looked where she had looked. Photographs of people he
didn't know, smiling, awkward people that looked like a
family that belonged to each other. He thought he recognised her in some of the faces but he couldn't be sure. And
then a picture of this huge pink house told a story all of its
own. Ludo's eyes drank in the details and character of the
House, all that the picture would give up, in fact, but he
thought despairingly the picture just wasn't big enough to
give up all it had. He flipped it over to read any inscription
someone might have put there for him. '*The Pink House.*
Hanville!!!'

'You rang me!' Ludo screamed back at her when he didn't
want to and then held himself down, angry with himself.

They were sitting in his car a few doors from the Pink
House. They were sitting outside number 27. Ella was working hard to keep her head steady and look straight ahead
through the windscreen. Of all the places Ludo could've
parked his car, she didn't know why she was surprised he
should've chosen this place, right slap bang outside the epi-
centre of her misery.

Her memory had always been that number 27 had burnt
to the ground. That there had been nothing left of it except
a pile of old bricks and scarred timber. But really it was
standing hollow and dark, shattered and spooky. It was like
someone who had gone through a war and now stood on
their last legs daring anyone to come and do their final best.
The windows had once been boarded up, but wind and

time had dealt with them and left the place open and
exposed. For all the years since the fire, nothing had been
done to the place. The family who had once lived there had
simply abandoned it, unable to put foot there even when the
fire and then the water had subsided.

'You told me your family was dead,' he was saying to her.
'Even though you could've asked me to be with you. I
thought you were dead or something.'

There was a tiny leak in her brain that allowed Ludo's
voice to register in there. She was back in the car with Ludo.

'Ell.' He was saying her name and she didn't know how
long he had been.

He placed a hand over hers but she wasn't going to
respond to him in any way. She sometimes did that. If she
wasn't happy with what he was talking about, if he had upset
her in any way, or even if it wasn't anything to do with him,
sometimes she didn't do the normal rational thing and
explain, sometimes she just sat there and let him guess and
suppose what the problem might be.

Ludo looked at Brownie's book on her lap. 'What's that?'

Again she didn't respond. She just sat there thinking long
and hard about something, weighing it in her mind, up,
down and around. Sitting there quietly with Brownie's book
on her lap, scared stiff to look left and holding her head
straight. Now she was wondering what she was doing. She
didn't have to go through any of this. She could go! Just
leave. She'd made a mistake coming back to Hanville, she
had been wrong to come running headlong back into that
fire when she had already run from it years ago. To run from

it, to cover the smell of it and to never look back at it was what she was thinking now. She had gained something, it hadn't been a total loss coming back, she had Brownie's book, maybe there was something in there that she could use for BrightWell's. There was nothing left here for her. And once more she had transport.

'Let's go.'

'Where?'

'Home!' Ella reached over her shoulder, pulled the seat belt around her and clipped herself in. She had made her decision. She was ready, that was how it was for her.

Ludo looked at her; he didn't get what she was on about. He didn't get any of it. Pointing behind, in the direction of the Pink House, he asked, 'To the House, you mean?'

'London!' Ella sat there looking out into the dark, waiting expectantly for Ludo to start the car.

'London?'

She wasn't going to respond to him. She didn't know why he had suddenly found the way to question her like this. Commendably – she thought – she was holding it down, she was doing her damn best not to rise up.

He thought she was weak, that was why he'd rushed to her. Ella Brightwell didn't have vulnerable times and it was a torture to her that she had revealed herself so pathetically. It looked like she was sitting in her seat as calm as anything, but it only looked that way. There was heat in the car. Ella was suffocating. There was like a fire of heat, leaving no place for either of them to breathe.

'Let's go,' she said and she said it like nothing before had ever happened. Like she'd never bled over him at a wedding, like she'd never lied about her past, like she had never ever sat in his sycamore tree virtually naked and kind of like Ludo didn't love her. Like she'd never begged him to help.

Still he made no move to start the car. He had wiped his face with his hands in a calming kind of way, he'd swallowed hard and fixed himself in his seat, but to start the car and to go, he made no move. He just wasn't going to do it and on that he had made up his mind, no matter what happened next.

'D'you want me to drive?'

It was his turn not to answer.

''Cause if you do, I will.'

Still nothing came from him. She was looking at him, waiting for him to kick into life. She didn't need to be feeling that she was losing him right now. He didn't need to go on with this new-found strength and closeness he'd been exhibiting lately. If he wanted to pick it up, say, next month, next week, tomorrow even, that would be fine. She could meet him and deal with him then, but today, right now she didn't need it. Had he any idea what she was going through while they were just sitting in his car? He was annoying her.

As the wait went on, Ella's mind failed her. The hinges on it buckled. Smoke was seeping out.

'Shall I, then?'

The shapes were shifting inside her, building up the way she had trained them to rescue her from any situation she didn't care for. The smoke had curled around her feet again and was rising up her legs, up the seat and circling her like a trail round and round as it had done before. Ella began to clear her throat. She glanced across at him to see if he could see her discomfort, to see if he was smelling and tasting it too. Ludo was aware of nothing, it seemed, except how he could help her and so help himself. The smell was settling in her nostrils, that musty, cheesy smell of a stale fire.

Six weeks after the fire, Ella had slid through the half-shored up back door. All around there was this musty smell she had daily smelt on Patrick since it had happened. All around living gothic horror. As she moved from room to room, she could hear the fire all around her as it begun to take hold again. She could hear the panic in the boys like it was happening for real, and the only thing she was able to hold on to was that it had happened six weeks ago and couldn't touch her now – for a twelve-year-old, Ella had way too much detachment.

She could hear the boys wanting to stay and put it out, wanting to call the fire brigade, an ambulance, someone – even Patrick had wanted to, but she had said no and she had run and in the end so had they both.

As Ella reached the stairs in number 27, she tried to mount them, to confront, to stare down something she knew would haunt her for ever if she didn't. She didn't really have the balls to do this but if there was anyone, be they twelve or grown, who could find them when they needed them, it was Ella. She knew the consequences of not looking it in the eye and she no way nohow wanted to be owned for the rest of her life. She took a deep breath, put one foot on the charred black step and her foot smashed clean through the step, which swallowed it. Ella screamed! She began to panic, pulling on her foot, desperate to release it. A hand reached out and touched her from behind. She flashed around ready to fight, scared because it had got to her before she could get to it, and there was Patrick crying his eyes out.

'Pinky, we got to tell!'

Ella saw the fear in him. She wasn't immune to it. It wasn't that she didn't see what her brother was going through, it wasn't that she didn't feel what he was going through, she just couldn't do it with him or allow him to do it on his own. She had to deny.

Ella grabbed hold of her older, stronger brother, forced him back against a wall, poking at his chest angrily until he was backed up with nowhere to go. She was warning him with all that she had.

'You open your fucking little mouth and I'm gonna kill you!'

The terror on Patrick's face would've been a joy to Ella had she not been there herself, and it looked like Patrick would never be able to do anything again after Ella had said that to him. He looked like suddenly he had found out this was all that life had for him and from now on he would have to close off and get by on the scraps of it.

'And you know I can,' she warned him with a little smile.

Quickly she undid her seat belt, opened her door and got out. She was walking around the car to the driver's door with

Brownie's book in her hand. The smell didn't leave her. Ludo's door wrenched open and she stood there waiting for him to get out. He got out of the car and stood in front of her. The two of them stood in the middle of the road, she unable to look at him, holding on to Brownie's yellowing book like the lifeline it was for her. And all Ludo knew was this: she was running, he had found her running, had not been able to stop her running, and he wondered what in the hell would.

'Ell!' He put his arms around her. 'I'll stay with you.' It was all he had.

She pushed him off her like he were some stranger who had accosted her in the street, got in the car, slammed the door and drove off, all before Ludo could even react. Ludo stood there watching his car scream away, cut left and disappear out of sight. He waited a few seconds like he expected her to come back. Then he turned back and started to walk towards the House. He stopped and looked down the road, still hoping for her. Then he continued on towards the House and when he got to the gate he saw Mirabel sitting on the front wall looking at him.

He stared at her and found he was smiling at her in his agony. He liked her, thought she was beautiful and had a peace about her. She jumped down off the wall, took his hand from his side, led him through the gate, down the side of the House and into it.

Three streets away Ella had stopped the car and wound down the windows trying to let the smell of fire out. Brownie's book had travelled on her lap like she was afraid to put it down and now she picked it up and smelt it, trying to get the smell of smoke out of her nostrils. So far, with all that had happened since lifting the book from the spice and herb cupboard, she hadn't yet had the chance to just sit, to just take in even the touch of it.

It looked like it was nothing. Like it could easily have been nothing and thrown in the rubbish like that. It had no reverence, no grandeur, it was just a tatty old yellowing book that smelt not of the cupboard where it had been all these years, but of Brownie. As soon as Ella put her nose to it and pulled in the smell of it, she knew it. A friendly smell, one of the best, friendliest smells in the whole wide world. She couldn't get enough of it and felt herself giddy with it, could've sunk clean away into it and did.

The cover was hanging off. A little chunk had been ripped off the top right-hand corner. It had no title, no name and was no bigger than a regular paperback book. What held her after the smell, though, before the smell even, was that as she laid her palm flat on the cover of it, a little heartbeat tickled the centre of her palm. Alarmed, like maybe she didn't expect it, Ella pulled her hand away and looked at it. She took it in again; innocuous to look at, trash-worthy, a book. That's all! Slowly she put her hand back to see if it was true and it was. Like a little butterfly maybe, in the dead centre of her palm, a little baby heartbeat tickling her. She gasped a giggle, covered her mouth, placed her palm back there and laughed again and again. She closed her eyes and lived it. This really was what her childhood had been built on. On this feeling, that inside, somewhere, someone, somehow had the answer to something.

Or maybe this was just some old book Brownie had stuffed at the back of her spice and herb cupboard and forgotten about? Maybe it was just nothing and she had made it whatever it was. Because sitting there in Ludo's car, it suddenly dawned on her that there was no way Brownie would write down recipes. Brownie just wasn't the kind of woman who would sit and write down a list of ingredients and then a method of preparation. Her cooking was done with feel, with emotion, with what she was about.

Cautiously, as if it were some treasured relic from an age past, Ella flicked the pages of the book. The movement moved her stomach with it and then she breathed out like she'd run a mile or something. As the pages had flicked open and shut from beginning to end, in a matter of seconds, the brightest light had flooded through to her eyes and it didn't even hurt her mind. A buzz was buzzing inside her, pumping round her and sending her heart up to her mouth. She had to go again; this time she had to savour the movement of the pages like one of her mother's meals. The change in tempo of the pages brought a change to the rhythm of her heartbeat. It brought a change to the speed of the world and everyone in it. As the pages flicked by her wide eyes, from between them began to fall a bunch of stuff. Things tumbled from between the pages, cascading into her lap like the charms from a charm bracelet. Sealed from the light for decades, they had been waiting for this very moment. She could see what they were, but had a million and one questions as to what the hell they were. There were small twigs, a bunch of them, some of them tied together. A bundle of curly hair. A black string, a shoelace. Clips of fingernails so tiny they were hardly there. Ribbons, the smallest and most delicate of blue ribbons ever; they looked like threads. Tentatively Ella reached down into her lap, put a finger and thumb among the lot and came up with a bunch of hair, and it was the most blameless bundle of anything she had ever felt. Warm between her fingers, and like something she had touched before. And she didn't understand anything and began to think that this was just so Brownie to have a book stuffed with the most disparate odds and ends. And whatever Ella didn't know about these bits, and that was everything, something was telling her they were beautiful things and they must lead somehow to Brownie's heart.

She opened the book at random and saw a tiny baby handprint in brown. Ella touched it and some of the outline flaked away. It was dried blood. A baby's handprint in dried blood that flaked away to the touch and it was there that was the centre of the heartbeat. She felt it stronger than ever as she touched the imprint and realised it lived right there, on the first page she had come to.

There were words in Brownie's hand. She had never seen her mother write anything down. In fact, she had often wondered if her mother could write, but without a doubt Ella knew this was her mother's hand. Reading, she heard Brownie's voice like Brownie were sitting right next to her.

'Compare to you brother Patrick, Kellit is a soft boy. Compare to you brother Johno, Kellit have so much to do I wonder if him ever going manage even a taste of it.' Brownie was writing to one of her children, which one Ella had no idea.

Him is a fine boy who have it in him that him must have everything and have everything immediately. Like a little boy running through life knocking into the corners of it. Him eagerness make you eager and make you know that there's things out there for you. But if him should ever get to understand that all he already have is all him suppose to have, him going love it all the more. The food I soothe him with is ackee and salt fish. Ackee needs a little patience and you have one of the most wonderful dish of food ever. First you put to soak over night as much salt fish as you need . . .

A slight ease came over Ella; Brownie had after all written down her recipes. Then it suddenly occurred to her that despite wanting to find out how her mother cooked, why it was the only thing she ever took seriously outside her children and Daddy Ned, Ella suddenly felt betrayed that Brownie had after all written them down. Ella didn't want to believe her mother had done this basic, normal thing in leaving behind something of a cookbook so anyone could just up and plunder what had made her her.

To talk to a boy like you brother Lambert you best cook up a pot of mackerel rundown. Make like you not cooking it for him alone 'cause him don't like to think you go to any trouble just for him. You set it before the whole table, everybody eat and when them all eat and gone you will find Lambert come up beside you washing plate and talking 'bout whatever him need to. With you brother you don't have to push at all, is like the gate open and you sure enough to step through. I look on him and I can see everything me and you daddy have for each other in him and I believe him don't have a piece of hurt inside him.

Ella turned a page, losing the thread of whether it was a cookbook or just some reflections by Brownie on her children. Whatever it was, Ella was quickly aware that the couple of pages she had already read were the most she had ever heard her mother express uninterruptedly in seventeen years of living with her.

For mackerel rundown you going need salt mackerel, coconut milk, onion, vinegar, tomato, pepper and lime juice and always a little love. (Ella smiled, her eyes settling on the last of Brownie's list.) Chop off the mackerel head them. Wash the fish in lime. Soak for some hours. When the fish half soak, you do you coconut milk in the usual way. Boil up the milk in a dutchy and just before it turn, add the pepper, add the tomato and onion. Add them mash up . . . (Brownie's tone switched in midsentence.) . . . today ah sit and ah look on you sister . . .

Just like that, Brownie had fallen out of the recipe and gone back to writing to whoever she was writing to. Ella turned the page hoping Brownie would straight away pick

up the recipe, but she didn't. Over the page the recipe did
not continue. Over the page there was other stuff. About
her. Ella's mood changed slightly and she sat firm and straight
in the seat, eager to see what Brownie would say about her.

Pinkette climb all the way up and go sit down with you
and she just looking out on you. Just sit down up there
looking for you. You already know this as a truth, but is
like you can see some of the whole world from up there.
And I have it in mind that she know it. Is a good time
now the three of we don't just sit and consider together. I
look on her and I know today not the day she going want
me join you and she, so I just sit down at the bottom of
the tree and consider.

Just as in life, Brownie was making no sense in death. Ella
continued reading, needing to make sense of it. 'I have it in
mind to tell her everything she need. She have a sense of you
already and she have a need for you already, but after that, I
don't know much bout what she can manage to—'
There came an excited knock on the windscreen, crashing into Ella's closeted world like a tornado into the shack of
an outhouse. Ella's head shot up from the book, her mode
switched to attack, ready to defend herself against the threat,
wherever it came from. Then and there she would've been
useless, though, because before she knew it the passenger
door opened and Althea was sitting next to her, grinning at
her.
'How you doing?'

Ella stared at her like she didn't know who she was, even though she saw that it was Althea. As Ella smiled at her, surreptitiously closing up the book and putting her hand over everything in her lap, it began to form in her mind that it was Althea sitting next to her. Althea, one of Patrick's pregnant women. She stared at Althea.

'You enjoying yourself?' Althea came straight out and asked.

Ella smiled at her, not because she wanted to, but because she couldn't think of anything to say.

'I don't mean right now, mind you. I mean if you enjoying yourself lifewise?'

Ella was clutching tightly the book and all its contents on her lap.

'The first thing I think when I see you, she enjoying herself lifewise?'

Ella didn't know one hell of what Althea was trying to ask her and she thought if she just ignored her, Athea would take the hint and go and leave her to get back to reading Brownie's book. But Althea remained smiling at Ella.

'No room not round there to park?'

'Round where?'

'By the House?'

Ella clicked on, started up the car, drove the car round the block and parked Ludo's car right where it had been before, right outside number 27.

'I like you, you know.'

'Do you?' Ella was being rude. It didn't take much for her to drag on her attitude.

'And once you dash 'way all this other foolishness, so will most people.'

Whatever Ella thought she had, she immediately lost and sat there suitably humbled.

'I say to Patrick, "I like you baby sister." You an' him don't really get on, do you?'

'What did he tell you?'

'Him don't talk 'bout you at all. Is only through Donna I really know Mamma Brownie and Daddy Ned have another child. Not even Mamma Brownie used to talk 'bout you.'

Ella didn't need to hear that Brownie had never mentioned her since the night she had left. She didn't need Althea droning on about how completely she had been removed from the family, she already had an idea it had been that way, she didn't need it confirmed to her. Truth was, it hurt her widely.

'I used to often wonder what it was that Mamma Brownie used to sit and consider on, you know, and once I know 'bout you, I get to understand is you.' Althea turned directly to Ella. 'You and Mamma Brownie did have something then?'

Ella couldn't answer Althea and began instead to open the car door and climb out. But it was too late, Althea had seen a tear streaking its way down Ella's face. So Brownie hadn't talked about her? She never would've believed Brownie was the type of woman to hold a grudge and banish her from her mind, but apparently she had done just that. Ella was by the car waiting for Althea to get out and slam the door shut so she could lock it.

She avoided number 27 and walked as calm as she could over to the Pink House. It was all lit up. There was singing coming from the sitting room and the sound of people at the back. There was the sound of a house full of people who knew about each other, who cared about each other, who belonged to each other. Brownie used to love it when it was full. Who were they kidding, thinking they could ward her off? Brownie was in there and in there large. Althea joined Ella, put her arm around her and guided her in through the front gate and up to the side of the House.

The women had loved Ludo straight away. A man who loved his food and didn't care that anyone could see he did. For the women it was the chance to feed a stranger and that was a joy to them. As soon as someone walked into their kitchens, a plate of food was placed before them. If it was someone new to them and their ways, if it was a white person, then they were eager to show off just how gorgeous their hands were. Sometimes they ran the most joke on a stranger, not because they didn't like the stranger, but because they loved the drama of it. Sometimes they ran the joke on a white person because they knew all that they had was infinitely more powerful than anything any white person could manage. This then was what both the women and the men were running in the kitchen of the Pink House and they were running it on poor Ludo.

Ludo had dutifully made himself, as instructed, comfortable at the table, opposite Poor Cousin Winston, in between the domino match and the continual storytelling. Ludo looked across at Poor Cousin Winston; he was eating up his food with a huge thing that looked like a shovel, but was in fact a spoon. He observed that whatever it was that Poor Cousin Winston was eating, he found it fine, because he hardly had time to raise a smile across the table in the direction of his fellow diner. And then Ludo realised that it wasn't only him that thought it, because one of the women called out a kind of chastise that Ludo didn't quite understand.

'Then Poor Cousin Winston, take time no, man! It a go run from you?'

Poor Cousin Winston nodded his head that he had heard what had been said to him, but he took no heed of it and continued in the same shovelling way.

'You know full well food the only thing dat sweet the boy,' one of the men came back, because he didn't see any need that just because they had a stranger in their midst, and a white stranger at that, they should show off and pretend their ways were otherwise. The man was Jackson. He smiled warmly at Ludo, who didn't quite understand what had gone on around him, though he suspected it would not have gone on had he not been there.

Before Ludo there suddenly appeared a knife and a fork, a mat, a coaster and then a huge plate of curry goat and rice. He had had this before at BrightWell's and it was one of his favourites. After the first time he'd tasted it, he'd begged Ella to cook it for him at home, but she never would. The only way he could eat it was at BrightWell's or from some takeaway.

'Curry goat and rice! My favourite!' Ludo announced,

stunningly proud of the fact that he knew what they had placed before him, that he wasn't some stuck-in-the-mud white man unfamiliar with the culture that had spawned the woman he so completely loved.

As Ludo waited for his food, the men had begun their part in the game. They had placed before him a shot glass and half a bottle of Wray and Nephew white rum. Sam Nugent had poured Ludo's shot, corked the bottle and sat back waiting for Ludo to try it. Ludo looked around the table and the kitchen; they were all waiting for him to try it. They were all waiting and he knew something was up. But then his plate of food arrived and he was able to divert from it. He smiled thanks to the women and tucked in. He took a forkful and stuffed it into his hungry mouth. Before he had even swallowed the first mouthful, he realised this was not quite the way Ella cooked it. It was similar, it smelt the same, it looked the same, but it was not the same. The one mouthful of goat nearly blew Ludo's head off, and the one sip of rum he had grabbed for in his haste to cool his mouth had left his stomach rotting right down to the pit of it. This was Jamaican cuisine at its brashest. This was Jamaican cuisine with all the heat of the island, with all the richness of the people. This was the food with none of the diluted nonsense Ella had brought to it. And so, as Ella walked into the kitchen with Althea, the men were having the most fun trying to get Ludo to drink more rum and the women were having the most fun trying to get him to eat more curry.

Miss Nugent was passing Ella with a long glass of cool ice water and placing it on the table in front of Ludo. She put it

on the table and then put an arm sympathetically around
Ludo. He grabbed at the ice water before him, sinking his
inflamed jaws into it. There was much laughing, even Ludo
could find some humour in it. Ella watched him. They liked
him. The people in and around the Pink House liked Ludo
and he liked them. After minutes in their company Ludo
seemed to fit in with them more than Ella had done in a lifetime. She was jealous. As he downed the ice water in one go,
Ludo's eyes caught sight of Ella and he stopped laughing at
himself, put the empty glass down and stood up. All around
him, though, everyone else was still laughing.

'She have a little cry,' Althea was telling him when she saw
the concern in his face.

Her words didn't console Ludo, they only alarmed him
more. For starters he couldn't believe Ella could ever have
anything named 'a little cry'. He'd never seen it. He knew
when she had left him in the car she was on her way somewhere, but he had never thought she was on he way to the
place where people went for 'little cries'. He didn't believe
she knew such a place existed, never mind how to get there.

Ludo stood up ready to go to her; she saw this and walked
calmly out into the passage. He followed her. In the passage
they were alone, but behind the closed sitting-room door
they could hear singing:

'What a friend we have in Jesus, all our sins and grief to
bear. What a privilege to carry everything to God in prayer.'

Ella was in front of him pacing up and down, trying to get
her head around something. Trying desperately to control
what she had lost control of. Ludo was watching her.

Eventually he asked, 'You all right?'

'Feel that' Ella thrust Brownie's book into his hand. Ludo looked at it, felt it and looked at her, trying to make sense of what she was on about. Really, that was all he ever did.

'Don't you feel anything?'

'Like, what?' He was trying his best.

'What does it feel like? What do you feel?'

'Feels like a book.' Ludo didn't know what she wanted from him.

She took the book from him, put her hand over it and felt again that same tickling little heartbeat. She put it back in his hand and placed his hand right where hers had been. 'You don't feel anything?'

He didn't have to answer for her to know he didn't.

Ella took the book from him and pushed it in her pocket. She was beginning to think she was going mad. She didn't know what she was doing, where she had gone wrong. She had had a plan but somehow it had been smashed. And it had been smashed because there was a saying that 'you could dig out your guts and replace it with dry trash', but all sensible people knew you couldn't live like that. Anyone who tried to had to one day stop and be shown just how wrong they were to even try.

'You don't feel anything?' She pleaded with him to join her.

Ludo shrugged.

'Nothing at all?'

Ludo put his arms around her and held her, trying to calm her. Trying to be with her. Surprisingly he felt her sink into him and he sank further into her, trying to soothe her with all the love he could muster. For Ella whatever he could muster right then and there was never going to be enough because she still didn't have her answers and, what was worse, she didn't even have the questions.

The sitting-room door flew open, the singing still going on behind it, and a fine-looking man wearing a dog collar was coming out, talking to Mirabel and her dolly. As soon as Ella saw him she froze. It was like every drop of blood in her body drained away. The man didn't see her, he was so busy and so calm in the way he was talking to Mirabel. Mirabel clung to him, Mirabel loved him and Ella wasn't surprised, because it was Johno. She hadn't seen him for nearly twenty years and then suddenly here he was in front of her like he'd just come up from some dark, disgusting place and the brightness all around him was what had kept him alive.

Ella took her time looking into his face. She didn't really want the shame it induced in her but just couldn't help herself. Her eyes just wanted to see his face again. Ludo still had his arm around her like he was protecting her. Johno stood tall and straight in front of her, not bent or bowed by his life. Mirabel was holding his hand and wondering what the hell was going on now. Ella's mind was shifting in and out at its usual speed. Firing off questions she couldn't answer at a pace that was self-defeating: questions about who he was, where he'd been and how he could stand up straight and tall and look so damn pleased and open.

The last time she'd seen him free was eighteen years ago, the day Johno had looked for her. He hadn't spent the

morning walking around Hanville trying to find something
of interest to occupy himself, he had looked for her.
Everything Ella had comforted herself with previously burnt
away as the lie it was, as she stood held by the peace in her
brother's face.

Ella had left Larry sitting on the wall outside the Pink House
that morning. He had called round bright and early for her,
but she'd still been running her ego trip and was still making
him suffer and had left him on the wall, his silly skin open
before her so she could see the hurt she had caused in him,
and she'd left him and gone 'bout her business.

   Larry had looked so vulnerable that morning. It was only
a week or so after the morning at the Bridge, the morning
he had arranged to meet Ella. By rights Larry should still
have been in bed, there were no two ways about it. He still
had a broken arm, his eyes were just fixing to go down and
he was badly bruised. Brownie had suggested Poor Little
Lost Son should stay with her that day. She had a feeling he
should rest up and spend the day drinking cornmeal porridge and fever-grass tea. But he wouldn't. He was after
making it up to Ella. He had been thoroughly disappointed
she wouldn't even speak to him yet again that morning. For
her to just ignore him like that and walk out, before he had
had even the chance to be near her. But Johno had come
down for his breakfast, seen Larry's ongoing plight and said
he had an idea where she might be spending the day. Larry
saw a chance; with her beloved Johno around he might get

back his special best friend. He decided to take it. Ever since she had come across him on the Bridge with Andrew Naylor, it had been his task every waking hour to figure out a way of working his way back to a point where she would forgive him. This morning, with Johno in tow, might just be it.

After finding Larry with Andrew Naylor, Ella had gone straight to Rose Farm with all she'd seen. It was like she came out singing that hymn and had but one thing in mind. She had known the outcome before she arrived there, she'd known the outcome as she had begun to tell, but it never stopped her and only as she walked away from the misery of the place did she regret. Momentarily she'd thought of finding Larry and telling him to leave Hanville now and never look back, but it was only momentarily. The fury she had unleashed on Larry was something she'd have to live with. She had set it off and she would sit back and wait for Larry to learn his lesson. He had slapped her; she was merely slapping him back.

Sitting in the tree, she watched them approach. She knew they'd come. They were her two best boys and one of them was up to making up to her, she was flying. She had that morning managed to climb to the middle of a particularly large apple tree that had been defeating her for a couple of months. It was in the park. An apple tree in a public park! There was a branch just on the opposite side that looked like it could hold her, but she couldn't figure out the route to get there without falling and breaking her neck. It was this that she was pondering on and she sat there eating bad apples for some time before she saw her boys coming through the park gates.

'Told you!' Johno said triumphantly to a sullen Larry who just couldn't settle in himself until they had found her. Even now they had, it made no difference until she had forgiven him.

Johno stepped forward first, looking up at her, losing her with the sun behind her until he shaded his eyes. A half-eaten apple was on its way down towards him; Johno stepped out of the way and then stepped back once it had landed, looking up at her again, shielding his eyes from the sun.

'What you doing up there?' Johno's words floated up to her.

'What you doing down there?' Ella threw back at him without even looking down at him, and especially without looking at Larry for even a minute.

'You going come down?' Johno asked her.

Ella knew Johno wasn't asking for his sake, there was no war going on between them. She knew he had come as mediator, so she made them wait, especially Larry, who, she noticed, could not take his eyes off her the whole time she refused to look at him. She stayed put, feeling superior, feeling that this, having her two best boys at her feet, one desperate to make up with her, was where life began and ended. And she ate four more apples before she felt sick and came down, knowing immediately there was no way she was going to be able to eat her snapper lunch.

'So what we going do today, Pinky?' Johno grinned as he undid the greaseproof paper to begin eating her lunch.

Ella was staring at Larry now and he was smiling at her, hoping this meant forgiveness was near, but it didn't mean that at all. It meant Ella was walking over him and he was letting her.

She could've done without going to the petrol station and tormenting Patrick that day. She had her two best boys to torment already, but she was greedy and one more would make her feel she had done an exceptional day's work. So in response to Johno's question, that was where they were going.

Patrick was in a good mood when they arrived, because Mr Heath had left him in charge for the first time. A thirteen-year-old idiot in charge of a petrol station, Ella stood back observing. Only in Hanville! It was then, as she looked angrily into the smug, happy face of her brother Patrick, who felt huge at being left in charge of all he surveyed, that Ella hatched the plan. That was why she came up with the idea, to bring him down a pace. She hated that look and she knew the only reason it was on his face was to put his foot on her neck. Her plan was this: Larry should steal a shelf of Marlboro from the petrol station where Patrick had been left in charge, and they should go back to the park and smoke them. That was all she had in mind. Get Patrick in trouble with his boss, get Larry to prove how sorry he was for what he had done and give herself something to do.

'No!' Patrick was putting his foot down and his foot had suddenly somehow slipped off Ella's neck. He wasn't about to let it happen; this time he was going to stand up to his tyrant of a sister and say no. He said it again. 'No!' And he looked to John to back him.

Johno couldn't say anything. He was half on Ella's side, half on Patrick's side, he was on everybody's side apart from his own and she knew it.

'Well, he can't carry them, not with a broken arm!' Patrick shouted when he knew he had lost Johno. And he was right, with Larry's broken arm there was no way he could carry a shelf of Marlboro. Not for anyone else or for himself, but he could carry them for Ella.

Quick as anything Larry rushed inside the shop and lodged a tray between his rigid arm and his good arm and emerged with the Marlboros and stood on the forecourt grinning. Whatever pain he was going through, and it was plenty as he held the tray up, it was nothing compared to the delight the look on Ella's face gave him when he saw it. Ella had triumphed over Larry and over Patrick too.

Patrick for one couldn't believe it; all he knew was that he would lose his job. All he knew was that Ella, 'cause he didn't blame Larry, would lose him his job and he hated her. Ella glared at Patrick, daring him to come over and hit her. Hitting Johno was something he never thought even once about, but hitting her! Ella knew it would take more than he had. She smiled at him, hoping that just this once he would lose his head and follow that streak of red that was urging him on, but he wouldn't.

Ella turned from him to Larry. 'Come on then.' And she was about to set off when she heard another 'no' behind her. It was Larry's voice.

Ella turned back, horrified that he should say no. That perhaps he didn't want to make it up to her as much as she had seen that he did. She looked at Patrick; he was smiling. He was thinking that Ella had defeated herself. He was joyous that Ella had dropped down in it and it had happened to her right in front of him.

'The Naylors have gone on holiday,' Larry added to his no.

At the mention of the name Naylor, Ella's attention perked up and she wondered what he was on about.

'Number twenty-seven's empty. We can go there and smoke them.' In his eagerness to prove himself, to win her back, to impress her, this was Larry's idea and Ella loved it, loved him and leapt on it. In the midst of them, Johno and Patrick had no idea what it meant.

When the fire started, it started with Larry and neither Patrick, Johno nor Ella could work out how. They had gone to Andrew Naylor's bedroom at Larry's insistence to smoke the Marlboro and while they were standing in front of a smiling picture of Andrew Naylor, the fire had started right there, with Larry. The fire seemed to come from Larry and they didn't know how. They ran. They all left him. They all ran, none of them looked back and none of them saw when Larry needed their help.

She lit a Marlboro and held the smoke deep inside, trying to warm herself. She was out in the yard of the Pink House alone. Chilly from the cool of the night, but preferring it to the smell of smoke she had left swarming round the inhabitants in the passage in the House. Brownie's clothes were fluttering but she tried to keep off them and sat instead on a large, flat stone at the root of the oak tree, trying to think and feel how it might go this time. She was learning to ignore the sounds in her stomach, was learning that they would live with her no matter what she did or didn't do for them so she was now doing nothing. All that was really on her mind was how it would go with Johno and, if it went badly, would she care? Beneath her jacket, cradled there where it was still beating in the rhythm of a heartbeat, the book felt like something that would protect her. She tapped at it, half for reassurance that it was firmly safe and half as a kind of talisman. As she thought on the idea of talking to Johno, the adrenaline skittered through her body, wiring her up so'til Ella had smoked two cigarettes before she knew she had even lit the third. She was nursing on that when the back door opened and Johno came out, bringing two glasses of something. She stood up to meet him.

'What is it?' she asked, unable to just take his offering and drink.

'Just take it no, man!' Johno smiled at her, offering it again.

She took it and tried to hide the fact that she put her nose in before her lips round it and eventually took a tentative sip. 'Orange and syrup!' She took in a gasp of air and everywhere about her seemed to warm and brighten in the instant.

And together they laughed and started upon a little nursery rhyme that was theirs. 'Orange and syrup, say the bells of Ja-maica. You owe me five cents, say the bells of Maypen. When will you pay me? say the bells of St Catherine. When I grow rich, say the bells of King-ston!' And they cracked up laughing and she drank down the rest of her orange and syrup in one go in a race with Johno, who purposely let her win the way he always had.

As she drank it down, her mouth smiling happily around the glass, Johno was watching her and was loving just doing that. When she finished, Ella became aware that he was and had been the whole time she'd had the glass turned to her head and he knew she didn't like it. She used to love being looked at but the pain he could see in her now wasn't worth the joy looking at her brought him.

Ella darkened and dropped back down on the large, flat

stone. She was kind of surprised he had managed to distract her in so complete a way with such a little thing. He really knew her, he was such a clever man, and she warned herself that she'd have to be careful or he would have her relaxed again before she knew it, letting out all kinds of stuff that she couldn't bear thinking about. He came and sat right next to her, smiling at her the whole time, and Ella tried to hide her discomfort with a smile that hardly cracked her face. Johno kicked back, reached for the half-smoked cigarette in her hand and dragged on it, holding the smoke deep inside himself, almost as deep as she could. Now she was looking at him.

'What?' Johno asked.

'You're a priest!'

With the smallest of movements he had managed to elicit yet another involuntary motion from her, again she noted it. And Johno dragged on the cigarette, finishing it before he spoke, and she noted that too.

'A vicar, get it right.'

She thought she'd been chastised when she hadn't been and her spirit shot up and stood between them, ready to defend herself. Johno put a hand on hers trying to calm her.

'Just something I picked up when I was away. Can't seem to shake it.'

She got it now, he was about to start with the accusations and the recriminations as she had known he would right from when she looked into his face a little while ago. She wondered what his line would be. If she were him she would go with blaming the two who had walked away from the whole mess with apparently everything intact and then she would detail exactly every minute of the time she had been away, describing every degrading incident she'd had to endure and every lonely sad second she had been made to live. Patrick must've had his blame years ago, now it was her turn.

She did want to hear how things were for him. How long Her Majesty's pleasure indeed had been for him, how he had gone from that to the church to sitting smoking Marlboros with her under the oak tree – she wondered if he knew they were Marlboros – but she had never had the courage to find out when she was younger and now she didn't know how to hear it without living the guilt in animated 3-D.

Patrick used to write to him at least. And go and see him too. The whole family used to go and see him; once or twice Ella made herself go but more than that she couldn't. The first time the Brightwells were fixing to go off and see Johno, Ella had a nose-bleed and had to stay home alone in bed. The second time they were fixing to go she had that morning fallen out of one of the neighbourhood trees, having forgotten the sequence of the branches, and had to spend the day in bed drinking tea and cornmeal porridge. The third time Aunt Julie bound Ella to her the day before, and they all set off to the prison healthy and fit. She stomached one more time before she went to Brownie and told her she would never go there again, she went to her mother in a kind of pleading way that Brownie had never seen before. She needed to play in the sun and climb trees, she didn't want to sit in a long room huddled around a table with

the whole Brightwell clan as they fired questions at Johno
about what the food was like or what the toilets were like.
She didn't need to see Johno dressed in a kind of serge blue
that looked so rough it probably cut his arse every time he sat
down. She had a course around the neighbourhood trees
that she estimated would take her six months and she was
working steadily on that.

When she discovered that Patrick wasn't only going along
with the family to see Johno, he was writing to him too, on
a regular basis, and what's more, Johno was writing back,
they were swapping stories about their lives – when she discovered all this, Ella flew into a rage and tried to warn
Patrick off doing it. She didn't want Patrick mending stuff
between himself and Johno. She wanted it left open and
flaming red the way it was between herself and Johno. But
Patrick wasn't having none of it. Although he had lost any
will to stand up to her since the fire, Patrick had also taken
from the whole event a kind of ease that made it all right.

As far as Ella was concerned, she could stand not to hear
better than she could stand hearing what and how it had
been for Johno. And she knew Johno would know this and
a kind of false ease came over her as she settled back into the
tree next to him and confidently told herself he wasn't there
to make things uncomfortable for her, he had never been
there for that.

'Well, you looking well,' Johno said after the longest time
summing her up.

Ella smiled. Even though it was the only way she wanted
to go with him right now, she never would have taken him

for small talk. She never would've taken him for a coward in
a crowd.

'And you running a restaurant, Donna say?'

'Just a little place really.' Ella was being patronising and
guarding herself against 'who does she think she is?'

'You think that got something to do with Mamma
Brownie?'

'I think it's got something to do with me.' Her spirit had
not subsided one bit then and all she could do to hide her
embarrassment was light another cigarette. Again he placed
his hand over hers but this time she pulled from beneath it,
got up and moved away to the other side of the yard. She
had wanted to do that for a long time.

She knew he was watching her, and she felt uncomfortable with Johno sitting and looking so calm, so together,
while she stood fraying all over the place. He was waiting,
she thought, waiting for her just to stop, take a breath and
talk to him. She suddenly couldn't stand the silence of the
gap he had given her, and so she just started talking.

'And Lambert?'

'Flying in from America first thing. Journalist. Doing
well.'

'Yeah, Mirabel gave me some of his cuttings.' Ella pulled
them out of her pocket and pretended to be interested in
them, but she clearly wasn't and wasn't fooling anyone. She
stuffed them back after what she thought was a suitable time
studying them.

'And Kellit's travelling back from Jamaica Donna said,'
Ella added.

'We all trying to do something,' Johno finished.

Ella knew the silence was renewing itself and so she went on chatting nonsense. 'So everything's ready for tomorrow, Donna says?' Ella thought it wasn't noticeable, but it was. And just like always he did his best to accommodate her.

'Yeah.'

'Poor Cousin Winston told me the wrong day.'

'Yeah.'

'I mean I would've come Friday, if I'd known. Coming like I did meant I had to leave the restaurant. And that's never good business.'

He was trying to calm her with his presence, with his eyes, trying to tell her that whatever she was feeling she could tell him and they would find a way to make it all right and they would find a way to be together, because whatever she was feeling was a justified feeling and Brownie had taught him that. She had taught Ella too but Ella had all the time been too busy running her own vapid lessons. So all he could do was sit and watch this show she was intent on performing for him. Changing costumes at will as she tried to dazzle him from the truth. Bigger, more elaborate costumes, and all the time he could see clearly through to the suit she was trying to hide from him, the one she was born with.

If he could see what she was hiding from him despite herself, it didn't make sense to go on in the pretence, he thought. He wasn't the same boy she had known all those years ago. He had spent eight years locked up. He had his faith that had heated him when he had nearly died from the

cold life had dropped him in. He had Brownie's voice guiding him hand in hand with his faith, but standing by calmly
to let a whirlwind exhaust itself on and around him was just
something he couldn't do, not even for her. And so he said
it. The way he had been brought up to just say it.

'You don't have to hide from me, you know, Pinky.'

For a second she played with the idea that he might be
right, that this might be the one person left from whom she
didn't have to hide. She pushed her fingers in and out of it,
round and round it, testing it and prodding it, poking it and
sizing it up to see if it could sustain her and work for her.
And maybe she was just on the verge of finding out that its
dimensions were sufficient, because suddenly she pulled back
from it and clamped down shut.

'I should find Ludo.'

She stepped away, heading for the back door. She didn't
know if he was coming up behind her, if he suddenly had
to go back inside and find someone too, and as she went
she found herself glancing slightly over her shoulder to see
if he was following her. He was. As she was making to
move faster, the distraction of him behind her, and possibly
something else too, made her take a wrong step. Ella
tripped and fell down on her hands and knees; the book
flew out of her pocket and everything she had cradled
moments before fell down in front of her. Before they had
even settled, before she could even realise how she was, Ella
was scurrying to reclaim them because no one else was
supposed to see them, no one else was supposed to touch
them and no one was ever supposed to see her this way. But

Johno had and was coming up quick behind her to help her.

'No! I can do it.'

He backed off and straightened up, watching her hands quickly gather up the things and stuff them back into the book. He held out a hand to help her to her feet and she took it and he pulled her upwards and looked at her.

'You cut you knee.'

'It's all right.'

'Donna must have something a Mamma's to put on it.'

Ella wasn't about to hang about listening to what Donna did or didn't have. She pushed forward and by him. It was like he decided he had watched enough of the show and hadn't found any of it fulfilling. As she was about to slip by him and out of his reach, Johno grabbed her arm and pulled her back where they'd come from. She didn't struggle and ask him what he thought he was doing. Her body had a kind of surrender around it as they headed back to the middle of the yard, but not her mind. Her mind was still racing and prompting and trying to arm her, ready for whatever was about to happen. She was right then, this was the reason she had been forced back to Hanville. To face off in the yard of the Pink House with Johno so that he could exorcise all his hurt on her and then move on with his life.

The moon wasn't full or anything, her breath wasn't frosting and neither could she hear it in her head. In terms of how scary this night she'd been running from for over half her life could've been, in reality the elements hadn't pandered to her drama. The light from the kitchen windows had sprayed out into the yard and flooded it yellow like the two of them were caught in a spotlight. Behind Ella the women in the kitchen were about their business, none of them particularly interested in what a long-lost sister was saying to her brother. They moved like black faceless patterns against an animation of colour. Ella had her back to the House as she stood in the yard waiting for Johno to say whatever he had first brought her out here to say and then blocked her from leaving to hear. He seemed to be having trouble beginning.

'I have to say something to you.'

Ella stuffed her hands in her pockets, half to stop them from shaking, half to feel the flutter against them. She thought he was taking a seriously long time and willed him to just begin his diatribe so she could take a breath and move on with the rest of whatever life he was about to leave her.

'I've been to BrightWell's.' He let it out like a plank of wood he'd been carrying across his back.

'What? When?' They were involuntary grunts that washed everything she'd been preparing clean out of her head.

'Three years ago. I had to be in London, I told Mamma and she said I should go and look for you. It's like I never wanted to. I had every kind of excuse not to but Mamma said I should. Said that all I was running was nothing if I didn't go and see you, and I knew she was Mamma and she was right. "Go and see Pinky!" Them was Mamma exact words.'

Ella's mind was with him but it was off some place else trying to grab at reason, trying to pluck a memory of seeing Johno three years ago. Had she welcomed him and sat him at a table and not even recognised her own brother? Had she served him almost rotting fried plantains, roast breadfruit and al dente cho-cho? Or fried fish with vinegar, onion and peppers around a ring of fried dumplings? Ella didn't know and it occurred to her that she was absolutely capable of such a thing but for the life of her she just couldn't remember.

'She wanted me to decide if I was going to just see you or go and speak to you. Mamma and her lessons!'

Ella nodded.

'I had this beard. Thicker than the way you see Patrick's. Coulda hide from the whole world in there.'

Ella nodded.

'I bought the razor, bought the shaving cream, got a nice new mirror, but in the end I never.'

Ella nodded.

'You were seeing to this group of people. Fussing over them, laughing and joking. You looked at me once but not long enough.'

Ella nodded, she just couldn't place the evening.

'Up until then I thought I knew what I was doing, that I'd worked out everything, but I hadn't. I hadn't, Pinky. I just hadn't.'

And that was the fight Ella had been running from? She had so many questions if that was it, she had so many questions if that wasn't it. But Johno simply kissed her and went inside.

Ludo was there. Pensively waiting for them to come in, sharing a drink with the men and a chat with the women, who were fascinated by him, like a fat little child who had landed in their midst and wanted all the attention they could feed and give him, but for the fact that he had one eye cracked to the door watching and waiting for Ella to come in and wondering in what kind of state she might be. When he saw it was Johno that came in, and there was no Ella coming up behind him, and then when Johno came over and shook his hand and said a few quiet words to him that the women in the kitchen strained to hear, even though they knew their business was elsewhere, definitely not around what was going on between a brother, a long-lost sister and her man, it worried him even more.

Johno was holding his hand, shaking it and smiling at the worried Ludo and kind of urging him to give her a moment. Ludo wasn't sure if he wanted to leave her out there on her own for even a moment. But when Johno let go of his hand, Ludo took up his seat again and the banter carried on either side and through him and all he could do was smile intermittently as his mind darted from the back door to the yard where she was.

Ella had sat back down on the flat stone, as heavy as one, it seemed. She thought she might follow Johno back inside, but she found herself sitting at the root of the oak tree looking up at the leaves as they tinkled in the light breeze that was getting up. There was altogether a kind of freshness in the air and it was taking with it her past fears. Brownie's clothes were hanging large as life on the line and tinkling the leaves awake above her. She hadn't picked the day it had started because she now knew the day had been charted and not by her.

Ella pushed gently on the door like she hoped it wouldn't give way, like it might force her back and bar her from entering, but it didn't. What little pressure she had applied made it open up before her like it had been expecting her. It was dark and degrees colder than outside. The only light that streamed in came through the half boarded-up windows and the light fixed itself at spangled points all around her. But the light never fell on the corners of the place and she wondered at the kind of hurt that had spent the years nursing itself in the darkness of those corners. She thought she could hear a breeze whistling around, the house was so big and vacant, but she didn't know whether she was imagining that. Every now and then, as her eyes travelled around the place, she could make out the odd word of graffiti where kids who had not lived the event, who only knew of it second-hand from parents, had tried in vain to claim the place. She tapped at her talisman throbbing for life in her pocket, working away for her like something she had lost for years, and with this she took a step forward. Her feet crunched down heavy and loud on something. She looked down and saw a stream of light showing her the debris underfoot. Above the roof had made a hole for itself like it thought that would free the smoke and the memories, and she realised the house had continued to destroy itself for all the years she had been gone.

As she had stood at the entrance, as she had moved from the yard of the Pink House down the road and around the back of the place, she had told herself that no matter what she found or smelt in there she would have to make it to the bedroom and face down whatever was in there tying her to the place. Whatever Johno and Brownie had designed to teach her, she felt sure that it was here. So now she was moving through it, taking the moment and living it instead of reflecting it away, wanting it all to touch her so it would leave her once and for all, wanting it all to be clear to her.

As she reached the place where the kitchen door had once been there was no door, but she pushed gently on that too and it swung open and she stepped through. The carpet was brown, with swirling patterns that interlocked and left each other at symmetrically exact points every time and then repeated. There was a snake of shoes along the wall that led up to the front door. The phone was on a table at the foot of the stairs. There was a football, a large rubber plant spiralling upwards, its leaves supported by canes, a couple of letters were on the mat by the door and it was just the home of a family, all of whom were away on holiday.

'Jamaica!' Larry said it like he was the only one who knew it, like everyone in Hanville didn't know where the Naylors had gone.

They'd gone for a month. Saved up for like three years and then gone for a month. Ella recalled every time they bumped into Brownie or Daddy Ned or Aunt Julie or anyone, the Naylors would always say how they were taking the whole family off to Jamaica for a month and how much it had cost them and they always beamed when they said it.

They were heading for the lounge, led by Ella, but Larry pushed past her and her brothers and stood at the bottom of the stairs clutching at the tray of Marlboro, smiling like for-giveness was only a heartbeat away and would come all the quicker if he embellished his apology with another twist. 'We can smoke them in Andrew's room!'

And before any of the Brightwells could respond, Larry was bounding up the stairs with the tray of cigarettes and no one could stop him.

Andrew's room was blue, with books, with a desk, a single bed and dozens of football posters and ten-penny football cards. As soon as they all piled in Patrick found the spirit of the adventure, jumped on the bed, bounced off, landing with a 'whow!' in front of the wall of football cards. Johno was studying what was going on between Ella and Larry but couldn't quite work it out and so left it. Larry was open-ing up a packet of cigarettes with one hand and Ella was settling into the thought that she had command over all of them and all of it. She remembered now that in the days and weeks after the fire she had toyed with the idea that Larry had started the fire on purpose, that he had meant to kill them all. She had believed that, or else what was that smile about? The one he grew before he struck the first match? But she really couldn't think he had wanted that and had instead settled on the idea that it was his broken arm that had contributed to his dropping the match. It had been an acci-dent. He had struck it, it had fallen out of his hand and he could do nothing. Somehow, though, there was no image of

Larry stamping out the fire in Ella's mind, of him trying to fight the fire back, even. And now the doubts were with her again. And as she pushed down yet another door she saw Larry standing in Andrew's blue room surrounded by books, a desk, a single bed, dozens of football posters and ten-penny football cards, and she thought she saw him drop another match deliberately.

Ella's stomach doubled over like someone had punched her in it and instinctively she made to take a step back but instead she swallowed and closed the door and stood in Andrew's room with her brothers, Larry and the rising fire. This was the face-off she had been running from.

Past her they ran, but she stood and would stand until the smoke was circling around her feet and tearing at the back of her throat. She called to him, wanted him to come with her, but he wouldn't, Larry wouldn't, and suddenly she was wondering how long she could stay there and wait for him without killing herself. How long could she call his name if he ignored her and decided to go his own way? Ella didn't know how she was supposed to do this on her own without him. He had brought a perfect harmony to her life, the two of them together, and she was never quite sure how he had managed to do it when he was just someone who squinted at the sun, had that wet pink skin, just someone she had met two years ago. He wouldn't come. Johno, and Patrick with the tray of Marlboro, intent even in the tragedy on safeguarding his job, were halfway down the stairs before she realised Larry wasn't going to ever come to her again.

Ella breathed out all the smoke that was trying to settle in her lungs and moved forward. She moved further into the blue room, allowing it all to touch her: the door banging shut behind Patrick and Johno as they fled, Larry striking match after match, falling and screaming as the fire appeared to tickle and play with him and then writhing in front of her, screaming for her help. She was about to reach down to do just that for a second time and try and drag him clear of the fire, but he was gone. Disappeared and gone for ever as quickly as he had appeared.

The room was black and now free of smoke and it would be whenever she remembered it again. She was standing at the half boarded-up window, looking down into the road where the Pink House lived. Ella punched at the remaining board and it fell away and down into the front yard and freed the last residue of all that had held her in number 27. From her pocket she pulled out the last anchor of her childhood and opened it.

I couldn't nurse her for two months couldn't even look 'pon her for all that time and not until you dream me and tell me her name could ah even get up outta the bed and see say me hair turn white.

I talk to you Daddy Ned and him is more than everything to me right now and always. Him hug me up with the fullest hand them I ever have round me in the biggest way I ever could have them. Some people have it in mind that when you look on him him is nothing much. That if you rub him even a little bit all that shine bright from him will gone for ever. But no, if you trouble that man him feel it deeper than all who know him could ever think. You love that man even a little bit and you find him give it right back to you warm and new like the bread of life. I have a feel for him, you see, I have a feel for him so'til I don't even need to put out me hand them to reach him 'cause him always there, wrap round me like the sweet warm Jamaican sun.

I get to understand that the hardest thing the two of we have is to understand what we should take from this thing sometimes I get to understand that you Daddy Ned already understand clearly and that is both the happiest thing for me and the saddest thing too.

Like when him wash me foot them or when him reach for a shirt and drop it over him back and gone to the factory for the day with him flask a tea and dish of food, leaving me one to take the teaching. I know full well I have to take the lesson and move through it, but sometimes is all I can do to stop meself going through the whole thing again and again to find out what me do wrong: like cook a wrong food at a wrong time, or make a wrong wish at the wrong time.

Sometimes I even consider I never hear when Him say stop and go no further cause surely Him must a done and then ah consider say I never even feel Him much less hear Him and so I consider why all me other lovely things was just that and more.

All a them come and them live and breathe in me hand and but every day a me life the lesson stand up before me like a man and tell me say I should take it and let it go.

And if I had was to tell the truth up till now and when I never will.

You Aunty Rosa keep on a ask me if me want go talk to you and more times than none it at me mouth to tell her I need nobody to talk to you and I know Pinky don't neither.

I know you and she know you and both a we live you and love you the way we suppose.

Is me: the three of we was in this thing together you and she the most blameless baby them I ever hold in me hand them so that leave me and all I can do sometimes to stop meself dropping down beneath the weight of it is to say you never was mine and to tell her you never was hers.

But sometimes she look 'pon me like she would ask the question who why or what.

And I know is me. I never reach for you, you see.

You sister she come first and them put her in me hand them and is like the whole wide world was fresh in her face and I never see that world before. Like the world just lay down in her face and all I could do was just look 'pon it.

But when me look for you is like me love did done. You come on a wave of red and you just slip away from me on that same colour.

You sister did have a cry in her that come deep from inside her telling the whole House to stop and listen. But you I never hear you and I never feel you either.

You Aunty Rose and you Aunt Julie take you up and I

know say if I did but reach for you right then you would be my little red boy but all that I could do come too late and by the time I look for you I never see you face till you eye them close, I never see you smile, never see you walk or talk not till me mind 'llow me.

Is a kinna thanks I give Him every day that Him 'llow me to see you through you sister who live life so full she live it for the two of you.

You and she is much the same like the two ends of one line that can't ever meet.

And with that the life in the book drained itself into Ella, fixing itself there.

Back in the yard of the Pink House, Ella heard herself saying, 'It's all right.'

Ludo was saying her name in a calm way, trying not to startle her, and she was saying in an equally light way, 'It's all right.' And again, 'It's all right.' And then touching his hand on her, 'It is, it's all right.' Like she was trying to make herself live that phrase. Everything was telling him it wasn't all right, though, not least her nose bleeding. Just little plops that were settling on her black skirt initially, that was what he'd seen from the window in the kitchen, that was what had made him race out saying her name, trying to calm her, and now the blood was junking out of her nose like anger.

He touched her face to see if she would know him because the way she looked was just telling him that it had all stopped for her and she could run no further down the road where he had first seen her face. He had watched her just sitting under the oak tree from the moment Johno had left her out there until now, and the blood funnelled over his hand and down on the book she'd been reading. He had watched her until he couldn't stand it for himself or for her and now he was desperate for her to trust him. All the drums, all the pretence, all the running had stopped and he wanted to know how she would come out of it. She was cold, she didn't know how cold she was, like she was drunk and running naked on a freezing night and couldn't tell the difference between being hot and being cold enough to kill. He began to wonder how long she had been like this without realising. He began to wonder how long he had let her remain out there knowing full well that everything wasn't all right with her and he began to get angry with himself. From his pocket he pulled out a handkerchief, corked her nose with it and then pulled her to her feet. The book fell away covered in blood, everything fell out of it and neither of them noticed. He was moving her to the back door to see her inside to the warmth and to try and stop the nosebleed.

'Come. Come.' He had his arm around her and she was planting one foot, then the other, in that deliberate, drunken kind of way, holding the handkerchief to her nose. Up the step of the back door he took her, into the crowded kitchen, and immediately they were in, the women wanted to help, wanted to tell him this was wrong with her, that was wrong with her, but he wouldn't allow any of them to be near her and backed them away, offending all but not caring. Whatever she needed, Ludo had to do it himself. He led her through the dining area, past the domino match and out into the passage, where he hoped he'd be left alone to do just that.

She was getting lower and lower within herself, and Ludo didn't know where he was going with her. There was singing coming from the sitting room. Coming up behind him was first Donna and then Mirabel. Whatever Ludo was going to do for Ella, he'd have to do it now, because the four of them were now sealed in the space between the stairs, the front door, the sitting-room door and the dining-room door, and if he didn't stand his ground he would be sidelined.

'Ludo?' Donna said, touching his shoulder.

'I can do it! I can help her!'

Donna backed off but stood by like a mother watching her child walk for the first time, positive the child will fall and fall dangerously, but knowing that the child must know for himself.

Ludo had decided to move upstairs. It was the only place left. He manoeuvred the two of them to the bottom of the stairs and before Ella's foot hit the bottom step, Ludo couldn't hold her, she just sank to her knees and lower still, calling his name, 'Ludo! Ludo!'

From the heart of the House there came the loudest bawling it had heard for possibly thirty years. Ludo had his arms around her and was struggling to hold her up. She was floundering so completely she was nearly on her knees in the middle of the passage when simultaneously the dining-room door flew open, the door to the sitting room flew open and a mass of people came out of each, concerned about her.

Aunt Julie was heading the group out of the dining room, Miss Nugent the posse from the sitting room, and Donna was at her side as Ludo decided the safest and easiest place for her was down on the floor. As he wrestled with himself, Ludo was thinking two things, would she be all right and she had called for him, would she be all right and she had called for him. He was afraid for her, for himself that he wouldn't be able to cope with what she would need from him, but never mind, she had called for him. All who were trying to sideline him in her best interest, all who were trying to help her with what they knew, he fought against and held on to her on the floor of the Pink House. He was not going to let her go.

Full of concern, Donna bent over Ella, touching her around the face like she knew what she was doing. Like she thought she was Brownie. And everyone was waiting for her wisdom; even Ludo, who kept looking from the one to the other, was waiting for Donna to say what it was.

'Is she all right?' Ludo asked when he couldn't wait any longer.

Donna shouted, 'Somebody boil up some cerrassee tea!' And Miss Nugent turned towards the kitchen immediately.

'Thirteen years she don't set foot in the place and she think seh she can just walk in here and no feel it seh her mamma dead!' one woman threw in.

'Bring her come.' Donna was mounting the stairs, not only because she thought Ella would do better with the comfort of a bed, but because she herself couldn't stand the bad-minded thoughts that were beginning to circulate down in the passage.

Ludo scooped Ella up into his arms and carried her up the stairs after Donna. As he went, he heard, 'Thirteen years is a long time!'

'A Brownie trouble her.' It was Aunt Julie.

'Brownie would never trouble not one a her children.' It was Miss Bee.

'Then how you explain dat?' Aunt Julie continued.

No one could. They all looked from one to the other, but none of these women who had the ability to meet you out in the street, take one look at you and tell you you were pregnant before you had even a suspicion of it yourself, not one of them could explain Ella's sudden collapse. None, that is, apart from Aunt Julie.

'You see! You spit in the sky and it shall fall in you face. My sister Brownie!'

Johno seemed to remember himself. 'Aunt Julie . . .' He was about to slap her hands for what she was suggesting but had to do it in a way where he still showed the respect her age commanded. But she knew what her nephew was about and cut him off. She wasn't going to be spoken to before people, in her own home, by a child.

'Boy, stand steady, you hear, and let big people believe what them believe.'

'She right!' Miss Tam said and then proceeded to canvass from the attending women just how right they thought she was. 'She wrong or she right? Eeeeh? She wrong or she right? She right!'

The sound of the murmur told Johno he had lost that argument and he was preparing to withdraw upstairs to see how Ella was when there came the clear sound of moving furniture and the House fell alarmingly quiet. Everyone looked up at the ceiling and listened again if what they'd heard was real. As they looked up at the ceiling, the fear inside them was multiplying at speed. Someone was moving furniture! They followed the sound and found the origins of it in the sitting room. As one they turned their eyes and heads around, lodged themselves in the sitting-room door-way and looked up at the ceiling The sitting-room ceiling was directly below Brownie and Daddy Ned's bedroom. Someone was moving furniture up there. There had been women who hadn't had the heart to rush and look what was the matter with Ella. Old women, infirm women, fat women, out-of-breath women, and they had remained seated in their chairs in the sitting room. Suddenly the fear that had been multiplying at speed in each of them gripped one of them so badly, it had to manifest itself somehow, and one of them shot to her feet and set about a great loud singing to drown out the duppy.

'When the shadow of this night 'as flown, I'll fly away. Through the hills of God's celestial home, I'll fly away.'

'Sing it, sister!' one of the men commanded.

And another woman got up ready for the chorus and began to smack a tambourine in perfect rhythm against the point where her wrist joined her palm, swaying her hips from side to side, dancing.

'I'll fly away, oh, glory . . .' And then everyone joined in.

Singing the roof off the House, even Aunt Julie, all in an attempt to keep the duppy from them. 'I'll fly away. When I die Hallelujah by and by, I'll fly away . . .' And so they all went on, even the men, singing at the top of their voices, swaying their hips and clapping their hands, all in the attempt to keep Brownie in her place.

Johno wasn't sure of what he had heard. His teaching was telling him there had to be some kind of explanation, but he also knew that Brownie had taught him something that had sustained him in his years away from her: to just be and accept what you're given. Johno couldn't. Yes, he had done better than any of Brownie's children in this, her most basic gift to her children, but in this instance he was failing. He would not, could not, believe that his dead mother was not at peace and was instead in her bedroom moving furniture.

He found himself mounting the stairs two by two to find out what was going on. But what if he opened his parents' bedroom door and saw his mother standing there with her arms out to him, beckoning him to come to her the way she used to? What if he pushed down the door and his dead mother asked him if she could cook something for him? He reached the top of the stairs and his hands were shaking. All of him was shaking. He felt like a darkness had invaded his body, that God had left him. He had not come up with any argument to counter Aunt Julie's. He had not just stood where he had stood and prayed, he had said no and had charged two by two up the stairs and was now standing outside his parents' room ready to enter. Singing was filling his ears from downstairs but he could still hear behind the door the furniture moving. Whatever they were up to in singing like that, it was having no effect. He had not finished fighting himself when Johno suddenly found he had taken everything in his hand, pushed down the door and there he found Daddy Ned struggling to move the bed back to where it had been. When Johno stepped into the room and saw Daddy Ned, Daddy Ned let go of the bed all defeated like and straightened up. Through his eyes he poured out his fear of life without his Brownie and Johno caught it and the two of them just stood there looking at each other, pouring out every ounce of pain inside of them and it was all about how they were ever going to live without this woman. Daddy Ned couldn't hold it, gave up and just let gravity take him down on the bed, where he began to shake. Whatever peace Ella had seen in her Daddy Ned earlier in the day, throughout it something had crept upon him and this was now who he was. This was what he was. Johno put his arms around his father and the two of them cried. Below them the singing seeped up through their feet trying to warm them.

A few doors along, in the room that was once Ella's and was now Mirabel's, Ella was being undressed by Donna down to her underwear. She laid her sister under the duvet and covered her. The room was dark save for a lamp turned to the far wall so its light was thrown back into the room. The night had long ago developed a chill, but for the people in and around the Pink House the temperature had risen. From downstairs they were being lulled by the singing. From a room down the passage a loud bawling was going on and Ludo was hovering, worried to the pit of his stomach.

Donna was taking it all in her stride and was sitting next to Ella on the bed, holding her hand. And Mirabel was at the open window looking out into the night, into the oak tree at something she wasn't afraid of.

'She going be all right,' Donna was telling Ludo. 'She going be quite all right. She always been our little Pinky who never really wanted to be. But we know she would come back to us.'

Ella didn't know it but she was now in the safest place she could ever have been. She had looked, found no place else and had settled on this best place ever.

'She been through a lot, you know,' Donna was telling him, like it had been she who had spent the last few years in Ella's life and not him. And the door pushed open and Miss Nugent came in with a cup of cerrassee tea.

'Sh–sh–she wake?' Miss Nugent asked.

'No. Look like she going run a fever.'

On hearing that, Ludo excited himself, especially when he saw that neither woman viewed the prospect of a fever as anything to be alarmed about. 'Shouldn't we call a doctor?'

'For what?' Donna asked him; it was a genuine question.

'But a fever!'

Donna smiled at him, placed her hands around his face and kissed him lightly on the lips. 'Darling. Is only the body telling her to stop.'

'St–st–stop an' go n–no fur–ther!' Nodding her head in agreement, Miss Nugent echoed the sentiment like she had lived it. And then again, 'St-stop an' go no fur-ther!' Like she had learnt it.

'No need to call any doctor.'

Ludo was listening hard to them, trying to catch the ease they were exuding, but it just wasn't working for him – whatever they knew, he didn't.

'Miss Nugent, Brownie have some bush bath I going boil up and bath her. You going come help me?'

'St-st-op an' go n-no further!' Miss Nugent was ready, nodding her head and swaying to the singing from down-stairs, singing the phrase 'stop an' go no further' like it was a song she needed.

The women were ready to leave the room and a bemused Ludo who was still up for calling the doctor.

'Oh, and hand that to the lad,' Donna said of Ludo, who was only just younger than her. She meant the cup of cer-rassee Miss Nugent had entered with. And then she said to him, 'Make sure you drink that up, you going need it if you going set up with her when we bath her done.'

Miss Nugent promptly slotted Ludo's bemused hands around the hot cup, smiled at him and left the room.

'Come, baby,' Donna said to Mirabel, and Mirabel left the window and whatever was holding and comforting her and left with her aunt.

Gingerly Ludo advanced on the bed, sat next to Ella and took her hand. She was hot. Donna was right, he had to submit because they seemed to know what they were doing. He fixed the covers around her, fixed them again and again and then had to consciously make himself stop. He took a sip of the tea he had been given, found it bitter and disgusting and abandoned it on the side table.

Ella was dreaming. She was sitting at the large oak table in the Pink House eating rice and peas and chicken and drinking carrot juice from a pint glass. It must have been Sunday, because Sunday was the only day they had rice and peas and chicken. The peas were usually red peas that were soaked overnight and then cooked with coconut milk, salt, thyme and water. To which was then added the rice, which was cooked until soft, and by then the rice had turned a glorious royal purple. This was Ella's favourite food. The peas generally went on early in the morning, were cooked by late morning, and dinner would then be ready around four. Wherever her adventures around Hanville took her on a Sunday, by half past three she was sure to be making her way back to the Pink House.

As she sat at the table, her stomach was fit to busting. She had been greedy, but she was eating on and eating on as though she would never taste the stuff on her plate ever again. It was like the food on her plate was Brownie herself and it was the most wonderful way Brownie had to express her love for them and she showed it proudly and generously. But for some reason, Brownie wasn't at the table, no one else was at the table in Ella's dream but herself and Daddy Ned. He was sitting opposite her waiting for her to finish. He had finished ages ago. A fast eater who always ate with a smile on his face as if he too understood that in the food on the table was the very soul of his beloved Brownie and he wanted to gobble it up before it disappeared. His smile meant he too had discovered that eating the food she had prepared was a way to stay close to her and hold on to her. It was like their secret. It was the thing that held them close and she didn't understand why she was dreaming about rice and peas and Daddy Ned.

Face to face with Brownie, that was what it always came down to. Face to face at the Old Yew Inn, Brownie holding Patrick's hand, unable to let him go, holding on to him like she thought the minute she let him go he would run, and the truth of the matter was, had she, he would have. Brownie had never looked as small as she had that night, Brownie had never cried as much as she did that night, because for Brownie it was like everything she had believed in was now up in the air. Everything she had taught her children was now suspect and so was Brownie's belief in herself. She had believed if she put herself into everything, especially her children, they would somehow always find their way back to a path they could live by. She had thought that somehow there was intrinsically a thing of beauty in all of them. Ella and Patrick had shaken Brownie and everything she believed in. But it would be all right if Ella, at that moment, before she walked out, just gave something to Brownie. If Ella did a simple thing like offer up an embrace to Brownie or some-one, just anyone. If Ella could just be it would be all right. But Ella offered her nothing except this: 'I'll go then.'

'Pinkette?' Brownie called after her.

Ella wouldn't stop. She continued down the road, heading for the Pink House to get her stuff and leave before her dis-grace had circulated around the whole town.

'Pinkette?' Brownie was moving after her. And she never called her youngest daughter's name again.

Ella marched on. The night was drawing in. If she was going to leave tonight, she would have to make it to the House quick, she was telling herself. The fact that she was rushing had nothing to do with the fact that Brownie was following her, it had to do with how quickly she could turn around and leave and get transport over the Bridge. But Brownie wanted answers and she had never wanted answers before, and Ella's haste had become plain straight running.

She had started out ahead of Brownie, almost a mile ahead of her as her mother saw to it that Patrick was all right. That his tears and sorrow would not consume him. When she set off after Ella she had half a mile to catch up – Ella was that scared and was moving that fast. For every one step Ella took, Brownie took two and was coming up behind, her eyes searching her out through the night. And Ella's eyes went backwards and forwards as she realised something was following her. Initially she couldn't really let herself believe it was her Brownie following her like that, chasing after her and terrifying her like that. But every time she looked back she couldn't discount it for sure – she couldn't tell one way or the other who it was. So it could've been Brownie! She ran faster, put her feet down harder. Common sense was screaming, 'Head for the Bridge, head for the Bridge, head for the Bridge!' But for some reason she had to go back to the Pink House and get her things. She had to leave with things and she had to walk out, she couldn't run and leave just like that. She had to walk out with her dignity or else what would she have? Who would she be? And how could she ever face her Brownie again? For her pains, Ella came face to face with someone in front of her. The shock of seeing someone standing in the road ahead of her stopped her dead in her tracks. There was only one person with a silhouette like that.

It was quiet. Ella could hear herself banging about in her head. After all her trying to tell herself her mother would not frighten her like this, it was after all her. Somehow Brownie had got past her and was now standing in the middle of the road ahead of her, waiting for Ella to come to her. Ella looked behind trying to work out how Brownie had done it. How had she managed to outrun her and get in front of her like that? There was no short cut. No second route. There was one way, Ella herself had taken it, Brownie had not overtaken her on the road, so how?

They were alone, on the edge of Badlands Woodlands, with the night closed in and no one for miles. Ella was jumping and shaking. The contrast between her and her surroundings couldn't have been more acute. While Brownie stood as calm as anything, arms out, inviting her daughter to please come forward with whatever explanation she chose, Ella made a wrong decision.

She jumped out of her sleep and found herself in the bath with Donna and Miss Nugent around her. The electric light had been switched off and there were candles flickering their light around the bath and the windowsill. There were four people in the bathroom, not counting Ella herself, and two of them were big on the walls and sometimes merged with the ceiling too. Large heads, still larger bodies that grew and shrank depending on which way they went in the candle-light. Bodies that looked like cartoons or maybe ghosts. They were ghosts! One of them, the one that looked like Miss Nugent, was hovering directly over Ella. Ella's big eyes were fixed on it, sure it was there for only one thing. It stopped for the shortest time above her and gave the anxiety in her time to breed in every pore. It drew back, did something in the corner and then came back above her, a dark, heavy mass above her in a golden room where she had been brought to die. It withdrew again, did something else in the corner and then came back. All the way there and back, here and there, Ella's eyes never leaving it. It was playing with her. The ghost on the ceiling was playing with her. And then to add to Ella's hysteria, the ghost on the ceiling joined up with the ghost in the corner that had so far shown itself to be calm, friendly even, and perhaps not interested in her. The two of them came together above her and you couldn't see where the one began and ended and it was like their work had begun. Now that they were joined together, Ella knew that this was it.

She lurched out of her sleep and found herself. She didn't know where she was, but she was in the bathroom. She didn't know how she had got there, but she was naked in the bath and Donna and Miss Nugent were there. Candlelight flickered around the bath and windowsill. Ella looked for the ghosts above her but they'd gone. She saw a big white sheet thrown over her, weighted on the far side of the bath with pebbles so it managed to stay out of the water and against the wall. At the side of the bath, her hand under the white sheet, was Donna. Ella looked down suspiciously, wondering what her hand was about underneath the sheet. When she felt it on her, she flailed about splashing and shrank away to the far side of the bath trying to get out of reach of it. Donna was able to calm her, not with words but with her spirit. It seemed to Ella that her body had submitted and now it was the turn of her mind. If she was ever going to get out of this with some semblance of sense and peace, she would have to just be. Donna looked like a safe bet. Like a poor little thing she allowed Donna to slide her back to the centre of the bath and begin her work, and Ella felt Donna's hand come around her body, soothing it cool with a warm clever sponge. Every time the sponge came at her, it took the pain in Ella. Every time the sponge came at her, it knew just where to touch her and so it took the fear that was in Ella. It was like bathing in a warm smell, a smell she remembered from her childhood. And it had her floating away wrapped warm and secure around a sweet image upon which she used to just be.

The smell was how Brownie used to bath her in a bath just like this. Donna and Miss Nugent had helped themselves to Brownie's stock of cerrassee, ackee, pimento, sage, velvet, guava, Jack-in-the-bush and lime leaves. Every time someone went Back Home, they would bring a fresh batch of leaves, which would be kept until necessary. They had boiled them up like they were going to make a tea and then poured the liquid into the hottest bathwater the bather could bear and into this they lowered Ella.

She was back in the bed. Dried and wrapped and then slipped into one of Brownie's huge nighties that only added to the way she was feeling, like that little girl. Once Donna and Miss Nugent had seen her secure, Ludo was let in again. Ludo wanted just to sit with her and she was surprised to find that she wanted him to.

She thought it was Friday morning. She thought it must be Friday morning proper. And when she woke it wasn't like she had woken from a fever-induced sleep, all drowsy and the like; her eyes simply opened and it was like she'd been waiting for this very moment. They scanned the room and Ludo was asleep on the floor with the duvet from the other bed dragged over him. The other bed was naked and empty at her toes. She didn't need to wonder why he hadn't slept on the other bed. She pulled the duvet down and saw Brownie's nightie looping around her and held it to herself. Flashes of last night, dreams of last night, nightmares of last night were before her eyes and they forced her out of the bed where she stepped over the sleeping Ludo, searching for her clothes, not realising she was already wearing them.

Standing at the top of the stairs, Ella sensed no movement in the House. She didn't know exactly where she was going, but she was going some place. A healing had begun last night and every step that took her bare feet down the carpet of the Pink House continued it. Past the family pictures that hung snaking their way up the wall, every other step looking behind for Mirabel who Ella was sure would find her any second, would somehow have the strength to hold her down screaming for the whole House to come and see who she had found up and about so early in the morning.

Ella was on the spot where she remembered Ludo had tried to hold her up last night. She was still wondering if it had been last night, but if it wasn't last night, then what was this bright morning before her if not Friday morning, the day her mother would be buried? She didn't even stop at the sitting-room door, she knew whatever she was doing wasn't connected with anything in there. At the dining-room door her hand faltered on the handle as she looked one more time up the stairs, past the pictures, checking for Mirabel.

Finally she squeezed down on the handle and cracked the door open and the knowledge that it was the last door she had to open fortified her. A deep amber singing voice jumped at her and she knew it would shake the whole House awake if she didn't close the door on it immediately. Ella's eyes darted back up the stairs checking if anyone had heard that voice. Her heart beat began to calm slightly when she saw no one. The only people up were her and whoever was singing. She listened at the door, trying to identify the voice. Like a poor lost little girl barefoot in Brownie's overlapping nightie, she stood straining to hear the pitch of the voice to know who it was. But there was not a sound now. The door was shut and Ella couldn't hear a thing from inside the dining room or the kitchen to tell her who it had been.

But nothing! Nothing but silence! It wasn't a heavy door. As a child all you had to do to find out business that wasn't yours was stand right where she stood and you heard every word, every emotion that poured out of anyone behind it. But not now, this time she couldn't hear a thing.

Again she squeezed down on the handle, cracked the door the meanest amount, and there was the singing again, loud as anything. In perfect tune, breathing warmth into her, and she was torn between keeping the sound in the kitchen and wanting the sound swarming around her. She forced her head round the door, poked it into the dining room, looked through to the kitchen, but could see no one. She could hear as clear as anything, but no one was visible.

The smell, though. There was a smell of food and it was coming from Brownie's kitchen. It was breakfast, she could smell breakfast. Someone had got up and was frying fritters and she could smell ackee and salt fish and fry fish. But if she didn't close the door right now! This second! For sure the whole Brightwell clan, led by Mirabel, would be down those stairs and down on her. And so she closed it. She knew the voice and knew the smells like the second she had heard and smelt them. It was Brownie's voice, they were Brownie's smells, inside Brownie's kitchen, filling it in death the way she had in life. It was Brownie all the way, holding her, taking care of her. It finally fell into her brain like a ten-pence piece in a long-empty slot machine that then kicked into life.

It was like opening a warm, welcoming music box, that was how it was when Ella pressed down the handle and slid through the crack in the door to emerge into the dining room. Sitting down at the table as quickly as she could, not afraid. The singing was everywhere. It reminded her of a kaleidoscope that she had played with as a child, trying to figure out how it gave such wonderful colours and shapes.

From the oak table Ella looked across into the kitchen and there was her mother. Not dead. Not gone from her, but still a part of her. Still waiting for her.

'Fritters, salt fish, goat fish or all?' Brownie smiled at her.

Ella smiled back. No matter what she said to her mother in response to this question, her mother always placed the whole lot on her plate and left her last daughter to find her way through it. And so it was, before Ella there arrived a pack of plates laden with the said food and Ella tucked in.

She knew how her mother had kneaded the flour that morning and worked the flour into hand-size dumplings that she had dropped into hot fat on a gentle heat, where they would cook and brown into the softest dumplings ever. Scaling the goat fish in the yard with flies dancing around her face and she laughing and joking like they were telling her something that only she could understand. And on watching her, Ella knew that that was exactly what they were doing. Gutting the guts out of the fish and dropping them plop into a bucket of cool lemon water. Heads as well. Two dozen. Her mother never fried less than two dozen goat fish on any occasion and if they had company or it was a special occasion, then there was more. Soaking the salt fish overnight in water and then mashing it into pieces to add to the fritter mix and the ackee in the dutchy. Even if the cooking had

not warranted her rising so early to prepare and have ready
for the family, her mother had to be there, first down in the
morning, living in the space that was her most precious
place.

Out of nowhere, Brownie's voice boomed around the
kitchen. 'Morning, Poor Little Lost Son!'

Ella stopped eating and her head spun up from the plates
of food before her and looked to the back door. There was
no one there. He had gone.

Climbing back up the stairs, she stopped midway. She
had lived and grown for seventeen years and ten days in the
Pink House and walked past these pictures for all those years.
Pictures of people she didn't know, running up the wall of
the stairs. All of them pale like ghosts in suits and stiff white
dresses against the backdrop of some banana walk, some
veranda. 'Stiffs', that was what she and Johno used to call
them. First there was a small old man with a fat face and fat
eyes that held you, who Daddy Ned looked the spit of.
Then a girl who had been taken when she was no more than
ten, people thought. Then another man, but younger this
time, who was posing in his best suit with a wife on his arm.
Now last on the wall hung a picture of Brownie.

Ludo was still asleep on the floor. She pulled the duvet
over him just that little bit more and sat by the open
window. The oak tree was brushing against the window like
it always used to. She moved to the window, opened it and
looked down. The drop looked scarier than it had ever
looked when she was a child. The branches looked less
sturdy than they had ever looked, the ledge thinner. She

hadn't climbed a tree since she couldn't remember, but she knew she could climb this one. She sat on the ledge, swung her feet through the window and was inches from the branches in front of her. She tucked the front hem of Brownie's looping nightie into her knickers and smiled at the branch calling to her.

Grab! She was holding on but with one precarious hand. And her mantra now was 'hold on, hold on, hold on!' She threw her other hand at the same branch and found she was holding on, swaying in the morning sun, with nothing but thin air below her and Brownie's nightie fluttering lightly around the back of her. There was a branch almost dead centre where she used to sit, and that was where she was heading. Between it and the branch she was swinging from, though, were branches that didn't look like they could hold a baby, never mind a grown woman. But there was a way over to that special branch. She used to know the sequence of this tree, the only question was could she remember it now? Crack! The branch holding her gave a little. It had evidently had enough of her questioning, her doubting and unwillingness to trust and be and just reach for the right branch. The oak tree was thinking on giving her up to the ground then, but she wouldn't panic. She closed her eyes and began to swing her legs back and forth as she tried for momentum to thrust out her legs to reach the branch up ahead. You got to the first branch, swung your legs, that gave you the momentum towards the next branch, whereupon you threw yourself at it and held on for dear life – that was what she remembered. Back and forth she went, pumping

her legs beneath her like a kid. When she hit the branch, she
hit it with her eyes closed, but felt it against her chest and it
was the best feeling in the whole wide world. She swung a
leg up over the branch and found herself astride it like riding
a horse, she swung her legs over to the same side, opened her
eyes and this was where she had sat before and could just be.

Ella was looking down from a height at the funeral gathered below her. Needless to say it wasn't raining. The weather forecaster, a cousin of the Brightwells who claimed to be able to read weather, had predicted torrential rain at precisely the hour Brownie was to be lowered into the ground. But it was nice. It wasn't bright and sun filled, but it was okay for a burial. People must have been stupid to think it would rain. Nothing ever rained on Brownie, even the rain was something to embrace something to find joy in.

They had chosen horses and a cart. Two sturdy looking black horses with black feathers in their heads, a freshly washed milk cart, Brownie's peach coloured coffin elegant on it and they all walked the mile across town behind it. Johno led the service and the singing at the graveside where the men were vying to mould up the grave. From one to the other Ella looked at them. A hoard of people that had stopped any traffic through Hanville for the day. There was her brother Lambert, fresh from America where life had taken him, sobbing, while his stoosh and far removed wife stood there wondering what it was all about, who all these people were. And Ella knew her. Kellit whose travels the funeral had interrupted. And it didn't surprise Ella to see again the principal crier among the family wasn't any of Brownie's children or Daddy Ned, but Aunt Julie. It seemed to Ella that Aunt Julie suddenly realised that Brownie had gone and whatever it was, had gone with her, and she missed it and would continue to. Next to Ella was Della, strapped into her chair, head flailing this way and that, black hat pushed hard down on her forehead. Ella reached over to her and didn't even think about it, she reached over to Della and pulled the hat off her head and immediately Della stopped the confusion and was calm. Ella thought she saw her sister smile but she couldn't be sure. As Ella went back to the congregation her eyes fell on Mirabel who was watching her from the other side of the grave. Ella looked at her and knew her for real now and wasn't afraid of who she was. In her acceptance, at the right moment, a hand reached across for her and instinctively Ella allowed herself to be found and held and held on to the hand in hers too. It was Ludo by her side.

'Sleep on beloved, sleep and take thy rest and lay thy head upon the Saviour's breast. We love you well, but Jesus loves you best. Good night. Good night. Good night.' They all sang.

On the island where Brownie was born and raised into a young woman, the island that had infused them all, there grew a herb that was locally called 'Shame O Lady'. The herb was so called on account that the leaves would close upon touch and reopen moments later when the union had broken. Now the union was made again, now even with a touch it could remain open, because now it was time.